FROST AND FIRE

CHRISTMAS AT HALL FARM ILLUSTRATED EDITION
BOOK 1

ANA ASHLEY

Frost and Fire- Christmas at Hall Farm Illustrated Edition, book 1
© 2025 by Ana Ashley
ISBN: 978-1-915031-64-8

Frost and Fire is a work of fiction. Names, characters, businesses, places events and incidents are either products of the author's imagination or used in a fictitious manner. Any resemblance to actual persons, living or dead, or actual events is purely coincidental.

Cover design: Ana Ashley

Illustration: Tal Lewin

Editor: Abbie Nicole

Join Ana's Facebook Group Café RoMMance for exclusive content, and to learn more about the latest books at anawritesmm.com!

To the romantics who know twinkle lights make excellent accomplices—conspiring with cocoa steam, crisp night air, and the shocking truth that the one who sparks your temper might be the one who sets your heart alight.

Merry Christmas,
Ana

ABOUT THIS BOOK

After decades of sold-out stadiums and never-ending tours, coming home to run my family's Vermont dairy farm was supposed to be peaceful. Instead, I'm being terrorized by my devastatingly attractive neighbor who's apparently declared war on me—one "gift" at a time.

A goat that won't leave my side. A rooster with a Napoleon complex. A hive of bees with serious attitude problems. The boy I remember as my best friend's sweet little brother has grown into a man with a serious grudge and zero intention of making my homecoming easy.

When a crisis threatens our small town's Christmas celebrations, we're forced to work together. Fighting our attraction while saving the holidays should be simple, right?

Too bad Taylen James has always been my greatest weakness.

Frost and Fire *is a brother's best friend, enemies-to-lovers*

Christmas romance with an age gap, small-town charm, and enough sexual tension to melt Vermont snow.

Christmas romance with an age gap, small-town charm, and enough sexual tension to melt Vermont snow.

1

———

BASTIAN

Post-gig chill is better than post-sex glow. I said what I said.

I'm sure I'd feel differently if I were getting sex on the regular, but I'm not. I can't remember the last time someone else's hands, mouth, or dick were anywhere near my body.

So watching my bandmates in the afterglow of a show, when the adrenaline has softened into something mellower but still electric? Pretty perfect.

There's a special kind of magic in these hours, when we're all sprawled around someone's hotel room, or in this case, Mik's living room, dissecting our favorite moments between bites of takeout.

We're Hall of Fame: Mik, on the guitar, Fox on bass, Stone on drums, and me, the voice. Four kids scouted to be the best rock band in the country, and we actually made it. And then there's Nikko, Fox's younger brother and our tour manager. He's as much a part of the band as we are.

I sit cross-legged, my back against Mik's plush couch, watching Fox, the only one of us who put his food on a plate, as he meticulously separates his curry into neat

3

sections. Some habits never change, even after twenty-five years of touring together.

Stone sprawls across an armchair, his perfectly manicured hands gesturing as he recounts the night's most memorable moment.

"I swear, who requests 'Sweet Home Alabama' at a Hall of Fame gig?" Stone's laugh fills the room. "Like we're some cover band at a county fair."

On the floor beside me, Nikko scrolls through his phone, occasionally reading out social media reactions to our impromptu set at The Academy, an old school building turned into a restaurant in the small town of Stillwater, Connecticut, where Mik decided to settle down.

"'The Hall of Fame secret gig was *life-changing*,'" he quotes, then snorts. "It was a restaurant gig, not Madison Square Garden."

"Hey, every show matters," I say, though my words get partially lost in a mouthful of green curry.

Nikko doesn't look up from his phone, his thumbs moving rapidly across the screen. "They're loving the impromptu gig. Small venue performances always get the best reactions."

The door swings open, and Mik enters with his boyfriend Tyler, their fingers loosely intertwined. Something in my chest tightens at the casual intimacy of the gesture. They look so right together, like a song finally finding its proper key. Mik's smile is brighter than I've seen it in years.

"Room for two more?" Mik asks, though he's already settling on the sofa with Tyler beside him.

Stone immediately sits up straighter, a wicked grin spreading across his face. "Well, well, well. Look who's back already." He checks his watch with exaggerated concern. "What's it been, two hours? Two and a half?"

Fox doesn't look up from his meticulously organized

plate, but I catch the slight smirk tugging at his lips. "Record time, really."

"Hey now," Nikko chimes in, setting his phone aside to join the assault, "we told you to take all the time you needed. All night, even. But here you are…"

"Missing us already?" Stone adds, his voice dripping with mock sympathy. "That's sweet, Thor. Really. But we thought you'd have better things to do than hang out with your band-mates tonight," he says, using the nickname we came up with for Mik because of his Scandinavian heritage.

Tyler's cheeks flush pink, but he's laughing as he buries his face against Mik's shoulder. Mik himself is turning an impressive shade of red, running his free hand through his hair in that nervous gesture we all know so well.

"Jesus Christ, you guys are worse than teenagers," Mik mutters, but there's no real heat in it.

"We're just saying," Fox adds mildly, finally looking up with those sharp amber eyes, "when a man gets the all-clear from his bandmates to celebrate properly with his guy, we expect a little more…commitment to the cause."

From somewhere near the hallway, a young voice pipes up. "La la la la la!"

Kay, Mik's teenage daughter, appears briefly in the door-way, hands clapped firmly over her ears, before dramatically spinning around and marching toward the kitchen. "I can't hear you! I'm getting juice."

The room erupts in laughter, and even I can't help but grin. It feels good, this easy ribbing between brothers. Normal. Like maybe we can face whatever comes next without losing the connection we have. Our brotherhood.

We fall into easy conversation about the show, about the way the crowd's energy filled that small space, about how different it felt from our arena tours. It's comfortable, famil-iar, until Stone suddenly tightens the lid on his container with a sharp snap. He sits up straighter, his usually playful demeanor replaced by something more serious.

"So," he says, his dark eyes scanning the room, "are we officially on hiatus?"

The question lands like a stone in still water. Nikko's thumb freezes mid-scroll, and Fox's fork hovers above his plate, his rice dripping onto the curry sauce. My shoulders tense, the curry sitting heavy in my stomach. We've all known this conversation was coming—hell, I've talked to Mik about it and even welcome the change—but knowing doesn't make it easier.

The silence stretches, thick and uncomfortable, broken only by the soft hum of the heating system. I look around at these men who have been my family for more than two decades, reading the weight of the moment in their faces. Even Tyler, the newest addition to our circle, seems to hold his breath.

Mik breaks the silence first. I envy his certainty, the way he can speak about the future like it's already written.

"I'm staying put," he says, his hand finding Tyler's. "Kay needs stability, and I need..." He glances at Tyler, a smile softening his features. "Well, I need this."

The weight of everyone's eyes shifts to me, and I fight the urge to squirm. My calloused fingers find a loose thread on my jeans, worrying it as I speak. "The farm needs me full-time now. Dad's health isn't great, and I can't keep splitting myself between two worlds."

Fox nods slowly, his amber-brown eyes thoughtful. "Taking time to figure things out isn't a bad thing," he says, still methodically organizing his food. "We've been running full-tilt for decades."

"I've got some production offers," Stone adds, but his voice lacks its usual swagger. "Studios in LA, Nashville. Nothing concrete yet."

Nikko's anxiety radiates off him in waves as he sets his phone down. His fingers drum against his thigh. "And what exactly happens to a tour manager when there's no tour to manage?"

The question hangs there, sharp and uncertain. I watch his features tighten, see the way Fox subtly shifts closer to his brother. Years of reading each other's cues makes the undercurrent of panic impossible to miss.

"Look," I start, "this will take some time to get used to. We should see it as an opportunity to evaluate what we want for our future, not just as a band, but as individuals. The farm will always be home to all of you." I turn to Tyler. "That includes you too, Ty."

Relief softens Stone's shoulders while excitement brightens his eyes. He's always loved the farm's recording studio. Fox's expression remains carefully neutral, but I catch the slight uptick at the corner of his mouth.

But it's Nikko who leans forward, his anxiety finding a new focus. "What exactly would I do there? Tour managing is my thing. Are you suggesting I go into farming?"

"You manage logistics better than anyone I know," I say, meeting his worried gaze. "A farm is just a different kind of tour. Feeding schedules instead of sound checks, equipment maintenance instead of guitar tech. The skills translate."

If he could throw daggers with his eyes, I'd be dead, so I raise my hands to clarify. "I'm only joking, but if you want to keep busy while you figure out what's next, I can help you with that. Or maybe another band?"

"And what about our identities?" Nikko presses. "We've been Hall of Fame for so long. Who are we without that?"

The question hits closer to home than I want to admit. I've been asking myself the same thing every time I look in the mirror lately, seeing the growing silver in my hair and wondering if I'm more Bastian Hall, the rock star, or Sebastian, the farmer's son. The answer changes depending on the day.

Kay reappears from the kitchen carrying an armload of snacks that would make a nutritionist weep. Chips, cookies, candy bars, and what looks like enough sugar to fuel a small concert. She dumps her haul on the coffee table with the satisfaction of someone who's just solved world hunger. "Thought you guys might want dessert," she announces cheerfully.

A collective groan rises from the room. Stone clutches his perfectly flat stomach with theatrical horror. "Do you know what processed sugar does to a man my age?" he mutters, but his hand is already reaching for a cookie.

Fox shakes his head disapprovingly while simultaneously muttering about how many extra miles he'll need to run tomorrow, yet somehow, a bag of gummy bears finds its way onto his lap.

Even Nikko, who usually supplies the band with healthier snacks to prevent sugar crashes, perks up at Kay's junk food selection. "Finally, someone who understands proper snack distribution." He grins, already reaching for a bag of chips. "And before anyone says anything about my choices, I'm still on the right side of forty, my metabolism can handle it."

Stone gives him the finger while Fox pushes his brother off the couch.

We're all getting older, all more conscious of what our bodies can and can't handle, but none of us can resist Kay's offerings. Some things never change. We're still just a bunch of guys who can't say no to junk food and good company.

Eventually, everyone drifts away to the guest rooms, leaving Mik and me alone. We start gathering empty containers of food and half-eaten bags of chips to take them to the kitchen. I don't need to see the way he glances at me to know he has something to say.

"Okay, let it out," I say, nudging him with my elbow as we cross the threshold into the kitchen.

He makes me wait until he's put everything away and then leans against the counter, crossing his arms.

"Are you sure we're doing the right thing?"

I lean against the sturdy oak kitchen table. One that is clearly meant to have a big family around it, just like the one at my parents' farm. "I've only ever been sure of one thing: music. But that was before I was away from home for months on end. Before I started missing calving season, or hearing that someone else was naming the calves. Why do you ask? Are you having a change of heart?"

Mik shakes his head. "Not at all. I need this. Kay needs this. But I do feel guilty that my wanting to settle down has forced this change on everyone."

"Maybe we all need it, but just haven't had a good enough reason to do it. If we'd given it a couple more winters, I would be the one doing it. Dad's health isn't what it used to be."

Mik nods his understanding. When we started, we were four kids filled with dreams and zero responsibilities, five when Nikko came to work with us. Since Kay was born, I've known we were on borrowed time. If we're honest with ourselves, Mik settling in one place to give Kay a chance at a normal life probably should have happened long before now.

"So," he says, his tone deliberately casual, "what about the farmer next door?"

The question catches me off guard. "What about him?"

"Last time I was in Vermont, things seemed a little tense."

"He's like fucking burdock in the pasture," I mutter.

I go back to the empty containers I carried in, scraping

off every tiny bit of food before placing them in the recycling bin. Anything to avoid meeting Mik's gaze, to avoid acknowledging the complicated tangle of emotions that comes with thoughts of Taylen Howard and the way his hostility burns like ice whenever our paths cross.

"I don't know what that means." Mik laughs. "I'd love to find out, but I have a sexy man in my bed upstairs and I've already left him alone too long. I'll see you in the morning."

"Sure thing." I drop the last of the containers into the trash and then wash my hands.

Tomorrow, I'll make my way home with the knowledge that I'm definitely there to stay. But right now, Vermont feels both too close and too far away, and Taylen… Taylen feels like a storm I'm not ready to weather.

2

TAYLEN

"The usual?" Joe asks from behind the bar, already reaching for the tap. His flannel shirt has more holes than fabric these days, but nobody would dare suggest he replace it. Some things in Winterberry are sacred.

"Make it the winter ale. Might as well embrace the season."

Joe slides the glass across the bar. "How's that new rotation working out? Heard you're trying something different with the east field."

Old Jim Turner's head turns at that, his weathered face creasing with interest. "That sustainable stuff you were talking about at the co-op meeting?"

I take a slow sip of ale, letting the hoppy notes linger on my tongue before answering. "Early days yet, but the soil samples are promising. Thinking of expanding it next season if the numbers hold."

"Always pushing boundaries, aren't you?" Joe wipes down the bar, his movements as familiar as the creek that runs through my orchard. "Your brother would've—"

"Been proud," I finish for him, the words automatic now

after all these years. The ale suddenly tastes bitter, but I force another swallow. "Yeah, I know."

A wave of greetings ripples through the tavern as Finn breezes in with that perpetually harried expression of someone juggling too many plates at once.

"You're late," I say as he slides onto the stool next to me. "Let me guess. Emergency tinsel shortage? Santa's elves unionizing?"

Finn ignores my ribbing, which is annoying because it's the best part of our Friday drinks. "You try coordinating three different church choirs for the tree lighting ceremony. Sister Margaret's convinced the Methodists are trying to upstage her sopranos. And it's not even Thanksgiving yet."

"Ah, yes, the great Christmas Carol Conspiracy of 2023." I signal Joe for another round. "Truly the crisis of our time."

"Mock all you want," Finn says as Joe delivers our drinks. "But someone has to make sure this town doesn't descend into holiday chaos. Did you know the craft fair committee is threatening to withdraw from the Christmas Festival? Apparently, the quilting circle felt underrepresented in the marketing materials for last year's festival."

I lean back as we both stand, spotting an empty booth near the window. "And naturally, Vermont's most eligible event coordinator is the only one who can prevent this catastrophe," I say as we slide onto the worn leather seats across from each other.

"Damn straight." Finn takes a long pull from his beer, then immediately grimaces at whatever notification just lit up his phone. "Oh god, now the elementary school principal wants to know if we can get live reindeer for the pageant."

"Can't you just stick antlers on some of the Petersons' goats? Or maybe not. Those things will eat anything, including the set pieces, probably."

That finally gets a genuine laugh out of him, his shoulders relaxing slightly. "You know, sometimes I miss when this town's biggest event was the annual pie contest."

"Truer words, my friend."

"Speaking of drama, how's the new irrigation system working out?"

I recognize the careful shift in his tone, the way he's testing the waters. Finn never asks about farm operations. Event planning is his calling, not agriculture, and he's always been grateful to have found his own path away from the family farm. "It's fine," I say slowly. "Why?"

"Just curious. You know, since you mentioned at the last agricultural committee meeting that you were looking to expand the sustainable practices program." He takes another sip of beer, too casual. "Might be good to have some fresh perspectives on that."

I narrow my eyes. "Fresh perspectives?"

"You know, other farmers who've implemented similar systems. People with experience in both traditional and modern methods." His phone lights up again, casting a shadow across his neutral expression. "Just thinking aloud."

"Uh-huh." I drain the last of my ale, letting the silence stretch between us. "And would these hypothetical farmers happen to have any musical experience? Perhaps a tendency toward dramatic entrances and leaving when things get tough?"

Finn winces. "Tay—"

"Save it." I wave to Joe for another round. "Let's talk about something that actually matters. Like how you're planning to prevent the annual gingerbread house competition from turning into a contact sport this year."

He allows the deflection and our conversation meanders through safer territory, such as the upcoming farmers' market schedule, and the latest gossip about which of the Morgan twins will get her hands first on the hot new veterinarian. Finn's phone continues its steady stream of interruptions, but he manages to keep at least seventy percent of his attention on our conversation.

"You know," I say, watching him respond to what must be his hundredth message of the night, "they do make this amazing thing called a *Do Not Disturb* setting these days. Revolutionary technology."

"Hilarious." Finn's fingers fly across the screen. "Some of us can't just turn off the world when the sun goes down."

Sadly, I can't see the screen of Finn's phone as I watch him type, pause, and type again.

I tap my empty glass against the table. "I'm starting to think you're seeing someone. The phone, the constant texting, the distracted smile. Should I be planning a shotgun wedding?"

Finn's head snaps up, his cheeks flushing slightly. "What? No. It's just…work stuff."

"Uh-huh." I lean forward, resting my elbows on the scarred wooden table. "Because the Christmas parade route really requires that many heart-eye emoji?"

"I don't use—" He stops, narrowing his eyes at my smirk. "You can't even see my screen from there."

"No, but I can see your face." I gesture to Joe for another round. "You've got that look."

"I so don't have a look." His phone buzzes again, and his eyes flick down automatically before he forces them back to me. "Besides, if we're talking about my love life, let's talk about yours too. How's that going?"

"Nonexistent, as you well know." I accept the fresh beer from Joe with a nod of thanks. "Unless you count my thriving relationship with the east field's soil composition."

"That's sad, Tay. Even for you." Finn sets his phone face-down on the table. A gesture that would be more meaningful if it didn't immediately light up again, illuminating the wood beneath it like a distress signal. "What about that guy from the farmers' market committee?"

"Nah."

Finn leans back, studying me with that too-knowing look that makes me want to slide under the table. "When was the last time you actually went on a date?"

The question hits a nerve I'd rather leave unpoked. "When was the last time you minded your own business?"

"Never. It's literally my job to know everyone's business." He picks up his phone again, but this time, his expression shifts from distracted to determined. "Actually, I might know someone—"

"No." The word comes out sharper than I intended, drawing glances from nearby tables. I lower my voice. "No setups. No blind dates. No well-meaning interventions in my romantic life."

"But—"

"The last time you tried to set me up, I spent three hours listening to someone explain their theory about how crop circles are actually alien square dance patterns."

Finn winces. "Okay, that was a miscalculation. But this is different. He's—"

"If you say 'perfect for me,' I'm going to dump this beer over your phone."

He holds up his hands in surrender, but something in his expression sets off warning bells in my head. That little twist at the corner of his mouth that means he's working up to something. I've known him long enough to recognize the signs.

"Fine, no setups." He picks up his phone again, scrolling with exaggerated casualness. "Though speaking of people coming back to town…"

My fingers tighten around my glass. "Since when were we

speaking of people coming back to town?" I chance, hoping he's not about to say what I think he's about to say.

"I just thought you should hear it from me first." He's still not looking at me, his voice carefully neutral. "My brother's coming back. For good this time, apparently."

The words hit like a sudden frost. I force my hand to relax before I shatter the glass, but I can feel the tension spreading through my body like ice across a pond. The last person I wanted to think about today was Sebastian Hall, but here we are.

"Inevitable, I suppose." My voice comes out steady, practiced. I've had years to perfect this particular lie. "The prodigal son returns to save the family farm. How very Lifetime movie of the week."

Finn's watching me now, reading every micro-expression I'm failing to hide. "He's been keeping up with farming practices, you know. Following all the latest developments. He's not coming back blind. Besides, the farm doesn't need saving. It needs managing."

A laugh escapes me. "Right. Between world tours and Grammy parties, I'm sure he found plenty of time to study herd health and breeding lines."

"You know," he starts, and I already want to stop him, "Bastian's been doing more than just keeping up. He's practically managing the farm part-time."

I can't help the derisive snort that escapes me. "Part-time management? Is that what we're calling flying in for two weeks between stadium shows?"

"He's been more involved than you think." Finn's voice takes on that diplomatic tone I've heard more than once at town meetings. "Did you know he's been working with agricultural scientists to develop new sustainable farming methods? I don't know much about it because farming isn't my thing, but the grass quality has improved. Apparently, good grass means happy cows and happy cows mean happy milk."

"Now that's a new concept right there." I snort and gesture to the bar around us. "You see these people? They're not theories or test cases or PR opportunities. They're our neighbors. Our community. They're not a project or something you can abandon when the next opportunity arises."

Finn gives me one of his knowing looks, the kind that makes me want to throw something at him. "Are we still talking about farming?"

"Don't." The warning in my voice is clear, but Finn's never been good at backing down.

"I'm just saying, maybe if you gave him a chance—"

"To what? Show me how much better he can do my job?" I laugh, but there's no humor in it. "I've spent fifteen years building something here, Finn. Something real. Something that works. I don't need Bastian or his 'interesting ideas' to tell me how to do it better."

"No one's saying you do." Finn's voice softens, and somehow that's worse than his arguments. "But collaboration isn't the same as competition."

"Easy for you to say. You're not the one who'll have to watch him waltz back in like he never left, like he didn't—" I stop myself, the words sticking in my throat.

The silence that follows is heavy with everything I'm not saying. Finn watches me with too much understanding, and I have to look away from the sympathy in his eyes. On the wall behind him, there's a faded photograph of two teenage boys sitting on a tractor, guitars in their laps, matching grins on their faces. I force my gaze back to my beer before the memories can take root.

"He's going to need help," Finn says finally, his voice gentle in a way that makes my teeth ache. "Whether he admits it or not."

"Then he should hire help. That's what normal farmers do when they need extra hands."

"Tay—"

"I mean it, Finn." I meet his eyes again, letting him see the steel beneath my surface. "Whatever grand plans Bastian has for revolutionizing farming in our little corner of Vermont, he can implement them without my input. I've got my own land to worry about."

Finn's phone lights up again, and this time when he glances at it, his expression shifts. It appears our time together is coming to an end.

"Just…try to keep an open mind?" he asks, though it's more a plea than a question. "For the community's sake, if nothing else."

I don't answer, but my silence says enough. Finn sighs and picks up his phone again. I sip my drink while he pays attention to the world outside these walls.

I swear he's hooking up with someone, but no matter how hard I've tried to figure out who, the man is like a closed vault.

He pockets his phone and turns to me, his expression apologetic.

"Go do your thing," I say. "I should head home anyway. Got an early morning tomorrow."

He pauses halfway through standing, his expression softening into something I don't want to examine too closely. "One day you're going to tell me about this beef you have with my brother."

"Today is not that day."

My best friend lets out a resigned sigh before leaving me for a better offer. I'd probably do the same if sex with anyone was on the table.

I put my hand in my pocket to pull out my wallet when

my fingers brush against the old guitar pick I still carry out of habit, smooth from years of worry.

"Last call." Joe's voice breaks through my reverie.

I tuck the pick back into my pocket and put enough money on the bar to cover the tab. "Thanks, Joe."

He nods. I walk away, steadier than I probably should be after… How many beers? I've lost count, but it doesn't matter. I've got work tomorrow, fields to tend, and the return of the man I've been in love with since forever to not think about.

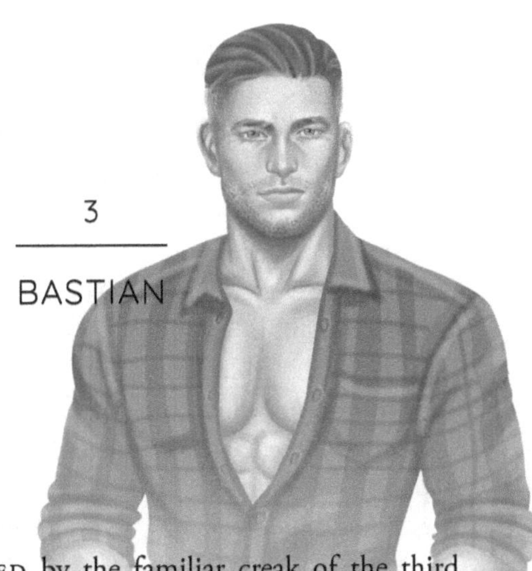

3

———

BASTIAN

MY YAWN IS SILENCED by the familiar creak of the third floorboard.

Home.

I could get it fixed, but I'd miss the sound as much as I hate hearing it every time I step on it, especially in the morning when every sound is amplified.

I move through to the farmhouse kitchen, ignoring the expensive coffee maker I bought for my parents last Christmas in favor of the old percolator. Stone is the only one who uses the machine to make all kinds of fancy coffee when he's around, which is reason enough to keep it.

The percolator gurgles to life, the coffee's aroma already beginning to chase away the lingering ghosts of sleep, when the floorboards announce my parents' approach. Mom's gentle footsteps, then Dad's slower, more measured tread. The change in his gait reminds me that he's one of the reasons I'm here.

"You're up early again," Mom says, like she has every day for the last two weeks.

"Farm schedule," I reply, reaching for three mugs without being asked. "Some habits stick with you for life."

Dad eases himself into his chair at the kitchen table, trying to hide the wince that crosses his weathered features. I pretend not to notice, just like I pretend not to see the way Mom's hand brushes his shoulder in silent support.

"That's not what you used to say when I had to drag you out of bed as a teenager," Dad says, accepting the coffee I place before him.

I sit at the table across from him with my own steaming cup. "It's been a while since I was one of those."

"I suppose that crazy schedule when you're on tour has kept you on your feet." He pauses and then looks straight at me. "Speaking of which, when's the next one?"

My jaw tightens. I wrap my hands around my own mug, feeling the heat seep into my palms. "The band's on hiatus. I told you."

"Hiatus isn't the same as finished, Sebastian."

I hate it when he full names me like I'm thirteen and need to be reminded that tractors aren't toys, like I've ever not fully respected the farm and our way of living.

"The farm needs consistency. Regular hands, regular schedule," he continues.

"Which is exactly what I'm offering." The coffee burns my tongue, but I welcome the sharp sensation.

"Honey," Mom starts, her voice gentle in that way that always precedes difficult truths. "We just want to make sure you've thought this through. The spotlight, the music… They've been your life for so long. We can always hire—"

"I've been a part of this family and this farm for much longer. The farm, the animals, the land, it's in my blood. The music was a dream I never expected to happen. I'm grateful for the life I've had, but it's okay to want a change." To need a change.

Dad's grunt tells me exactly what he thinks of that statement. I catch the look my parents exchange, heavy with years of complicity and love.

"I'm here to stay," I say, softer now but no less determined. "I know you have doubts. But this isn't temporary."

"If you're sure, son," Dad says.

"It'll be nice having you here for the holidays," Mom adds and then stands, placing her cup in the sink and walking toward the pantry. "Time to let out my frustrations on bread dough."

I laugh. "Mom, you're the most chill person I know."

"That's because I bake every day."

My dad raises his cup to drink his coffee, hiding his smile.

"And I should get going." I stand and place my mug next to Mom's in the sink. "Dad, I'll see you in the office later, okay?"

"Sure thing, boss."

I grab my coat and head outside, trying to remember that this change must be hard for him too. Even though he knows he needs to slow down, it's not easy breaking the habits of a lifetime, especially when he'd expected me to join him in running the business much earlier.

I might be twenty-five years late, but I'm here.

The snow crunches beneath my boots, each step leaving a print in the fresh powder. I fill my lungs with fresh air.

We're mostly a dairy farm, so the closer I get to the barn, the less fresh the air smells, but there's always an underlying scent of apple, thanks to the orchard next door.

The barn looms ahead, its familiar silhouette a darker shadow against the lightening sky.

I hum one of my favorite songs from our last album. One that's about coming home. I wrote it with Mik before everything changed. It's about finding home everywhere we are, as long as our people are with us. Little did we know.

A small shape materializes from a gap between the fence posts, and I stop short. A goat—a goat?—stands in my path, its white coat almost invisible against the snow except for a ridiculous red ribbon tied around its neck. The animal regards me with an expression that can only be described as smug.

"Where did you come from?" I ask, and it responds with a bleat that sounds suspiciously like laughter and trots forward to headbutt my leg with surprising gentleness.

That's when I notice the tag dangling from the ribbon. I crouch, already narrowing the list of possible culprits to a single person.

Gouta—because every wannabe farmer needs a
GOAT mentor.

"Very funny, Taylen," I say to the empty air. The goat—Gouta, apparently—bleats again and presses against my hand like a demanding cat.

I stand, intending to continue my walk to the barn, but Gouta has other ideas. She follows at my heels, her tiny hooves leaving delicate prints alongside my boot tracks.

"Go home," I tell her, trying to sound stern. She responds by skipping ahead of me, then turning to wait with what I swear is an expectant expression. "Your dad is on the other side of that fence," I add, already knowing it's pointless.

Despite myself, my eyes are drawn to her coat, checking for signs of neglect or poor health. She's clearly well-fed, her coat thick and healthy for the winter weather. Trust Taylen to make even his pranks are impeccably responsible.

"Fine," I sigh as we reach the barn door. "But don't think

this means you're staying." Gouta prances in place, her hooves leaving little dance steps in the snow. I fight back a smile, already knowing I'm fighting a losing battle. "And don't tell Taylen I said that."

The goat's answering bleat sounds like a promise she has no intention of keeping.

The barn door slides open with a familiar groan, releasing a rush of warm air scented with hay and livestock.

I remove my glove and run my hand along the nearest stall, feeling the worn wood beneath my fingers. The grain is smooth from years of use, but I notice spots where the finish has worn away, leaving the wood vulnerable to moisture. Another item for my growing list of things to fix.

Gouta follows as I move deeper into the barn, her presence oddly comforting in the quiet morning air. She pauses when I do, as if she's conducting her own inspection.

"Water trough needs cleaning," I murmur, more to myself than my small companion. The goat bleats in agreement. "And that hinge is going to need replacing before it gives out entirely."

A soft cough draws my attention to one of the stalls. Inside, Buttercup, one of our younger calves, stands with her head slightly lowered. I approach slowly, speaking in low tones.

"Hey there, beautiful." My hand finds the spot behind her ears that she loves, and she leans into the touch. "That doesn't sound too good, does it?"

The cough doesn't sound serious, probably just the dry winter air, but I'll keep an eye on it in case it gets worse. Maybe I'll call the new vet anyway. It'll give me a chance to meet him.

Next door, Daisy pokes her head over the stall door, demanding her share of attention. Her sister Clover follows suit from across the aisle, and suddenly I'm surrounded by eager faces and hopeful moos.

"Yes, yes, I see you all." I move from stall to stall, greeting each by name, checking water levels and feed supplies, and topping up where needed. My body falls into the rhythm of the work, and I only pause when I remember to turn on the old radio my dad keeps in the barn because he insists the cows love the morning shows.

The insulation above the north stalls is showing signs of wear. More items for the list. The draft isn't bad now, but it will be once real winter hits. I pull out my phone and start making notes: insulation, hinge replacement, water system cleaning. The list grows, but instead of feeling overwhelming, it feels right. These are problems I know how to solve.

A soft headbutt against my leg reminds me I'm not alone. Gouta looks up at me with dark eyes that are too knowing for a goat.

"What do you think?" I ask, reaching down to scratch between her horns. "Think we can get this all done before Thanksgiving?"

She responds by leaning into my touch, her presence steady and unexpectedly reassuring.

"Yeah," I say, patting her head one final time. "I think we can too."

The morning light streams through the high windows now, casting long beams across the barn floor. It's time to let the girls out into the pasture.

I unlatch the heavy gate that leads to the pasture and then swing it wide. The cows file out in their usual order, Daisy first as always, followed by Clover and the rest. Gouta dances around their legs excitedly, clearly hoping for some playful interaction, but the massive animals barely acknowledge her presence as they lumber toward the frosted grass.

I see him before he sees me as I'm closing the gate. A dark figure leaning against the fence line, his posture too carefully casual to be accidental. The morning sun catches in his hair, turning the brown strands almost golden.

Gouta trots ahead of me, betraying our approach with an excited bleat. Taylen's head turns, and I watch his expression shift from genuine warmth at the sight of the goat to something more neutral when his eyes meet mine.

"Didn't expect to see you still here after two whole weeks," he calls out as I approach. "You're usually gone by now."

The words sting more than they should, probably because there's truth in them, but it's also not a fair comment. I came home as often as I could, and definitely more than all of my band mates together, since the farm became the unofficial Hall of Fame safe retreat from the public eye.

I stop a few feet from the fence, close enough to see the stubble on his jaw, the way his light-blue eyes catch the sunlight.

"Things change," I say, aiming for casual but hearing the defensive edge in my voice.

"Do they?" His smile doesn't reach his eyes. "Or do they just look different for a while before going back to how they've always been?"

Gouta headbutts my leg before trotting over to Taylen's side of the fence. Traitor.

"This goat's probably got more farming experience than you do," he says, reaching down to scratch behind her ears before picking her up like she's a baby. The movement pulls his Henley tight across his shoulders, and I force my eyes away. Why is he not wearing a coat like a sensible human?

"You don't know anything about my experience," I counter, stepping closer to the fence. The air between us feels charged. I know why, but regardless of what's in the past, we used to sort of be friends.

"I know enough." His voice drops lower, and something in his tone makes my skin prickle. "I know farming takes more than money and good intentions. It takes staying power."

"You think I don't know that?" The words come out sharper than intended. I take a deep breath to stop myself from saying something I'll regret later.

He looks up then, and for a moment, our eyes lock. The morning sun casts shadows across his face, highlighting the stubborn set of his jaw, the slight part of his lips. Heat that has nothing to do with anger coils in my stomach, and I have to remember who he is.

"I'm not going anywhere, Taylen. Get used to seeing me across this fence."

His eyes narrow slightly, and I see something flash across his face. Frustration, maybe, or something else entirely. The moment stretches between us, taut as a wire.

Gouta's sudden bleat breaks the tension. Taylen puts her back on the ground, and she bounces between us, head held high as if proud of her intervention. Despite everything, I find myself fighting back a smile.

"Keep the goat," Taylen says, pushing off from the fence. "She's got good instincts about people. Usually." He turns to leave, then pauses. "Try not to prove her wrong."

I watch him walk away, my weak eyes noticing the way his jeans frame the perfect shape of his ass from his narrow waist to the thickness of his thighs.

"I didn't mean it like that, J," I whisper, looking up at the sky, hoping that wherever he is, my best friend won't start haunting me for appreciating what years of hard work have done for his brother.

Gouta presses against my leg, and I reach down to pat her head absently.

"Don't worry," I tell her, my voice carrying across the silent field. "I won't prove you wrong."

4

———

TAYLEN

MY MUSCLES SCREAM at me as I walk the shortcut between my land and the Halls', toward their farmhouse.

Serves me right for channeling all my restless energy into work after my encounter with Bastian this morning.

The basket of apples Sylvie asked for weighs heavy in my arms. Macintosh and Honeycrisp, handpicked for one of my favorite people in the whole world.

My fingers flex around the basket handle, already numb despite my gloves. The split-rail fence emerges through the light snowfall, weathered wood marking the boundary between their land and mine. I used to hop that fence daily as a kid, racing my brother to the old oak tree that stands near the corner.

Even with our twelve-year age gap, Jackson always made me feel like we were best friends. He was the kind of big brother who made time to teach me all the things our dad taught him.

Somewhere on the tree, initials are carved into the bark. J.H. and B.H. for Jackson Howard and Bastian Hall.

When I was thirteen and Bastian came home from one of

31

his tours, he brought me a present from Europe. A snow globe with a camera inside. Photography was my obsession at that age, and I'd been shocked that Bastian had remembered such a small detail from a kid who was just his best friend's younger brother.

Of course that turned my small crush into a new obsession. After Bastian left a couple of weeks later, I added my initials to theirs.

I used to think that having the same initial in my surname as Bastian was a sign that we were meant to be together. When Jackson saw it weeks later, he teased me endlessly about it, but he never broke the promise he made to not tell Bastian.

Sometimes I wonder what it would be like if we were running the farm together, if he were still here and not buried on the north side of the orchard.

I push those thoughts away as I approach the farmhouse. The Halls never lock their door during daylight hours—never have, probably never will. That trust in their community and neighbors is part of what makes them who they are.

I close my eyes, drawing in a breath. Somewhere inside, Bastian is probably moving through the rooms like he never left, like twenty-five years of absence can be erased by good intentions and a change of address. The thought makes my fingers tighten around the basket handle until the wood creaks in protest.

I put my hand against the door, knowing all it needs is a little push to open. This isn't about Bastian or the past or the way my stomach knots every time I see him across a fence line. I'm just here to bring Sylvie the apples she asked for, something I've done countless times since I was a kid.

I push the door and step inside, leaving the quiet of the snow-covered world behind.

The kitchen is filled with the scent of cinnamon and

coffee. Sylvie stands at the counter, her hands dusted with flour, while Bastian leans against the sink in that casual way that draws my eyes to his bulging arm muscles and makes my mouth water despite my brain's protests. Their conversation drops away as I enter, but not before I catch the thread of it.

"I knew they wouldn't stay away from your cooking for long," Bastian is saying. "Stone's already asking about your apple pie."

I clear my throat, announcing my presence properly. "Speaking of apples..." I lift the basket slightly, drawing Sylvie's attention.

"Oh, Taylen!" Her face lights up as she wipes her hands on her apron. "Perfect timing. I was just telling Bastian about our plans for Thanksgiving." She gives me a hug. "Which reminds me, you'll join us this year, won't you? The whole band's coming."

It's impossible to miss Bastian's subtle shift in posture. His shoulders draw back slightly, his weight shifting away from my direction.

"I wouldn't want to impose," I say, though with Bastian's reaction, I'm tempted to accept the invitation just to piss him off.

"Nonsense. You're family." The words land heavily on my chest. Family isn't a word I hear often these days, especially not when it includes me.

Ever since my parents retired to Florida years ago, it's been just me, and despite the frequent calls and their annual visit in the summer, sometimes it does feel like I don't have a family of my own.

I set the basket on the counter, taking the chance to steal another glance at Bastian. His jaw moves silently under his salt-and-pepper beard, the muscle there jumping like he's working extra hard to hold back words. "Well," I say, deliberately maintaining eye contact with him, "in that case, I'd love to come."

Sylvie claps her hands together, sending a small flour cloud into the air. "Wonderful! It'll be just like old times. A full house, everyone together."

Bastian pushes off from the sink. "I should check on the heifers," he says, but I wonder if it's just an excuse to leave. "Thanks for the apples, Taylen." My name sounds strange coming from his mouth, formal and distant.

"Any time," I reply, matching his tone. Our eyes meet briefly, and I catch something there, frustration maybe, or annoyance, before he looks away.

Sylvie watches him go, her expression softening into something that reminds me of my mom. "Okay, how about a slice of fresh cinnamon bread? I won't take no for an answer."

Knowing it's pointless to refuse, and because she's the closest I'll get to having a present parent, I take a seat at the large table.

Steam rises in delicate curls from the bread, carrying the scent of cinnamon and comfort across the kitchen table. Sylvie gives me the heel, my favorite piece since childhood, without asking, and a cup of steaming coffee.

"So," she says, settling into her chair with her own slice and mug, "tell me about your plans for the Thanksgiving market. I need the scoop so I can get my hands on your best stuff before everyone gets here." Her reading glasses hang from a chain around her neck, swinging slightly as she leans forward. "Griffin mentioned something about special ciders this year?"

I tear off a piece of bread, letting its warmth seep into my fingers. "Three new varieties. There's a spiced apple-pear that's been aging since September, and I've been experimenting with adding cranberries to the traditional hard cider." The bread melts on my tongue, perfect as always.

"Plus, a nonalcoholic mulled cider that I think the kids will like. Both pair nicely with one of your cheeses."

"I'll ask Griffin to place our stalls next to each other." She pauses, glancing around to make sure no one is listening. "Though I do hope he doesn't put us anywhere near Margaret Thornfield. That woman has been telling everyone who'll listen that her preserves are made from some ancient family recipe, when I know for a fact she bought those jars from the general store in Millbrook and just switched the labels."

I laugh as I eat another piece of my bread. Sylvie's not wrong about Margaret.

We sit in comfortable silence for a moment, the kitchen quiet except for the tick of the old wall clock. Sylvie's presence has always been like this, steady, nurturing. It's no wonder Hall of Fame is known for retiring to an *undisclosed* location in rural Vermont.

If only the public knew.

It's not even hard to not bump into them in town when they're around, but somehow, from the very start, there was this unspoken rule among the townspeople that Winterberry could be known for a lot of things, but not for hosting the biggest rock band in the country between tours.

"And the orchard?" she asks, pulling me out of my cinnamon bread and Bastian fog. "Everything ready for winter?"

"Almost. Got the last of the frost protection up yesterday. Just need to finish pruning the younger trees." I wrap my hands around the warm mug. "Jackson would laugh at how obsessive I've gotten about it all."

Her hand covers mine briefly, a touch so gentle it almost breaks me. "He'd be proud, honey. So proud."

I swallow hard against the sudden tightness in my throat. "Yeah, well, someone had to keep his dream alive."

Sylvie refills our cups without comment, letting the

moment settle. When she speaks again, her voice carries that particular mix of wisdom and kindness that's uniquely hers. "You're doing a great job of that. Just don't forget about your own dreams."

I consider her words for a moment. My dream was to run the orchard with Jackson and expand it. Grow the byproduct side, while he focused on the fruit and soil quality, and generally making sure that year after year, we have the best apples in the state.

"Sometimes dreams have to change."

She squeezes my hand again but doesn't say anything else.

When Bastian comes back into the house and goes straight up the stairs without saying a word, I make my excuses and leave.

My house greets me with shadows and silence. I don't bother flipping on the lights. Instead, I head up to my room and sit on the chair in the corner. The one that offers me a perfect view of the corner of the house next door, where Bastian's room used to be.

A light is on, but after all the renovations and additions they've made, I'm sure that room is no longer the same as I remember.

My house is smaller than the Halls', but somehow less cozy. Even while growing up there was never the permanent smell of baked bread or the warm light of a fireplace in the winter.

My mom is a great mom, but she was never a homemaker. She loved her job in town, and any time she was home, you could find her in the garden tending to her flowers. Cooking or baking was just a chore for her, one that I remember Jackson shared with her because he loved doing those things.

She hated the smell of wood burning, so we have a very

expensive heating system that I don't bother using now that it's just me in the house.

I should be exhausted. Twelve hours of pruning apple trees, repairing irrigation lines, and dealing with a broken sprayer should have me dead to the world by now. Instead, I'm sitting here wide awake, my body bone-tired but my mind racing like a dog chasing its own tail. The silence presses in from all sides, making the house feel bigger and emptier than it actually is. Maybe what I need isn't sleep. Maybe I need something quick and uncomplicated to burn off this restless energy. Something that doesn't require explanations or morning-after conversations. I reach for my phone on the nightstand.

The dating app's interface glows too bright in the dim room. I swipe left on a guy whose profile reads *Looking for my country boy*. Hard pass on the fetishization of farm life. Left on a shirtless gym selfie with no bio. Left, left, left.

I ignore the inbox because the least uncomplicated thing I could do tonight is hook up with someone I've been with before. No, thank you.

I close the app and stare at the screensaver. A photo of Jackson grinning, his baseball cap pushed back on his head, dirt smudged across one cheek.

"What would you say about all this?" I mutter to the image. "About your best friend coming home to stay, about me being invited to Thanksgiving dinner like nothing's changed?" I laugh, but it comes out hollow. "About me sitting here talking to a picture instead of having a life. Dating."

The photo offers no answers, just Jackson's frozen smile and the memories of everything we never got to say. I close the app and open my messages instead, quickly typing one to Finn before I can think better of it.

TAYLEN:

Need a drink. Meet at Joe's?

I push myself off the chair, grabbing my keys and wallet before I get a reply. Finn's my ride or die. He'll be there.

Hopefully, by the time I come back, tonight in a cab or tomorrow after crashing at Finn's, I'll be out of this weird funk that's been chasing me for weeks.

Or maybe Finn's right. Maybe I do need to talk about it. About Bastian, about Jackson, about all the hurt and regrets.

But first, I need a drink.

5

———

BASTIAN

THE HEAT of the shower pounds against my shoulders, but it does little to ease the deep ache in my muscles.

I brace my hands against the tile wall, letting the water cascade down my back.

There's being stage fit and farm fit. I've managed both most of my life, but damn, I'm starting to feel every single one of my forty-five years.

Gouta's bleats drift through the bathroom window, a sound that pierces what I'd hoped would be my first moment of solitude today. I left her in the barn with the cows just an hour ago, even made her a special bed of fresh hay, but apparently, she has other plans. Now she's out there calling for me like some sort of four-legged conscience. I can't decide if she's a gift or a taunt from Taylen—probably both, knowing him.

Taylen.

Huh, that man.

My mind is stuck on the way he looked this morning, leaning against the fence in just that Henley, like the cold couldn't touch him. Even with his hair sticking up every-

39

where when he came into the farmhouse kitchen with his apples, he couldn't have looked more like someone I'd happily have in my bed.

Twelve years younger and somehow, he makes me feel like the rookie, like I'm the one who needs to prove himself. This stupid attraction is inconvenient at best, inappropriate at worst. He's Jackson's little brother, for Christ's sake.

I turn off the water with more force than necessary. Water drips from my hair onto my bare shoulders as I step into my bedroom, towel secure around my waist.

The sight that greets me almost makes me jump. Gouta, whom I thought was outside, is currently curled like a white cloud on my pillow, looking entirely too pleased with herself.

"This is not a petting zoo," I tell her, trying to sound stern. She responds by stretching luxuriously across my pillow, her red ribbon—which she's refusing to let me take off—slightly askew. "The barn has perfectly good hay. Fresh, even."

She blinks at me with those oddly intelligent eyes, then settles deeper into my pillow. The moonlight catches her white coat, making her look almost angelic. That is, if angels were small, stubborn goats with boundary issues.

I sigh and cross to the bed, reaching out to scratch behind her ears. Her fur is soft under my fingers, and she leans into the touch with a contented sound that's almost a purr. "You're as bad as your dad," I murmur, then catch myself. Dad? If Taylen is her dad, what does that make me?

The last thing I need is to start thinking about Taylen while standing here in just a towel, so I move with purpose toward my dresser.

I pull out jeans and a flannel shirt, aware of Gouta's watchful gaze.

What I need right now is noise, conversation, something

to drown out the thoughts that keep circling back to this morning and Taylen's challenging smirk.

"Come on," I tell Gouta as I finish dressing. "You're going outside because I need some human company."

She bleats what sounds suspiciously like an argument and refuses to hop off the bed.

"Fine," I say, grabbing the pillow from under her. She follows me to the living room, where I place the pillow on my couch, prancing like this was her plan all along. "Please don't eat my stuff while I'm gone," I plead as I grab my coat and head to the door.

Joe's looks exactly the same as it did when I was finally allowed inside for my first alcoholic drink. Same neon beer signs, same scarred wooden bar, same people sitting on the same stools. The familiar scent of stale beer and wood polish wraps around me as I push through the door.

A chorus of greetings rises from the usual crowd. Not the screaming of fans, but the quiet acknowledgment of neighbors. Old Jim raises his glass from his perpetual spot at the end of the bar, while the Peterson sisters pause their eternal argument about fence lines to wave. I love this as much as I love the cheering of the fans.

"The usual?" Joe asks, already reaching for a glass.

"The usual," I reply, settling onto a barstool that feels like it's been waiting for me.

Ellie from the feed store leans over, her gray hair escaping its practical bun. "How're those Holstein heifers settling in? And I heard you switched to that new mineral supplement for the milking herd."

The conversation flows easily into talk of milk production and feed costs. Nobody here cares about platinum records or stadium tours. Here, I'm just another farmer trying to keep my herd healthy and productive.

Joe slides a bowl of peanuts my way, his movement practiced and smooth. "Good to have you back properly," he says, voice gruff with sincerity. "Place needs more young blood taking up the old ways."

"Thanks, Joe."

He waves me off. "Anyway, don't want to keep you. You're probably here for Finn."

The sound of familiar laughter draws my attention to a corner booth, where Finn and Taylen huddle over what looks like far too many empty glasses. Taylen's head is thrown back, his throat exposed in a way that makes my mouth go dry. His usual sharp edges have been softened by alcohol, making him look younger, more like the kid I remember.

Finn leans close, his hand on Taylen's arm. Are they… together?

It's none of my business, but I don't recall my brother ever mentioning that he's seeing someone, or even the last time he mentioned a guy. My mom would have spilled the beans by now. Right? *Especially* if Finn and Taylen were together.

I chew the salty peanuts, trying to ignore them, but my eyes keep going back to the same corner. So much for coming out to find some inner peace and good conversation.

Taylen waves off whatever Finn's saying, his movements loose and uncoordinated. His Henley has slipped to reveal the edge of a tattoo I can't make out from this distance. I watch as he reaches for his glass again, missing slightly before correcting.

Finn's protectiveness is obvious in the way he shifts closer, trying to block Taylen from the rest of the bar's view. But Taylen just laughs again, the sound brittle and wrong, and signals for another round.

My feet are moving before I think too hard about it. Whatever's going on, whatever's driven Taylen to drink himself into this state, I can't just watch from the sidelines.

Not when he's Jackson's little brother. Not when he's…whatever he is to my brother.

Finn spots me first, relief flooding his features. "Bastian, perfect timing," he says, cutting off whatever Taylen was about to say.

Taylen's head swivels toward me, his eyes taking too long to focus. "Well, if it isn't the progi…pro…prodi…gal… prodigal farmer," he drawls, words slurring slightly.

"Tay," Finn warns, but Taylen just laughs, the sound sharp and hollow. "It's time for you to go home."

"Sssnot. Ssstime for another round. I want the Christmas beer because it's my favrorite."

Finn sighs and turns to me. "He can't drive like this. Usually, he'd crash with me, but that's not possible right now. Can you take him home?"

I step close enough to smell the beer on Taylen's breath. "Sure."

"I don't need a babysitter," Taylen argues, but his attempt to stand ends with him grabbing the table for balance.

"No," I agree, reaching out to steady him. "But you do need a ride."

His body is warm against mine as I help him up, and I try not to think about how perfectly he fits against my side. If he's my brother's boyfriend, I definitely need these thoughts to take a long walk off a short pier. It's one thing to stay away from Taylen to respect someone who isn't here, but another to consider the feelings of someone who is very much here and who I would do anything for.

Finn mouths a silent "thank you" as he gathers his things, already pulling out his phone. "Don't worry about his truck," Finn says. "I'll have someone bring it by in the morning."

"Sure. Does he have a coat?" I ask.

Finn looks at me and shakes his head like he's had this conversation too many times.

I slip off my coat and drape it around Taylen's shoulders.

"'M not cold," Taylen protests, but he doesn't shrug it off. The coat hangs loose on his smaller frame, sleeves covering his hands completely.

"Sure you're not," I murmur, keeping one arm around his waist as we navigate toward the door. He stumbles slightly, and I tighten my grip. "Easy there."

Getting him into the truck proves to be an exercise in patience and upper-body strength. He's all loose limbs and uncoordinated movements, like a puppet with half its strings cut.

"Seatbelt," I remind him once he's finally settled, but his coordination is shot. I lean across him to pull the belt across his chest, trying not to notice how his breath catches or the way his eyes track my movements.

"You smell good," he says quietly, so close I can feel the words against my ear. "Like…like wood smoke and something else."

I close the passenger door and lean against the truck for a second. The chill of the night doesn't do much to stop my body's reaction to being so close to him.

You need to get a fucking grip, Sebastian.

I take a deep, steadying breath and go around the truck to the driver's seat.

As I start the engine, Taylen slumps against the window and pulls my coat tighter around his body. Is he sniffing it?

The drive passes in relative silence, broken only by Taylen's occasional mumbles and the soft country station playing on the radio. I keep glancing over at him, worried he might get sick, but he just stares out at the passing streetlights.

As I focus on the road ahead, my mind goes into a different space.

The last time I was at Taylen's house was the day I left for a tour and went to say goodbye to my best friend. That was the last time I saw Jackson. Every time I think of that day, I wish I'd given him a tighter hug, looked into his eyes a little longer. Fuck, I wish for things that have no point being wished for because nothing could have changed what happened.

The memory sits heavy in my chest as I pull onto the shared track leading to the farms. Taylen's breathing has evened out beside me, his face peaceful in a way it never is when he's awake.

I debate the right call. Taking him home means dealing with pain I'm not ready to face. But the alternative…

The truck's headlights cut through the darkness as I make my decision.

Taylen shifts in his seat, head lolling against the window, and something in my chest tightens at how vulnerable he looks.

The familiar curves of the farm road appear ahead, lined with snow-dusted trees that glow silver in the moonlight.

My parents' farmhouse comes into view, but before I get there, I take a turn to my place. The cabin is my sanctuary. Even my band brothers don't come in when they're on the farm. Bringing someone inside, especially the next-door neighbor who seems to have a beef with me, I must be out of my mind.

I park the truck and cut the engine, letting silence settle around us. Taylen's breathing, steady and deep, is the only sound in the stillness.

I unlock the front door and turn the lights on before going back to the truck to get Taylen. Surprisingly, he's a little more cooperative this time. Probably because he's half-asleep.

Somehow, he manages to use the bathroom on his own,

but when he comes out, he's wearing nothing but his boxer shorts.

Gouta's bleat draws me out of my stupefied state as I unashamedly ogle Taylen's body. The way his broad chest tapers to a slim waist, the tattoos he has scattered all over his chest and arms. It shouldn't come as news to me that the kid I remember chasing me and his brother around the farm is very much no longer a kid.

In fact, I know how much he is no longer a kid.

Oblivious to my thoughts, Taylen lies down on my bed and pulls the covers over his body, muttering, "Goodnight, rockstar," before a soft snore fills the silence. Gouta jumps on the bed and curls up against Taylen.

I turn the light out and head to the living room. At least I won't have to share the couch.

6

———

TAYLEN

My skull feels like it's being split open with an axe, each throb a new strike against bone. The unfamiliar mattress beneath me is too soft, the blanket too heavy, the morning light streaming through unknown windows too bright. Everything feels wrong, including the fact that I'm wearing nothing but my underwear in a strange wooden room that smells of pine and coffee.

I groan and press my palms against my eyes, trying to piece together the fragments of last night. There was Joe's Bar, Finn's concerned face, too many beers, and then…nothing. Just a black hole where my memory should be. The room spins slightly as I attempt to sit up, my stomach lurching in protest.

The walls around me are bare wood, unfinished but smooth, giving the space a cabin feel. Through the window, I see snow-covered fields stretching toward the tree line. Familiar territory, but from an angle I don't recognize.

My clothes are nowhere in sight, and panic starts to creep in around the edges of my hangover. Where the hell am I? This isn't Finn's guest room with its wall of vintage concert

47

posters. This isn't my house with its perpetual smell of apples and cider. This is…

The sound of footsteps makes me freeze. Heavy boots on wooden floors, coming closer. I clutch the blanket tighter, suddenly very aware of my near-naked state, as a figure appears in the doorway.

Bastian fills the frame, wearing a red-and-black checked shirt that stretches across his shoulders in a way that makes my mouth go dry despite my cottony hangover. His jeans, perpetually worn through at the knees, fit him like they were painted on. He looks exhausted, with dark circles shadowing his eyes, his usual perfect posture slightly slumped.

"Where am I?" My voice comes out rough, like I've been gargling gravel.

He leans against the doorframe, crossing his arms. The movement pulls his shirt tighter, and I force my eyes back to his face. "My place," he says simply.

"Your…" I blink, trying to process this information through the fog in my brain. "This isn't your place."

He shifts his weight, and I catch a flash of something in his expression. Defensiveness, maybe, or irritation. "I own my place. I should know what it looks like."

My thoughts tumble around in my head, pieces of memories I can't quite assemble.

"Did we…?" I start, then stop, unsure how to phrase the question burning in my throat. "I mean, did anything happen…last night?"

"Like what?"

"Like…?" I point at me and then at him.

His expression shifts from tired to annoyed in an instant. "It shouldn't surprise me that you think I'd take advantage of someone that drunk, but then again, you do have a habit of underestimating me."

He turns and disappears from my line of sight, returning

a moment later with a mug of coffee and two white pills that he places on the bedside table with more force than necessary. The coffee sloshes slightly, a few drops escaping onto the wooden surface.

"Take those, drink the coffee. Gouta wants to see you. I have work to do. See yourself out," he says, already turning away.

Before I can say anything else, he's gone, his footsteps echoing down the hall.

I stare at the coffee cup, steam rising in lazy spirals. The mug is plain white ceramic, utilitarian, nothing like the collection of band-themed mugs his mother keeps in the main house. This space feels almost deliberately different.

My head throbs again, a reminder that I'm still very much hungover and possibly still a little drunk. I reach for the pills, trying not to think about the possibility of Bastian's hands on me last night, removing my clothes while I was passed out. Trying not to imagine him carrying me to this bed, or sleeping just a room away while I was nearly naked under his blankets.

I'm not sure these are memories I want in my head, so I grab the cup.

The coffee is perfect. Strong and black with a little sugar, exactly how I like it. Of course he would get my coffee right. Little Mr. Perfect.

I take a sip and close my eyes, letting the warmth spread through my chest. The pine scent is stronger now, mixing with the coffee aroma and something else. A smell I *do* remember from last night. Bastian.

This is his space, his sanctuary, and I'm an intruder here.

The thought sits heavy in my stomach, alongside the whiskey and regret from last night. I need to get out of here, need to put distance between myself and this room that smells like him, this bed where he laid me down, these walls that have seen a side of him I'm not meant to know.

But first, I need to stop feeling like my head is going to explode. I swallow the pills and sink back against the pillows, telling myself the lingering warmth in my chest is just from the coffee.

The click of hooves on hardwood makes me look up just as Gouta trots through the open doorway like she owns the place, her red ribbon slightly askew. She spots me and lets out a pleased bleat before launching herself onto the bed with the grace of a much smaller animal.

"Easy there." I laugh despite my headache as she head-butts my shoulder affectionately. "Look at you, acting all domesticated. You're supposed to be teaching Bastian about farming, not learning house-pet manners."

She settles against my side, warm and solid, her presence oddly comforting in this unfamiliar space.

"I'm a legend," I tell her, running my hand along her soft fur. "Spent weeks training you to be the perfect farm menace, and instead, you've gone and turned into a lap dog. Jackson would never let me live this down."

Her only response is to press closer, demanding more attention. The coffee and pills are starting to take effect, the sharp edges of my hangover softening into something more manageable. I spot my clothes from last night folded neatly on a chair by the window.

"Come on, girl," I say, gently nudging Gouta aside so I can stand.

My legs are steadier than I expected as I cross to the chair and pull on my jeans. They smell faintly of laundry detergent. The thought of Bastian doing laundry while I slept makes me uncomfortable in ways I don't examine too closely.

Once dressed, I take in the rest of the cabin properly. The bedroom opens directly into an open-plan living space, the kitchen along one wall flowing into a modest living room centered around a massive stone fireplace. The stones look old, like they might have been salvaged from somewhere else on the property, each one unique and weathered.

The kitchen is sparse but functional, full of high-quality basics without any of the fancy gadgets I would expect someone like him to have.

Someone like him.

Rich? Successful? Used to the good things in life?

I'm starting to think I don't actually know Bastian, or what someone *like him* is like.

A French press sits in pride of place on the counter, alongside a grinder full of fresh beans. No dishwasher, just a deep farmhouse sink beneath a window that looks out toward another building. That must be the recording studio Finn told me about.

Gouta follows as I move through the space. The living room furniture is simple but comfortable-looking, with a deep leather couch that's seen better days, a reading chair angled toward the fireplace, and a coffee table that looks handmade.

What catches my eye is what's missing. There's no television, no laptop, none of the usual trappings of modern life.

The walls hold a few framed photographs of the band in their early days, all baby faces and big dreams, a shot of the whole Hall family at Christmas, maybe ten years ago, and one of Jackson and Bastian on the old tractor, guitars in hand. The same one that hangs proudly at Joe's.

My throat tightens at that one. I remember taking it, remember Jackson asking me to redo it over and over again, while Bastian pretended to be annoyed at having to pose.

Also noticeably absent are any signs of Bastian's success. No platinum records, no awards, no magazine covers. It's like he's created a space deliberately separate from that part of his life.

This is the perfect place to build his life. Close enough to his family but with some separation. I don't want to think about Bastian bringing men here, but the image forms unbidden in my mind. Bastian pressing some nameless man against that leather couch, those capable hands sliding under clothes, that mouth… My phone rings, startling me out of thoughts I definitely shouldn't be having.

Finn's name flashes on the screen, and I've never been more grateful for his terrible timing. Gouta headbutts my leg as I answer, clearly annoyed that I've stopped petting her.

"You're alive." Finn's voice comes through, tinged with equal parts relief and amusement. "I was starting to worry."

I sink onto the couch, trying not to think about who else might have sat here, what might have happened on these cushions. "Barely," I mutter, scratching Gouta's ears as she settles at my feet. "So why exactly didn't I crash at your place last night?" I keep my voice casual, but I know I'm not sober enough to get away with it.

Finn's pause lasts a beat too long. "Work stuff."

"At midnight?" I press, remembering fragments of last night—Finn checking his phone repeatedly, wearing the concerned look he gets when he's trying to manage too many situations at once.

"Um…" he starts, and I can picture him running a hand through his hair the way he does when he's uncomfortable. "I'm having some work done, and the place is a mess. Last thing I needed was you stepping on a rusty nail in the middle of the night and getting some…um…rusty infection."

I pretend that I believe him because my head hurts too much. "You could have just said that," I mutter. "Instead of pawning me off on your brother."

"First of all, you weren't pawned off. Bastian offered. And

second"—his voice softens slightly—"maybe it wasn't the worst thing to have someone looking out for you last night. You were in pretty rough shape, Tay."

I grunt noncommittally, refusing to examine too closely why I was drinking so heavily in the first place. "I don't even remember seeing him at the bar."

"He came in late. You were…enthusiastically explaining your theories about sustainable farming to anyone who'd listen."

Heat creeps up my neck. "Please tell me I didn't try to lecture Bastian about farming."

Finn's laugh does nothing to ease my embarrassment. "No, but you did tell Old Jim that his fence-line theories were, and I quote, 'more outdated than your flannel collection.'"

"Christ." I press my free hand against my eyes. "I'm never drinking again."

"That's what you said last time," Finn reminds me, then his tone turns serious. "Look, I've got to run. You going to be okay?"

"Yeah." I sigh, standing as Gouta protests the loss of her pillow. "Thanks for…you know."

"That's what friends are for. Even if sometimes being a friend means calling in backup."

We end the call, and I pocket my phone, taking one last look around the cabin.

Outside, the air is crisp enough to soften the remaining edges of my hangover.

There are no signs of Bastian, so I allow my curiosity to take me toward the recording studio. The building is a modern structure with large windows. It looks out of place next to the rustic cabin.

The windows are clear enough to see inside. A guitar rests on the couch, papers scattered across a desk, coffee cups on every available surface. Signs of recent and regular use that make my jaw clench. So much for coming back to be a full-time farmer.

"All for show," I mutter, turning away from the evidence of Bastian's real priorities. "Just like everything else."

Movement near the barn catches my attention. Bastian's tall frame is easy to spot, his shoulders set in that familiar line as he works. The cows are out in the pasture, which means he's probably doing the morning cleaning.

He straightens as I approach, wiping his hands on his jeans. Those gray eyes meet mine, and for a moment, I forget what I came here to say, distracted by the way the morning light catches the growing silver in his hair.

"Thanks," I force out, my voice colder than the air between us. "For last night."

His eyebrows draw together slightly. "You already said that."

"Did I? Must have been too drunk to remember." The words come out sharp, pointed. "Kind of like how I must be too drunk to notice you're not exactly sticking to the whole 'full-time farmer' story."

"What's your problem?" He turns to face me fully, his height advantage more noticeable now that we're close.

"People who lie." I gesture toward the studio. "Especially people who claim they're here to stay while keeping their escape route well-maintained."

Something flashes in his eyes. "You don't know what you're talking about."

"Don't I?" I step close enough to smell his hay-and-leather scent. My neck hurts from looking up to meet his eyes. "I must have mistaken farm invoices and paperwork in your studio for music sheets. My bad."

His jaw tightens, and I see his hands clench at his sides. Good. Let him feel a fraction of the anger I've been carrying.

"You don't get to judge my choices," he says, voice low and controlled. "You don't know anything about why I'm here or what I'm doing."

"I know enough." I turn away, unable to look at him anymore without saying things I might regret. "Thanks again for the hospitality. Next time, just leave me in the truck."

I walk away without looking back, my boots leaving deep prints in the snow. Each step puts distance between us, but does nothing to ease the knot in my chest.

Behind me, I hear the barn door close with more force than necessary, and I tell myself the satisfaction I feel is because I've exposed his lies, not because I've managed to crack that perfect control of his.

I glance behind me, expecting to see Gouta following, but she's not there.

Traitor.

Just like my heart, which can't stop hoping that, for once, what it wants is within reach, only to get crushed over and over again.

Because Bastian is going to leave. Because he always leaves.

7

———

BASTIAN

I slam the post driver down with a satisfying thunk, sending vibrations up my arms. Each impact drives the fence post deeper into the frozen earth. This is the kind of back-breaking work I know I'm going to feel for the next few days.

I've picked the farthest corner of our property for this morning's work, where the tree line borders Mt. Philo State Park. As far from Taylen's orchard as I can get without actually leaving Hall land. The irony that I'm running away while trying to prove I'm here to stay isn't lost on me.

Sweat trickles down my back despite the November chill, my flannel shirt sticking uncomfortably between my shoulder blades. The physical strain feels good, necessary, and my muscles burn with each lift and drop of the driver.

"You know, you could help instead of just lying there judging my technique," I say to Gouta, who's sprawled across a bale of hay like she's holding court. Her red ribbon is somehow still perfectly attached in place despite her active morning of following me around the farm.

She bleats in response, shifting to a more comfortable position but making no move to actually assist.

"Right, I forgot. You're management now, not labor." I pause to wipe my forehead with the back of my glove. "Must be nice having job security while the rest of us actually work for a living."

Gouta's answering sound is distinctly unimpressed. She fixes me with those smart eyes that seem far too knowing for a goat, like she can see straight through all my pretenses to whatever's really driving me to work myself into the ground this morning.

"Don't give me that look," I mutter, returning to the fence post. "Some of us process things by doing actual work instead of lounging around looking judgmental."

Speaking of judgmental, Taylen's words—the ones I've been trying to drown out with heavy work for days—come back to me. His claim that I'm filling my days with farm work while plotting my escape in the evenings.

I laugh at that. My "escape route."

Thump

"If you'd bothered to ask questions instead of jumping to conclusions, you would have found out that those mugs are the result of too many late nights listening to demo recordings from local musicians who can't afford studio time."

Thump.

"Kids who dream of making it, just like I once did."

Thump.

"The scattered papers aren't contracts for my next tour, or sheet music, for that matter. They're notes about sustainable farming techniques I've been researching."

Thump.

"But *you* don't want explanations. *You* want me to be the villain in whatever story you've been telling yourself about me. It's easier for *you* to believe I'm just playing at being a farmer than to consider that maybe, just maybe, the hurt *you* feel, I'm feeling it too, dammit." I'm just too much of a coward to reach out.

I put the post driver down and stretch my back, staring into the Adirondack Mountains in the distance, and wondering if I have it in me to be the bigger person and reach out to Taylen to talk. An actual conversation kind of talk.

The crunch of tires on gravel pulls my attention from the view. A car weaves down the access road like the driver's either lost or is past the age when one should be driving.

I recognize Stone's driving style before I see him. No one else would treat a rental with such care. The car comes to a slow stop, and even Gouta bleats her disapproval. Stone emerges first, his designer boots instantly coated in mud.

"Shit," he mutters, staring down at his feet. "These boots cost more than most people's rent. Why does the countryside have to be so fucking messy?" He looks up at me, replacing his scowl with his trademark grin. "Surprise!"

Behind him, Nikko unfolds from the passenger seat.

"You're early," I say, but I'm already moving to meet them, the post driver forgotten in the snow. Stone pulls me into a hug that smells of expensive cologne.

"Mom's redecorating again," he explains, grimacing. "And you know I'm not compatible with dust. And this one"—he jerks a thumb at Nikko—"was wearing a hole in his apartment floor."

Nikko shrugs. "Empty calendar makes me twitchy. Plus, your mom's cooking beats takeout any day." Then he points at Gouta. "Who's that?"

"That's my new workplace supervisor. Pretty useless. Has an attitude and a fashion sense more exquisite than Stone's," I joke. Stone leans over to mock-punch me in the gut. "But she's cute, I guess. Her name's Gouta."

As if summoned, Gouta descends from her resting place and comes over like the lap dog she thinks she is.

"Oh my god, she's adorable," Nikko says.

Stone gets one look at Gouta and takes a deliberate step backward. "Nope. Absolutely not. I don't do farm animals. They're unpredictable and they smell."

But Gouta has already zeroed in on him like a heat-seeking missile. She trots right up to his expensive boots and begins investigating them with the thorough interest of a customs agent.

"Get it away from me," Stone says, his voice climbing an octave. "These are Italian leather."

"She's just being friendly," I say, trying not to laugh as Gouta starts nibbling at Stone's bootlaces. "She has excellent taste in accessories."

Nikko crouches and extends his hand. Gouta immediately abandons Stone's boots in favor of Nikko's attention, nuzzling against his palm like she's known him for years.

"Traitor," Stone mutters, then looks around at the scattered fence posts and tools. "So this is what you're getting busy with these days?"

"I am a farmer," I say, sounding more defensive than intended. "This is my life now."

"Right. Well, your life now needs coffee and central heating, so can we go inside? Or even better, let's hit Joe's. I can feel my extremities going numb."

I pick up the post driver and throw it into the back of my truck. "Where's Fox?"

Stone looks at Nikko and then back at me. "We thought he was here."

"Here?" I laugh. "Why would he be here?"

"He left California two weeks ago," Nikko says, his usual swagger dampened by concern. "Like he had ants in his pants that were busier than mine. Just packed his bags and took off."

The uneasy feeling in my gut grows. Fox is many things, but unpredictable isn't one of them. Twenty-five years of touring together, and I've never known him to make an impulsive move. Everything he does is calculated, considered.

"Did he say anything else?" I press, watching Nikko's face for a tell.

"Just that he'd see us at Thanksgiving," Nikko admits. "So he should be arriving any time now, I guess."

"I bet he's hooking up with someone," Stone says.

Nikko snorts. "My brother?"

"Just because he doesn't talk about the guys he fucks, like the rest of us, doesn't mean he's not getting any," Stone says, and I nod my agreement. Some people just happen to be private about their sex lives.

"Weren't we going to Joe's?" Nikko asks, changing the subject.

"Man, I'm starving. You know I don't do plane food, and the thought of Joe's wings is giving me a boner," Stone says, heading back to the rental. "We'll drop this at the house first. No way I'm paying the insurance deductible if someone dings it in Joe's parking lot."

I leave Gouta in my cabin, much to her protest, but I tell her it's the warm cabin or the barn, so she soon settles on the pillow that now lives on my couch just for her Goaty Highness. I drive over to pick up Stone and Nikko from the farmhouse.

I haven't been in town since the night I ended up bringing Taylen home, so I'm surprised to see Main Street's Christmas lights already strung between lampposts, despite it not even being Thanksgiving yet.

A figure near the bookstore catches my eye. Tall, lean,

with a distinctive black leather jacket. My heart jumps before my brain catches up.

"Did you see—" I start, but when I look again, the sidewalk is empty.

"See what?" Nikko asks.

"Nothing. It was probably my imagination." Because there's no way Fox would be in Winterberry without telling us. Where would he even stay, if not at the farmhouse?

I pull up at Joe's and push Fox's non-sighting from my mind.

When we get inside, Joe greets us with his familiar wave.

"Pick a booth," he calls out, already reaching for glasses. "I'll bring over some wings and your usuals."

"Make mine nonalcoholic," I add. "I'm driving."

We slide into our usual corner booth, the vinyl seats creaking in welcome. Stone immediately pulls out his phone, grimacing at whatever he sees on the screen. "Daisy's at it again," he says, and I already dread what our agent is up to now. "Three emails just today about studio time. The woman doesn't understand the concept of a break."

Nikko leans over to peek at the screen. "What's she pushing for now?"

"A studio album." Stone scrolls through the messages. "Apparently, we 'don't want to get forgotten.'" His air quotes drip with sarcasm.

Joe arrives with our drinks and a massive plate of wings.

"We're not deciding anything without everyone here," I say firmly, reaching for a wing. "That includes Fox and Mik."

Stone sets his phone face-down on the table. "Agreed. But Daisy won't wait forever."

"She'll wait," Nikko says with unexpected firmness.

The certainty in his voice surprises me, but he's right. We've earned the right to take this break, to figure out what comes next on our own terms. If only we could figure out what those terms are.

"The farm comes first right now," I admit, the words feeling right on my tongue. "Dad needs help with the transition, even if he won't admit it."

Stone nods understanding, but Nikko's look reminds me that this wasn't his choice.

"Anyway, what about Winterberry's holiday events?" Stone asks, clearly trying to change the subject. "This is my favorite season here. I don't want to miss the markets."

"You'll have to talk to Finn about that," I say, grateful for the shift in topic. "He's got his finger on every pulse in town. Pretty sure he knows what color underwear the mayor's wearing on any given day."

Stone's eyes light up with genuine interest. "Is he still running the winter festival? Because last year's mulled wine was incredible."

"Still running everything," I confirm.

"Can't wait for Thanksgiving," Stone says. "I've upped my workouts and been living on air to prepare for your mom's food." But then he picks up a chicken wing and sucks on it until he pulls out just the bone from his mouth.

"Course you have." I laugh. "Don't worry. Mom's making enough food for twenty people."

Nikko perks up. "The sage stuffing?"

"And Dad's smoked turkey," I add, watching them both light up like kids. "He's already prepping the wood chips."

"God, I've missed real holidays," Stone sighs. "LA Thanksgiving is all about who can serve the most pretentious organic free-range whatever. Give me Sylvie's cooking any day."

The warmth of their enthusiasm feels good. This is what we needed, a chance to remember who we are beyond the music, beyond the fame. A chance to just be us again.

The door to the bar swings open, letting in a burst of cold air and Taylen Howard. He pauses when he sees me, his expression freezing like the winter wind outside, before deliberately turning toward the bar.

He hands Joe some paperwork. Their conversation is too low to hear over the bar's usual noise. A moment later, Taylen disappears back outside, returning with a box full of glass jars, probably the apple butter or the chutney Mom raves about so much. Joe takes the box toward the kitchen with an approving nod, and a moment later, Joe's wife and bar chef, Barbara, comes out and gives Taylen a hug.

Taylen's gaze sweeps over our booth again as he turns to leave, but this time, his eyes lock onto mine with an intensity that makes the air between us crackle. The look he gives me is arctic, his light-blue eyes holding mine a beat too long. Probably cursing my presence in this world.

When I look away, Stone's eyes are on me.

"Well," Stone drawls once the door swings shut. "That was interesting."

"Shut up," I mutter, but Nikko's already leaning forward with a gleam in his eye that means trouble.

"Want to tell us what that was about?" he asks, his instincts clearly sensing a story.

"Nothing to tell." I drain my ginger ale, wishing it were something stronger. "Just neighbor stuff."

"Uh-huh." Stone smirks. "Is that what the kids are calling it these days?"

Their teasing is familiar, comfortable, but it can't quite ease the tension Taylen left behind.

Maybe that conversation needs to happen sooner rather than later.

When I get home to another one of Taylen's "well-intended" gifts, I'm of two minds about barging into his place and giving him a piece of my mind.

The only problem is that first I need to figure out where to keep the two heritage chickens in the fancy coop in the middle of my kitchen.

The label on the roof reads: *These ladies will teach you about responsibility.*

I turn to Gouta, who's staring at me like she's innocent in all this and slightly scared of our new roommates.

"This is your fault. You let him in, didn't you?"

8

———

TAYLEN

THE CROW SLICES through my dreams, dragging me into consciousness.

"What the fuck is that noise?"

The clock on my bedside table reads three-seventeen a.m. The sound comes again, more insistent.

I fumble for the flashlight I keep by my bed, nearly knocking over my water glass in the process. The room is cool without the central heat running. I rely on residual warmth from the living room fireplace filtering through the old vents, but it's not enough to chase away November's chill completely. I pull on sweatpants but don't bother with a shirt, grabbing the heavy winter coat that hangs by the door and zipping it over my bare skin as another crow pierces through the pre-dawn silence.

The November air bites at my face as I stumble across the yard toward the barn.

When I see the door unlocked, my heart rate spikes. We don't get many break-ins out here, but it's not unheard of. Thieves looking for equipment, tools, and anything they can fence. I curse myself for not grabbing something, a baseball

67

bat or a wrench, before rushing out here half-dressed and defenseless.

But the crowing continues, louder now, more insistent, and burglars don't usually leave livestock behind. Unless...

My suspicions are proven correct when I spot the note attached to the door of the closed-off section inside the barn where I keep my chickens during the winter months.

I snatch the note from the door, my relief at avoiding an actual break-in quickly replaced by irritation.

Meet Elvis. He's got strong opinions about every-thing. You should get along like a hen house on fire.

Inside the enclosed area, my hens huddle together on their roosts, looking thoroughly unimpressed with their new roommate. And there, strutting across the floor like he owns the place, is the source of my rude awakening, a magnificent Barred Rock rooster.

Elvis tilts his head to study me with one beady eye before letting loose another ear-splitting crow. My jaw clenches automatically.

"You might want to fix your internal clock to this time zone, my friend. I need another couple of hours of sleep, and you might want to make friends with the girls because they outnumber you."

Elvis raises his head in defiance, as though he couldn't give two shits about what I'm saying.

I'll admit this is a masterful counterplay. Perfectly legal, undeniably useful, and absolutely impossible to complain about without looking ungrateful.

"Well played, Bastian," I mutter as Elvis struts past me to inspect his new domain. "Well played."

A week later, my hands shake slightly as I arrange the last jar of apple butter, the glass catching the warm morning sunlight. Seven days of three a.m. wake-up calls have left me running on fumes and stubbornness, but I'll be damned if I let it show at the biggest market day of the year.

The market fills the town square, vendor stalls arranged in neat rows radiating out from the central gazebo where the Winterberry Senior Brass Band plays Christmas music. Steam rises from coffee cups, and breaths mingle with the crisp morning air. I straighten my display of Honeycrisps to keep busy. Whatever happens, I can't stop, or I might just fall asleep on my feet.

"You look like death warmed over, dear," Mrs. Whitaker observes as she inspects my cider selection. Her dark curls peek out from under a hand-knitted hat that probably predates my birth. "Not sleeping well?"

"Just pre-holiday preparations," I lie smoothly as she picks two bottles of cider and places a bunch of apples in a bag. "You know how it is this time of year."

She clucks her tongue, clearly unconvinced, but pays for her stuff and moves on. Around me, the market pulses with its usual energy. Kids darting between stalls, old-timers gathered by the mulled cider cart debating snow forecasts, vendors calling out their specials like carnival barkers at a county fair.

I stifle another yawn as I restock the empty spaces in my display. My muscles protest every movement, a week's worth of sleep deprivation settling into my bones like winter frost. But I maintain my professional smile, making change and small talk on autopilot while mentally calculating how many more hours until I can collapse into bed.

A young couple stops to sample my new spiced cider, and I launch into my practiced pitch about traditional mulling methods. My voice sounds strange in my ears, too bright and brittle, but they nod appreciatively and buy two bottles. Small victories.

The morning stretches on, marked by the steady stream of customers and the gradually emptying displays. I focus on each transaction with fierce determination, refusing to let Bastian's revenge tactic impact my business.

From the corner of my eye, I catch Sylvie bustling around her stall next to mine, her hands quick and efficient as she weighs out cheese, restocks milk bottles, and wraps squares of her famous home-churned butter. Her garden produce, winter squash, root vegetables, and preserved goods from her summer allotment create a colorful display that draws a steady line of customers.

Every few minutes, I feel her concerned gaze drift my way, but the constant flow of people buying her dairy products and vegetables keeps her too busy to come over and interrogate me properly.

Fuck, I'm tired. So tired that the coins in my cash box start to blur together, forcing me to count each transaction twice. So tired that I catch myself swaying slightly between customers, my body seeking rest even while standing. Still, I persist. Because that's what I do. I endure, I adapt, I overcome. Even if overcoming means surviving a week of predawn wake-up calls courtesy of an overly enthusiastic rooster named Elvis.

I'm rearranging my display after running out of apple butter when my ears pick up a name mentioned by someone in passing. I look up and spot them easily, thanks to Bastian's height. Mik is talking to him and holding hands with a guy who must be his boyfriend Tyler. Ahead of them, Kay greets the locals she knows from years of coming to Winterberry with her father.

My stomach does an uncomfortable flip that I blame on lack of sleep rather than the way Sebastian's expensive-looking coat stretches across his shoulders in a perfect fit. And it definitely has nothing to do with the way his permanently ripped jeans draw my eyes to the skin beneath.

Kay reaches my stall first, her face lighting up with genuine warmth. "Taylen!" She practically vibrates with excitement, her hands already reaching for the sample cups of cider. "How are you? Nan said we had to come try your new spiced cider. She says it's the best."

My exhaustion lifts slightly in the face of her enthusiasm, and I love how she calls Sylvie Nan, even though they're not blood-related. I'll give it to Bastian. He's created a tight-knit family with that rock band of his.

"You've grown at least three inches since I saw you in the summer," I tell her, pouring a sample of the spiced cider. "Pretty soon you'll be taller than your dad."

"Not likely," Mik laughs, catching up with his daughter. "Taylen, I don't think you've officially met Tyler yet," he says. "Tyler, this is Taylen Howard. He grows the best apples in Vermont. His farm is next to Bastian's."

Tyler reaches out to shake my hand. "Nice to meet you, Taylen. Will you be at Thanksgiving tomorrow?"

"Sure will," I reply with a smile that turns into a yawn I manage to stifle.

"Oh my god, this is amazing. Dad, Tyler, you have to try this!" Kay says, pointing at the nonalcoholic cider.

I pour more samples, careful to avoid meeting Bastian's gaze as he hangs back from the group. But I can feel his eyes on me. The weight of his attention feels like static electricity on my skin.

Tyler asks about the cider-making process with interest and buys a couple of jars of my spiced-apple chutney.

"Can we see the honey stand?" Kay asks. "I want to get some for Grandma's Christmas box."

As they move away, Sebastian remains behind. The dark circles under my eyes suddenly feel more pronounced under his scrutiny, and I fight the urge to either snap at him or simply collapse in exhaustion.

"Elvis working out for you?" Sebastian's voice carries that particular tone that makes me want to either punch him or kiss him. A combination that's becoming distressingly familiar the longer he keeps not leaving Vermont.

I force my expression into one of casual appreciation, ignoring how his proximity makes my skin prickle. "He's great, actually. Really whipped the flock into shape. Egg production is up fifteen percent." The lie rolls off my tongue smoothly, though my bloodshot eyes probably tell a different story.

"I appreciate the thoughtful gift," I continue, unable to stop the word vomit. "Shows you know your poultry. Although, I'll take some credit for that. Moira and Myrtle have clearly been good teachers."

Sebastian's knowing look tells me he sees right through my act. I swallow dry as he steps closer, and his scent—hay, leather, and pine—fills my nose, making it hard to maintain my composure.

"Glad to hear it," he says, his voice dropping lower. "He's a champion Barred Rock. Thought you might appreciate his…strong leadership qualities."

Our eyes lock, and the market noise fades into the background. The air between us crackles with the kind of energy that turns sand into glass. I grip the table edge harder, my knuckles tight with the effort of not reaching for him.

We stand there, locked in a standoff, neither willing to

break first. His eyes drop briefly to my lips before snapping back up, and I feel the look like a physical touch. The market could burn down around us, and I'm not sure I'd notice.

"Taylen Howard, you look absolutely exhausted!" Sylvie's voice cuts through the tension, and as if I've been electrocuted, I take a step back, unsure of how I came to be so close to Bastian. "I promised your ma I'd keep an eye on you. Do I need to watch you more closely?"

Her hand touches my arm, gentle but insistent, as she studies my face with the kind of attention that makes lying futile. "I'm fine, Mrs. Hall," I say, straightening my posture and forcing energy into my voice. "Just busy."

She doesn't look convinced, but shifts topics with practiced grace. "You're still coming for Thanksgiving tomorrow, right?"

"Wouldn't miss it," I reply, watching Bastian's expression. His jaw tightens slightly, the only tell in his otherwise perfect poker face. "Can't wait to have your apple pie. I hope there will be leftovers."

As they leave—Sylvie with a maternal pat on my arm and Sebastian with one last loaded glance—I'm left wondering how I'll survive Thanksgiving dinner on minimal sleep with both Elvis and Bastian in my life.

Finn appears twenty minutes later, making his usual rounds with his tablet in hand and that harried expression that's become his permanent feature during festival season. He stops at each vendor stall, checking that everyone is okay and taking any feedback we might have. When he reaches my table, I'm down to my last few jars of apple chutney and maybe a dozen apples.

"Good day?" he asks, eyeing my nearly empty display with satisfaction. "Looks like you'll sell out completely."

"Best market day I've had all season," I admit, grateful for something positive to focus on. "Should be completely sold out within the hour."

Finn makes a note on his tablet and then glances at his mom's stand.

Something feels off. Usually, he'd comment on my obvious fatigue. The dark circles under my eyes are impossible to miss, and my best friend has never been one to ignore when something's out of whack with me.

"You still up for dinner and drinks after I pack up?" I ask, watching his face carefully. "Joe's? I could use the company after the week I've had."

Finn glances around the market square with visible discomfort, his eyes darting around, clearly avoiding mine. "I can't tonight. Got a bunch of work to catch up on. Rain check?"

The excuse feels hollow, especially coming from someone who's never missed our post-market tradition unless he was literally dying.

"Sure," I say slowly. "Rain check."

Under normal circumstances, I'd press him for details, demand to know what's really going on. But exhaustion weighs heavy on my shoulders, and I'm too tired to argue with my best friend about whatever secret he's keeping. If Finn wants to be mysterious about his sudden unavailability, that's his choice.

"Besides," he adds, "I'll see you at Thanksgiving."

And with that, I'm left alone in my almost-empty stall.

As the market winds down around us, everyone packing up their remaining stock and customers drifting away, I find myself looking forward to just one thing: going home and sleeping until Elvis forces me awake tomorrow morning.

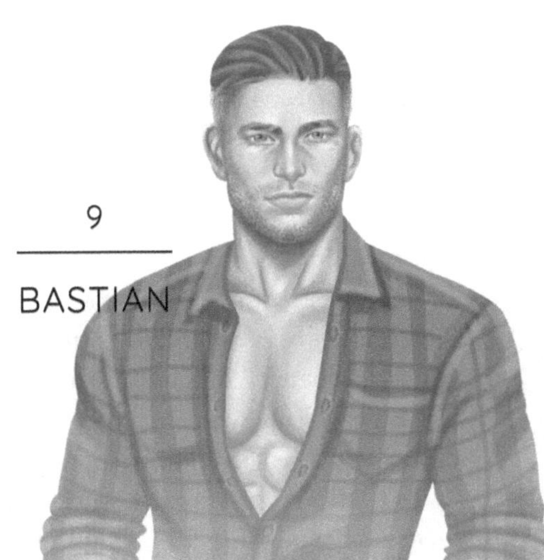

9

———

BASTIAN

I pause before I enter the farmhouse through the kitchen, wondering when someone last used the front door.

Taking a deep breath, I prepare myself for the chaos I know I'm going to find inside. For over twenty years, I lived surrounded by people. My band brothers, crew, fans, the press, you name it.

In the last few weeks, I've gotten used to the solitude I only ever get when I hide in my recording studio, writing songs with Mik.

Do I miss the chaos? Yes.

Am I ready to face a whole day of it, which also includes Taylen Howard in very close proximity? Hell no.

Gouta nudges me on my leg.

"Yeah, yeah, we're going in. You know, for a farm animal, you're way too happy to not be on the farm part."

She bleats her reply, trotting past me and going inside.

The farmhouse kitchen is filled with the sounds of clattering pots and familiar voices. Countless years of coming home for Thanksgiving, and I'll never not be surprised by the controlled chaos of Mom's Thanksgiving prep.

I stop in the doorway as I process the scene before me. Stone is fighting with a potato peeler while Nikko dodges flying peels. Kay perches on a counter, sorting fresh herbs, while Tyler and Mik work in perfect sync, chopping vegetables and trading secret smiles. And then there's Fox, looking relaxed and healthy, his silver-streaked hair longer than when I last saw him.

My feet carry me across the room, and I pull Fox into a tight hug, breathing in the familiar scent of leather mixed with his cologne. "When did you get in? Where the hell have you been?" The words come out rougher than intended, weeks of worry bleeding through.

Fox returns the embrace with equal force. "This morning. There was something I've wanted to pursue for a long time but never had the chance."

"And has it worked?"

"It's a work in progress," he says, his amber eyes holding secrets I can't quite read.

Before I can press further, Mom appears between us, brandishing a wooden spoon like a conductor's baton. "Questions later, potatoes now!" Her tone means no argument.

I try flattery as a diversion tactic. "Is that a new apron? The color really brings out your—"

"Nice try. Your dad has trademarked that one, and look what that's gotten him. A lifetime of turkey smoking outside in the cold." She points the spoon at a mountain of vegetables awaiting prep. "You're not getting out of kitchen duty that easily. It's bad enough that your brother is late."

Movement through the window catches my eye. A familiar figure crosses the boundary between our properties, and my heart does that uncomfortable thing it always does whenever Taylen appears. He looks exhausted even from this distance, his shoulders slumped under the weight of sleepless nights.

Despite having to manage the farm, two chickens that refuse to live anywhere but my living room, and being constantly shadowed by a goat who thinks she's a pet, things haven't been too bad.

We have enough help around the farm that I can distribute the jobs and focus on what needs to be done by me, and despite my efforts to live independently, I know I wouldn't hear the end of it if I didn't have dinner with my parents every day.

Taylen doesn't have those things.

Guilt gnaws at me, so before I talk myself out of it, and before my plan becomes too obvious, I turn back toward the door.

"We need more firewood," I announce, perhaps too quickly. Mom raises an eyebrow but doesn't comment as I head out, grateful for the excuse to escape.

Gouta, who was curled up on top of the blanket in the basket my mom set up for her in the kitchen, stands up, bleats some sort of announcement, and then follows me out.

Despite my boots crunching in the snow, Taylen doesn't notice me until I'm almost right in front of him.

He looks worse up close, the dark circles under his eyes like bruises against his winter-pale skin. He startles when he spots me, the curly waves of his hair falling slightly onto his eyes. Elvis has done his job too well. The thought brings me a lot less satisfaction than I expected.

"You look like hell," I say.

He tries to straighten his posture, a futile attempt at his usual defiance. "I'm fine. Just busy with holiday prep."

"Right." I step close enough to catch the slight sway in his stance. "And I'm sure the three a.m. wake-up calls have nothing to do with it."

A flash of his old fire sparks in those tired eyes. "Elvis is a great addition to the flock." The stubborn set of his jaw would be more convincing if he weren't clearly fighting to keep his eyes open.

"Come on," I say, making a split-second decision. "We need to talk."

I expect resistance, but he follows me without argument, his boots dragging slightly in the snow.

The path feels longer with Taylen beside me, our breath creating twin clouds in the cold air. He stumbles once, and my hand shoots out to steady him before I can think better of it. The contact sends electricity up my arm, even through layers of winter clothing.

"Why are we going to your studio?" His voice carries a thread of suspicion, but he doesn't pull away from my steadying grip.

"Because," I say, leading him toward the modern building that's caused so much tension between us, "I want to show you something."

The studio feels different with Taylen in it, smaller somehow. He stands in the center of the room, taking in the changes in the space. The coffee cups are now clean and stashed nicely next to the coffee maker, and the previously messy stacks of papers are now in a neat pile on the coffee table.

Gouta circles us a couple of times until she decides we're not doing anything exciting and goes back out, probably back to the farmhouse where she knows my mom will feed her scraps.

I shake my head. One month, I'm singing to a crowd of thousands of people, and the next, I'm living with a spoiled goat that can outdiva Stone.

"What do you want, Bastian?" Taylen's voice is filled with exhaustion and apprehension.

"Take a look," I say, gesturing to the paperwork.

He sinks onto the couch and picks up the nearest folder. I watch his face as he reads, seeing the moment understanding begins to dawn.

"Bastian…"

"I've been developing these plans for over a year. Working with agricultural experts, studying successful co-ops across the country."

The plans detail everything from sustainable farming practices to community involvement. In a nutshell, ways to combine traditional methods with new developments to create efficiency and lower costs.

"I…" He looks up at me, genuine surprise softening his features. "I owe you an apology."

I sit beside him, close enough to feel the warmth radiating from his body but not quite touching. "I didn't show you this so you can apologize, Taylen. I just wanted you to…" I sigh. "Being a rockstar is only glamorous on paper."

He looks up from the reports and raises an eyebrow.

"Okay, fine," I relent. "It's been pretty good. The money, the fame, doing something I know I was born to do. I'm luckier than most people. But all of that hasn't come without the other side."

"You mean being hunted by the press all the time? Screaming fans and all that?"

I shake my head. "Playing a full set for a full stadium, burning more calories than I can consume in a day, crashing, and doing it all over the next day for months. Coming home and finding I missed so much stuff, and trying to catch up while everyone else is on vacation somewhere sunny. Repeat that for two decades."

Taylen looks so tired. He leans on the back of the couch, letting his head rest on the soft cushion. "You liked it though, right? You always looked so happy in the interviews."

The thought that he watched our interviews or kept up with the band surprises me.

"I wouldn't change it for the world. My point is, I know what commitment looks like, Taylen, and just like I didn't quit on music, I'm not quitting on the farm."

"You did quit music." His lips curl into a smile, and with him looking so relaxed, I have to consciously keep my hands in my lap because I want nothing more than to touch him.

I don't want to tell him that while we're not touring, I can't bear the thought that this is it. Hall of Fame will never make music again. I'm not sure I can be myself without music. I just have to figure out how to do it without impacting my work on the farm. And that's not a conversation I'm ready to have right now.

Taylen glances again at the report. His fingers trace the edge of a detailed irrigation diagram. "These are good plans," he admits. "Really good."

"I want to help revitalize local agriculture while honoring traditional methods. Combine my business experience with practical knowledge like yours."

Something shifts in his expression, a warmth I've never seen before directed at me. "You're really serious about this."

"I'm here to stay," I promise, holding his gaze. "And it's not just about succeeding. It's about helping everyone succeed."

He nods slowly, and I see the last of his defenses crumbling just before his eyes close and he falls asleep.

I grab the blanket that drapes over the arm of the couch and cover Taylen with it. He stirs a little, like he's making himself comfortable.

"Thank you, rockstar."

I pull my phone out and drop Fox a message to explain my absence. I don't even care that he doesn't seem to buy it.

I'll make it up to my mom, but right now, Taylen is the one I need to make up to.

Taking the reports from his hands, I get comfortable and continue reading through the new information I haven't worked on yet. Eventually, my own early mornings catch up with me, and I fall asleep.

I'm jolted awake when the studio door flies open with teenage enthusiasm, Kay coming in with her bossy face on. I've known that girl since she was born. The only one who can maybe compete with Kay's bossiness might be Gouta.

Gouta trots in behind Kay, red ribbon slightly askew, looking entirely too pleased with herself.

"There you are!" Kay announces, seemingly oblivious to Taylen sleeping beside me. "Nan says dinner's almost ready, and Gouta was looking for you guys."

As if on cue, the goat launches herself onto the couch between Taylen and me, her hooves narrowly missing the papers spread across the coffee table. She settles herself like royalty claiming a throne, butting her head against both of us in turn.

Taylen laughs at the rude awakening, his fingers finding that spot behind Gouta's ears that makes her melt. "I'm still your favorite," he mutters fondly. "But you were supposed to be teaching him about farming, not cuddling on his furniture."

He yawns and rubs the sleep off his face. "Christ, I'm so sorry. I didn't mean to fall asleep. I promise the reports weren't that boring."

I laugh. "Sure, sure. Do you feel more rested though?"

"Yeah. Thanks."

"We should head back," I suggest, standing and offering him my hand. He hesitates for just a moment before taking it, his palm warm against mine as I help him up. The contact lingers a heartbeat longer than necessary.

Kay's already bouncing back toward the door, Gouta trotting after her like an oversized puppy. Our conversation still feels unfinished. There are questions I want to ask, but with Taylen, I need to take baby steps.

"Coming?" Kay calls from outside, her voice carrying on the crisp air.

Taylen follows me out into the snow, and we walk toward the warmth of the farmhouse, our shoulders nearly touching with each step.

10

TAYLEN

We're silent as we make our way to the farmhouse, the only sounds coming from the snow crunching under our boots and Gouta's happy trot beside Kay.

Each step takes me further away from Bastian's studio and our easy conversation, probably the first we've ever had.

I steal a glance at him from the corner of my eye. His profile is sharp against the winter light, all strong lines and silver-touched dark hair that makes my fingers itch with the urge to touch. His beard isn't as well-groomed now as when he was showing up in TV interviews all the time or being followed around by the press.

Sebastian Hall, the dairy farmer, couldn't be further from the spotlight.

Damn him for being good at this.

I've spent weeks convincing myself he's just playing at being a farmer, that his real commitment is still to his music career because I'm too scared he'll leave again when all I want is to get close.

But those plans in his studio aren't the work of someone killing time between tours. They're thorough, practical, and show a deep understanding of the challenges facing small farms like ours.

The realization settles in my chest uncomfortably. I've been nursing my resentment like a familiar friend, using it as armor against the feelings I've carried since I was too young to know better. But standing in that studio, watching him explain his vision for collaborative farming initiatives with genuine passion lighting his eyes, that armor developed some serious cracks.

This is dangerous territory. When it comes to Bastian Hall, I've always had a weakness. Even when I was thirteen and he was just Jackson's cool friend who played guitar and sang like an angel, there was something about him. Twenty years later, he's become more attractive, more accomplished, and apparently more committed to staying in Vermont than I ever gave him credit for.

Holding on to how much I felt his absence after Jackson died was needed to protect my heart from falling for him. Who knew that a chat and a short nap were all it would take to make me change my tune?

The warmth of the farmhouse kitchen wraps around me with scents of sage and butter and the ghost of traditions I thought I'd lost forever. My parents called earlier to wish me a Happy Thanksgiving. The conversation was short because they were getting ready to join their friends for a community dinner. A phone call is nice, but it will never be the same as having them here with me.

I don't resent them and their choice to move to a warmer climate, but I miss them.

All conversation stops as we enter. Stone's eyebrows climb toward his hairline while Nikko's grin spreads slow and knowing across his face. My neck burns under their scrutiny, and I resist the urge to check if my shirt is buttoned properly or my hair is sticking up at odd angles from falling asleep on the couch.

"Sorry we're late. Hope you didn't wait on us," I say, trying my best to keep a steady voice that doesn't give away my thoughts. "Bastian was just showing me…um—"

"I bumped into Taylen on my way to get wood for the fire, and it dawned on me that he hasn't seen my new chickens," he says.

I see Kay's smile from the corner of my eye, but she doesn't say anything. I knew I always liked that kid for a reason.

"Nonsense," Sylvie reassures. "You're both right on time. But Bastian is on cleanup duty."

He laughs and walks toward the large table. I follow him, weaving between the counter and the already-seated guests.

"Hi, Henry," I say to his dad as I pass him. "Good to see you."

"You too, son. Glad you could join the mad house."

I chuckle. "For Sylvie's cooking and your turkey? You can be as mad as a bag of hammers and I'd still join you."

The only chair I can take without disrupting everyone's places is right beside Bastian. Of course it is. I slide into the seat, hyperaware of how close our shoulders are, how the wooden chair creaks slightly as I settle my weight.

The kitchen table groans under its burden of a multitude of dishes. A massive golden turkey at the center, surrounded by dishes filled with stuffing, potatoes, and various vegetable offerings. Everything smells exactly like childhood memories, like holidays and happy times before I ended up rattling alone in my family home.

The empty chair beside Sylvie draws my eye. "Where's Finn?" I whisper to Bastian.

"You're his best friend," he says, passing me the mashed potatoes. "Shouldn't you know?"

I take the dish and spoon a generous portion onto my plate. "I'm his drinking buddy and crisis counselor. You're his brother." I grab the green beans and add some to my plate. "The one who actually grew up with him."

"I'm the brother who was on tour for most of his adult life," Bastian counters, reaching for the cranberry sauce. "You're the one who's been here through everything."

"Fair point." I pass him the stuffing. "But you're still family."

"And you're the person he trusts with his secrets." Bastian's eyes meet mine briefly before he looks away. "You're telling me you don't know whose mysterious texts he's been sneaking off to answer."

I pause mid-reach for the rolls. "You noticed that too?"

"Kind of hard to miss when my own brother starts acting like he's running a covert operation."

"Well," I say, settling back in my chair with a sigh, "I think we've established that neither of us has any idea where Finn is right now."

I'm reaching for the slices of carved turkey when the kitchen door crashes open with enough force to rattle the windows in their frames.

Winter air invades the kitchen's warmth as Finn bursts in, his hair a wild tangle, cheeks flushed red from more than just cold. His eyes are wide with the kind of panic I haven't seen since the Apple Festival was canceled because of a freak storm a few years ago.

He doesn't even pause to remove his coat, the words tumbling out of him. "Christmas is ruined!"

My fork freezes halfway to my mouth, matched by similar poses around the table. Sylvie rises partway from her chair, pulling Finn to take the empty seat next to hers. "Griffin, honey, what's wrong?"

Finn gasps for breath, his usual composure scattered like

leaves in a storm. "There's a major gas leak under the town square. They found it this morning after someone reported a smell when they were walking their dog." He runs a hand through his already disheveled hair. "The whole area's cordoned off and they're starting emergency repairs tomorrow."

"How long?" Stone asks.

"Four weeks, minimum." Finn finally sheds his coat, dropping into the chair. "The entire square will be unusable through the holiday season."

The implications settle over the table like fog on a winter morning. Four weeks. The heart of our town, sealed off during the busiest season of the year. The Winterberry Christmas Festival runs for two solid weeks before Christmas. I think of all the small vendors who depend on holiday sales, of the traditions that make our community what it is. That includes Bastian and me.

"Tell me you're joking," I say, though I already know he isn't. Finn takes his responsibilities as the town's events coordinator too seriously for this to be a prank.

His response is to let his head fall forward into his hands. "I wish I were."

Henry puts a hand on Finn's shoulder. "Have some food, son. I'm sure it'll all sort itself out."

Everyone slowly resumes their dinner, but it's clear the festive mood is gone. Even the guys who didn't grow up here have spent enough time on the farm to know the impact of something like this on the town.

I watch Finn push his food around his plate. He ticks off each compromised event on his fingers like he's counting casualties.

"The Christmas market's completely shot. All the vendor layouts were designed specifically for the square." His fork makes another circuit around his untouched turkey. "The tree lighting ceremony can't happen in its traditional spot. The outdoor concert series?" He lets out a hollow laugh. "Impossible."

Sylvie passes him a warm roll that he accepts automatically but doesn't eat. "The parade route's compromised too. We'd have to redirect through residential streets, and the floats can't make those tight turns." His voice grows more strained with each item. "The only things we can still do are the indoor events because they were always going to be in the community center. But everything else…"

I think of Mrs. Peterson's handmade wreaths, of the Morgan twins' baked goods stall, of all the small businesses that depend on holiday tourism. My own cider sales will take a hit, though I'm better positioned than most with my regular distribution channels.

"The whole town is counting on these events," Finn continues, his words heavy with responsibility. "It's not just about tradition. People plan their whole year around this income. The tourism boost carries some businesses through the lean winter months."

I catch Bastian watching me, his expression thoughtful. Something passes between us. This is exactly the kind of challenge his plans were designed to address, though neither of us could have predicted it would come so soon or so dramatically.

"The timing couldn't be worse," Finn adds, finally giving up the pretense of eating. "Four weeks before Christmas, and suddenly half our holiday traditions are impossible."

"What about the high school football field?" Henry suggests. "It's big enough, and it's already set up for crowds."

Finn shakes his head. "The power grid out there can't handle holiday lighting. We'd need generators, which means permits, which means time we don't have."

Tyler leans forward, looking at Mik and then turning to

Finn. "How about splitting the events between different venues? We have similar challenges in Stillwater with space allocation for large events. Last year, we ran a fundraiser at the community center, a concert in the park, and a small market in the town square. All on the same weekend."

"That would create a traffic nightmare," Finn points out gently. "Most people out here don't live in town. Everyone drives in."

Each idea dies a quick death, torn apart by logistics and practicality. I find myself watching Fox instead of contributing. He hasn't said a word since Finn's announcement, his focus entirely on his plate as he methodically separates his food into neat sections.

Finn keeps glancing in Fox's direction between shooting down suggestions, like he's hoping Fox will come up with the solution no one's thought of yet.

The evening has transformed from celebration to crisis management, and we're no closer to a solution than when he first burst through the door.

Fox continues his silent contemplation of his plate, though I notice his methodical eating has slowed to almost nothing. Whatever's going on in his head, he's not sharing it yet, which isn't surprising. Fox has always been the quiet one in the band.

Finn's fork hits his plate with enough force to make me jump. His eyes lock onto mine with an intensity that makes me want to check my shirt for stains, then shift to Bastian with growing excitement.

"Wait," he says, his voice carrying that particular tone that usually precedes either brilliance or disaster. "Maybe you two can help."

Everyone's attention swings toward us like a spotlight. Bastian shifts in his chair beside me.

Understanding dawns slowly, then all at once. The land

on the south side of our properties shares a border where both of us have fallow fields lying empty for the winter. I picture the spot where our fence line runs, that wide expanse where Bastian's land and mine back onto each other. The access roads from both properties could easily accommodate traffic flow.

I turn to find Bastian watching me. "We could," I say slowly. "The infrastructure's already there, and with both properties combined..."

His lack of an immediate answer tells me we're not on the same page with this.

Anger suddenly builds in my chest, and it takes everything in me not to shout at him or storm out.

For all the plans Bastian has to help the community, when things get tough, he's not actually willing to help.

It hits me. He doesn't need to.

Unlike everyone else in Winterberry, Sebastian Hall is a multimillionaire. He needs our community a lot less than we need him.

I realize then that I was wrong about him all along. This was never about Bastian Hall staying in Winterberry. This is about whether Bastian Hall belongs in Winterberry.

11

BASTIAN

WHAT THE FUCK is wrong with me?

One moment, my brain is thinking *hell no* to Finn's ridiculous plan to host the town's Christmas celebrations here, and the next, it's like someone pulled the power cable attached to my brain. I'm no longer able to put together words in an order that makes sense.

Because I'm remembering all over again how blue Taylen's eyes are. And how the short stubble on his face makes him look older. Or how the shape of his nose is just like Jackson's, as is the curly brown hair.

Because when he looked at me and I didn't see the usual hate, I saw something else.

But the longer I stare into Taylen's beautiful blue eyes, the more his expression changes into something I recognize more. He's pissed off.

"It's a ridiculous idea," I blurt out, finally finding my voice.

But Finn is already on his feet, his excitement practically vibrating through the air as he gestures toward invisible maps only he can see. "Think about it. The access road from our property connects directly to Route 7, and Taylen's service road could handle overflow parking. We remove the fence temporarily, set up the market stalls on the flat area by the orchard…"

I watch in growing dismay as my bandmates lean forward, caught up in Finn's enthusiasm. Stone's eyes light up with that particular gleam that usually precedes our most questionable decisions. Nikko's already pulling out his phone, like he does when we're brainstorming tour schedules.

My gaze keeps drifting to Taylen, waiting for him to object, to point out the hundred ways this could go wrong. But he sits there with his jaw set in that stubborn line I've come to recognize, deliberately nodding along as Finn details where the Christmas tree could go. The defiant gleam in his eyes makes it clear he's agreeing just to spite me, and my stomach twists with something that isn't entirely dread.

"The views of Mt. Philo would make it all feel magical," Finn continues, punctuating each point with increasingly dramatic hand gestures. "The natural amphitheater effect of the valley would be perfect for the carol singers. And imagine the lighting opportunities with all those apple trees!"

"It would solve the vendor space issue," Taylen adds quietly but with confidence. "The terrain's actually ideal for temporary structures."

I sit there, my turkey growing cold, as my sanctuary transforms into a festival ground in their collective imagination.

The chair scrapes against the floor as I push back slightly, needing some distance from their enthusiasm. I press my hands flat against the table as I gather my thoughts, forcing my voice into the calm, reasonable tone I've perfected over years of band meetings and contract negotiations.

"There are serious concerns we need to consider," I begin, measuring each word carefully. "The media attention alone could be devastating. One tweet about Hall of Fame hosting a Christmas festival, and we'll have fans descending on the farm from every state."

Stone waves this off with a casual flick of his wrist. "Please, we've managed bigger crowds."

"Not here," I counter, my frustration leaking through. "The farm's infrastructure isn't built for that kind of traffic." This is our sanctuary. Don't they get that once this comes out, it'll be impossible for us to blend in with the locals like we've done for years? Everything will change.

I glance at Taylen, silently pleading for support, but he just gives a small shrug that sends rage crawling up my neck. "The orchard handles harvest festival crowds," he offers, and I have to clench my jaw to keep from snapping at him.

"That's different, and you know it," I say between gritted teeth. "We're talking about insurance liability for hundreds of people on active farmland. What happens when some kid decides to climb over the fence and get into the equipment barn? Or someone breaks into the barn and lets the cows out?"

Nikko's already typing on his phone. "I can have our insurance guys look at temporary event coverage. We've done similar things for outdoor concerts."

The betrayal of my own team stings, but it's Taylen's continued thoughtful silence that really gets under my skin. He should be backing me up on this, should understand the risks to both our properties.

"And the timing," I press on, desperately. "Christmas is weeks away. The festival is supposed to start on the second weekend in December. There's no way we could coordinate something this big that fast."

"That's literally my job," Finn interjects, his excitement apparently immune to my concerns. "Give me two days to draft a proper plan. We can make this work."

I look around the table at their eager faces, feeling increasingly cornered. Even Mom's watching me with that particular expression that means she thinks I'm being unnecessarily difficult. Only Fox remains neutral, methodically finishing his dinner like we're discussing the weather instead of upending my entire life.

"I'll think about it," I finally concede, though the words taste bitter on my tongue. But from the triumphant gleam in Finn's eye, I suspect this battle was lost the moment he burst through the door with his crisis.

Mom stands with the same energy she's used all her life to break up our arguments. "Why don't you all retire to the living room? Bastian and I will clean up here before we have dessert."

"That sounds like a great idea," Dad says, sharing a look with Mom.

Everyone drifts away from the table until it's just Mom and me left in the kitchen.

Even though I know what's coming, I still have hope that the only reason she asked me to stay behind is because I didn't help with the dinner prep.

When I see the way she looks at me like she's considering what to say, I know I'm right.

"How are things going between you and Taylen?" Mom asks softly, as if she has no agenda.

"Fine," I manage, focusing intently on drying a serving plate that's already bone dry. "Why wouldn't they be?"

She hums thoughtfully as she loads the dishwasher, her movements efficient but unhurried. The silence stretches until I have to fill it. "We're neighbors. We're civil. That's all there is to it."

"Jackson would have wanted you two to get along," she says quietly, and the mention of my best friend hits me like a physical blow. "He always said you were more alike than either of you would admit."

My grip tightens on the dish towel until my knuckles turn white. "Mom, don't."

"Don't what?" She pauses, turning to face me with that gentle persistence that's impossible to escape. "Don't mention your best friend? Don't notice how you've been avoiding Taylen for years? Or don't point out that you've been carrying guilt that doesn't belong to you?"

"You don't know what you're talking about." The words come out sharper than intended, but she doesn't flinch.

"I know you left for a tour the same week Jackson died," she says softly. "I know you couldn't make it back for the funeral. And I know you've been punishing yourself for it ever since."

The plate in my hands becomes suddenly fragile, and I set it down carefully before I can drop it. "I should have been here."

"You were living your dream, and you had a job to do. Jackson was so proud of you, Sebastian. He wouldn't have wanted you to give that up, and he certainly wouldn't have wanted you to carry this around for twelve years."

"But I wasn't here," I repeat, my voice barely above a whisper. "When he needed me most, when Taylen needed—"

"Taylen had his parents, had us, had the whole town." Mom's hand finds my shoulder, warm and grounding. "What he didn't have was you torturing yourself from afar, unable to grieve properly because you were so busy feeling guilty."

I lean against the counter, the fight draining out of me. "I don't know how to be around him without seeing Jackson. Without remembering."

"Maybe that's not such a bad thing," she suggests. "Maybe remembering Jackson together is exactly what you both need. But you can't do that while you're keeping Taylen at arm's length."

"It's not that simple."

"Isn't it?" She turns back to the dishes, but I can feel her attention still focused on me. "Or are you afraid that if you let yourself get close to Taylen, you'll have to admit there's more there than just shared grief?"

The observation lands too close to home, and I busy myself with wiping down the counters. "I don't know what you mean."

"Sebastian Hall, I raised you. I've seen the way you look at that boy."

"He's not a boy anymore, Mom."

"No," she agrees, a knowing smile playing at her lips. "He's not. And that's part of the problem, isn't it?"

But she's already turning to face me, her eyes soft with an understanding I'm not ready for. "You can't keep holding yourself apart from everything that reminds you of him. And you can't keep pretending there's nothing between you and Taylen except old grief."

The words settle in my chest like stones, heavy with a truth I've been avoiding. I focus on folding the dish towel, buying time I don't really need. We both know she's right, but admitting it feels dangerous, like opening a door I'm not sure I can close again.

Not to mention, he doesn't trust me and seems to hate my guts. Both things I can't entirely blame him for.

When we finish, she excuses herself and goes upstairs to freshen up. The noises coming from the living room should be inviting. My bandmates and my family are watching football on TV on Thanksgiving, just like any other regular family.

But I'm wound too tight to join them.

The hallway offers a temporary escape. I lean against the

wall, letting the solid structure take my weight as everything else threatens to collapse around me.

My chest feels too tight, each breath a conscious effort against the pressure building inside. I close my eyes, but that only makes the images clearer. Market stalls sprawling across my fields, crowds trampling paths through the snow, music and laughter drowning out the quiet I've fought so hard to protect.

The farm has always been my sanctuary, the one place I could just be myself without the weight of public expectations. Even during the height of our fame, it remained untouched, preserved like a photograph of simpler times. Now Finn wants to throw open the gates, invite the whole town in, and transform our private space into a public celebration.

I clench and unclench my fists, hoping the motion will help me calm down. The logical part of my brain understands why Finn wants to do this. The town needs this. The community that's sheltered and protected us all these years is asking for help. Refusing would mean watching small businesses struggle through the winter, seeing holiday traditions wither like unpicked fruit.

But it's not just about the festival. Mom's words echo in my head, mixing with memories of Jackson's laugh and the way Taylen looked at me in the studio this afternoon.

Footsteps approach from the living room. I don't need to open my eyes to know it's Nikko. He's always had a knack for finding me in these moments of retreat.

"Hey," he says, his voice carrying that particular tone that means he's about to offer an escape route. "Local band's playing at Joe's tonight." He pauses, letting the information settle. "Could be interesting."

"Interesting how?"

"Well," he drawls, leaning against the opposite wall, "they

might need some expert advice. And Joe's has that new winter ale you like." His smile turns knowing. "Plus, it's somewhere that isn't here."

The offer tempts me. A few hours away from family expectations and Taylen's unsettling presence, lost in music that has nothing to do with my own complicated history. But I hear movement from the kitchen, the soft pad of familiar footsteps approaching.

"You should go." Taylen's voice comes from behind me, startling us both. "I need to head home anyway. Early morning with Elvis."

I turn to find him watching me with an expression I can't quite read, exhaustion and something else playing across his features. The mention of the rooster brings an unexpected smile to my lips.

"You started it," I remind him, and for a moment, the tension between us shifts into something lighter.

"Come on," Nikko interrupts, clearly sensing an opportunity. "One drink. We can talk about anything except Christmas festivals and farming."

Maybe a few hours' distance is exactly what I need to face all this tomorrow.

"All right," I concede, pushing off from the wall. "One drink."

12

———

TAYLEN

THE GRAVEL PATH BETWEEN THE HALLS' farm and my house feels longer tonight. The warmth of their kitchen clings to my clothes even as Vermont's November wind tries to steal it away, leaving me caught between two temperatures, two worlds, much like I'm caught between anger at Bastian's stubborn refusal and an unwelcome understanding of his fears.

His refusal wasn't a surprise. I know him well enough by now to recognize when he's building walls. But something about it burns in my chest all the same.

The porch light I left on casts a weak light on the steps I've climbed for what feels like a hundred years and a dozen lives. I fish my keys from my pocket and open the front door.

Inside, darkness wraps around me, the silence hitting harder after the hours spent in the warmth of the Halls' kitchen, where even quiet moments carry the weight of long-established family traditions.

My coat lands on the wrought-iron rack, followed by my scarf. I remove my boots and then make my way to the kitchen.

The bottle of whiskey waits on the counter where I left it last night. I pour two fingers neat, then, after a moment's consideration, add a third. The first sip burns, but the second goes down easier, spreading warmth through my chest that almost matches what I left behind when I decided it would be too hard to follow Bastian and the band to Joe's.

As much as I know the guys from years of having them around on and off, between tours and album recordings, I'm not part of the group.

I roll the tension from my shoulders, feeling each knot and tight muscle protest. Bastian's refusal to help save the festival sits heavy in my gut. All his talk about coming home to stay, about being part of the community again, crumbled in the face of actual commitment.

I push away from the counter, taking the whiskey glass with me, and head up to my room. The leather couch in the corner accepts my weight with a familiar creak, its worn surface cool against my palms.

The brass lamp beside me needs polishing, but its tarnished surface feels right tonight, matching my mood. In its weak light, the framed photograph beside it takes on an almost sepia tone, though I know its true colors by heart. Jackson's blue denim shirt, my teenage self's ridiculous attempt at facial hair, and the trees with their golden autumn leaves behind us.

Three weeks. The anniversary looms like storm clouds on the horizon, heavy with memories I both chase and flee. Twelve years shouldn't feel like yesterday, but grief has its own timeline.

I clench my fingers around the crystal glass, watching the amber liquid swirl around, bringing back memories I've tried to forget.

Seven years ago, I ran from grief like it was something I could outpace if I just moved fast enough, drove far enough, drank deep enough. Burlington's lights promised anonymity, its bars offering temporary refuge.

"You were wrong, J," I whisper to the photo, to the quiet room, to the shadows and memories around me. "Some things can't be fixed just because you want them to be."

But even as the words leave my lips, I know they taste like lies. Because seven years of distance haven't dulled the way my heart kicks when Bastian enters a room, haven't erased the current that runs between us, haven't changed the fact that every argument, every tension, every moment of friction carries an undertone of something else entirely.

The nightclub throbs around me, bass vibrating through my bones like a second heartbeat. Strobing lights slice through the artificial fog. I press my glass against my lips, letting the whiskey burn away the taste of grief that's followed me to Burlington, though even here, three hours from home, I can't quite shake the ghost of Jackson's absence.

Five years and his loss still feels as raw as the night the police knocked on our door to tell us a kid without a driver's license or insurance rammed my brother's truck off the road and directly into the path of an old oak tree.

Bodies press against me from all sides, a living tide of perfume and sweat and desperation. I've lost count of how many bars I've tried tonight, each one offering the same false promise of forgetting. This one's bigger than the others, more crowded, the kind of place where faces blur and names become irrelevant. Perfect for someone trying to disappear.

I push away from the bar, letting the crowd swallow me. Dancing bodies create currents and swirls, and I let myself be carried along, neither fighting nor following. The lights paint everything in stark colors, making the world feel less real, more like a fever dream I might wake from to find everything unchanged.

That's when I see him.

At first, I think it's the whiskey playing tricks, but I recognize the way he holds himself, the broad shoulders, the ripped jeans, the hands shoved deep in his jeans pockets. The baseball cap is pulled low, but I'd know that profile anywhere, having spent years pretending not to study it at every given chance.

He looks up, and our eyes lock across the dancefloor. The moment stretches as recognition floods his features, followed by something else before his usual careful mask slips into place.

I should leave, but I stay still, not even swaying to the rhythm of the music.

The anger in my chest tangles with something else, something I've spent years pretending doesn't exist. Attraction hums under my skin like electricity. Even now, raw with grief and drunk on whiskey, I can't quite ignore how the club lights catch the angles of his face, how his presence draws my eyes even in disguise.

The music swells around me, and I close my eyes against the assault of memory and sensation. Five years of running from the complicated tangle of emotions that Bastian Hall stirs in me. Five years of pretending I don't check tour schedules, don't follow his success, don't feel his absence like a physical thing.

When I open my eyes again, he's closer, though still separated by a sea of dancing bodies. The cap shadows his face, but I feel the weight of his attention like a physical touch. The anger rises again, sharp and bitter on my tongue. How dare he be here, in my chosen escape? How dare he look at me with concern after years of silence? Because he may have come home, but he never came back to me. We were meant to be friends. I guess we weren't.

But beneath the anger, beneath the grief and whiskey and pounding bass, something else pulses in time with the music. Something that reminds me of summer evenings and laughter.

Something that's been there since before Jackson's death, before fame and fortune took him away.

He takes another step forward, and the movement breaks whatever spell holds me in place. My feet carry me forward before my brain can object, moving through the press of bodies like water finding its path downstream.

The music shifts into something slower, heavier with bass, as I reach him. Up close, his height advantage is more pronounced, forcing me to tilt my head slightly to meet his gray eyes beneath the cap's brim. Neither of us speaks. Instead, we let the music fill the space between us.

His hand finds my hip with careful intent, and the touch burns through my shirt like a brand. The anger that drove me forward melts into something else entirely as we begin to move together, letting the rhythm guide us. Each point of contact sends electricity through my system as his fingers splay against my waist, his thigh brushes mine, and his breath is warm against my temple.

I should feel guilty for wanting this, for letting attraction override grief and anger, but the alcohol in my blood makes everything simmer instead of burn.

"I want you," he murmurs against my ear, his voice rough with something more than just club noise. The words vibrate through me, settling low in my stomach. His fingers tighten on my hip, pulling me closer until our bodies align from chest to knee.

My response gets lost in the music, but he must read something in my eyes because suddenly we're moving through the crowd, his hand wrapped around mine like he's afraid I'll disappear. The emergency exit appears through the press of bodies, and then cold air hits my face as we stumble into the alley behind the club.

Brick scrapes against my back as Bastian crowds me against the wall, his hands bracketing my head, his body a solid wall of heat against the night's chill. For a moment, we just breathe, sharing air in the narrow space between us, the music now a muffled heartbeat through the metal door.

"I need you so badly," he rasps, and the raw honesty in his voice undoes something in my chest. His cap falls from his head as he leans in, his intention clear in the way his gaze drops to my mouth. Five years of grief and anger dissolve in the space between one heartbeat and the next as his lips brush mine.

The kiss tastes like whiskey and want, like summer evenings and winter storms. My fingers tangle in his hair, pulling him closer as years of attraction ignite under my skin. His tongue traces the seam of my lips, and I open for him, letting everything else fall away.

His thigh presses between mine as the kiss deepens, and I arch into the contact, seeking more contact, more heat, more of everything he's offering. His hands slide from the wall to my waist, fingers finding skin where my shirt has ridden up. Each touch feels like a question and an answer, like salvation and damnation wrapped in one desperate moment.

The sharp click of radio static shatters our bubble.

"Mr. Hall?" A voice cuts through the night, professional and firm.

Bastian tears himself away, chest heaving, as two suited figures materialize from the shadows. Their earpieces glint in the security light, marking them as part of his entourage rather than club security. One moves to Bastian's side while the other steps between us, creating distance where moments ago there was none.

"I'm sorry," he says.

I watch, still pressed against the brick wall, as they guide him toward the mouth of the alley where I see a black SUV waiting. The second guard remains, his bulk blocking any attempt to follow, though his expression holds more sympathy than threat.

The SUV's door closes with a sound like finality, its taillights disappearing into Burlington's night, leaving me with brick dust on my jacket and the ghost of Bastian's touch on my skin.

The memory releases me back into my bedroom, leaving my skin burning with phantom touches from seven years ago.

I move to the edge of my bed, letting the cool air from the cracked window chase away the last traces of Burlington's back alley. But my body remembers—god, does it remember—every point of contact, every touch, every moment of connection before reality intervened. The ghost of his hands on my hips heightened with today's closeness in his studio and at the dinner table.

I sweep a hand through my hair, my defenses crumbling as understanding floods in. This thing between Bastian and me was never just about Jackson's death or local rivalry. The electricity that crackles between us is seven years of unfinished business.

But with Finn's plans to host the Christmas Festival here, I know I'm going to have to fight Bastian or work with him. I just don't know which option is worse.

13

BASTIAN

THE BAND STARTS A NEW SONG, and I add a notch on my mental board. This would be a cool game if I hadn't noticed the not-so-discreet glances between my bandmates. The only ones not engaging are Finn and Fox.

Finn is glued to his phone, probably already planning the Christmas Festival move, even though it hasn't been officially decided.

And Fox? He's quieter than usual. It's like he's with us, but he's not really here.

Stone breaks first. "So…" He draws out the word until it has three syllables. "Are we going to talk about how you and Taylen were practically setting the table on fire with those looks?"

It took them three and a half songs. They must be getting old.

I keep my eyes fixed on my ginger ale, watching bubbles rise to the surface. "There were no looks."

"Oh, honey." Stone laughs. "I've seen less heat between actual flames."

Nikko leans forward. "I thought Sylvie was going to force

you both into a timeout. The tension was thick enough to scoop with one of her serving spoons."

"Can we not do this?" The words come out sharper than intended, but they just exchange amused glances.

"Do what?" Stone asks innocently. "Discuss the obvious sparks flying between you and a certain incredibly attractive orchard owner? The way you practically stopped breathing when he reached across you for the green beans?"

My fingers tighten around my glass. "You're imagining things."

"Am I imagining how you couldn't take your eyes off him?" Nikko joins in, his smile growing. "Because I distinctly remember you missing your mouth with your fork."

"Like I said, there were no looks, and the fork thing did not happen."

"Oh, honey." Stone laughs. "We're not just talking about the looks. We're talking about the way you two practically combusted when Finn brought up the Christmas Festival. I thought the table was going to catch fire."

Finn leans forward, grinning, like he knows something I don't know. "You looked ready to either strangle him or—"

"Don't," I warn, but Stone's already laughing.

"Or drag him somewhere private and work out all that aggression," Stone finishes, his eyes gleaming with mischief. "Tell me I'm wrong. Tell me you weren't thinking about it."

My fingers tighten around my glass. "You're imagining things."

"Am I imagining how you couldn't stop staring at him when he was agreeing with Finn just to piss you off?" Nikko joins in, his smile growing.

"He wasn't…doing that," I say, but there's no heat in it.

"All that fire has to go somewhere," Stone drawls, leaning back in his chair. "And I'm betting angry sex with Taylen Howard would be absolutely explosive."

"Jesus, Stone." I think I need something stronger than my current drink. "We barely tolerate each other. He's made it pretty clear how he feels about me being back."

Nikko raises an eyebrow. "Is that why he couldn't stop watching you during dinner? Because he barely tolerates you?"

"Can we talk about literally anything else?"

A heavy hand lands on my shoulder, and I look up to find Mik standing up. "Come on," he says quietly. "Let's get some air."

I follow him to the bar, grateful for the escape. Mik signals Joe for fresh drinks, and moments later, two whiskey glasses appear in front of us. We take the drinks and step outside. It's too cold, but a sip of the drink soon sorts that out.

"You know they mean well," Mik says finally, turning his glass slowly between his hands. "They just want you to be happy."

I stare into my own drink. "I am happy. The farm is doing well. The transition is going smoothly—"

"That's not what I mean, and you know it." Mik's voice is gentle but firm. "I watch you, Bastian. I see how you light up when he's around, even when you're arguing. *Especially* when you're arguing."

"It's complicated," I mutter, but the words feel inadequate to describe the tangle of emotions that surface whenever Taylen is near.

"It always is." Mik takes a slow sip of his whiskey. "You know, I almost lost Tyler because I was too scared to bring him into our world. Too afraid of what might happen if I reached for something real."

I glance at him, knowing exactly how much they fought to be together. Twenty-five years apart and so much personal loss before they found each other again. Mik and Tyler have the kind of love that songs are written about, and I can't help but feel a little jealous.

The whiskey burns going down, but it's nothing compared to the heat that blooms in my chest when I think about Taylen.

"I don't know how to handle this," I admit quietly. "Every time I think I have a grip on my feelings, he does or says something that throws me completely off balance. And there's so much history, so many complications…"

"There always are." Mik's hand finds my shoulder again, squeezing gently. "But sometimes the complicated things are worth fighting for. Sometimes they're the only things worth fighting for."

I close my eyes, letting his words sink in. "I'll think about it."

He gives my shoulder one final squeeze before pushing away from the brick wall outside the bar. "Good. Now let's get back. I believe it's Fox's turn to be interrogated."

When we return to the table, Fox is studying his phone with unusual intensity while Finn leans across from his seat, gesturing animatedly about something. They both look up as we approach, Finn's words cutting off mid-sentence.

"Everything okay?" I ask, sliding back into my seat.

"Just picking Fox's brain about sound system logistics," Finn says smoothly. "Figured he'd know about power requirements for outdoor setups."

Fox nods, pocketing his phone. "Basic stuff. Nothing complicated."

Nikko appears with a tray of drinks, distributing glasses like an experienced bartender.

The local band has shifted to slower songs, their melodies wrapping around my thoughts like smoke, making it harder to keep memories at bay. Seven years is a long time to pretend a kiss never happened, but alcohol has a way of making buried things surface.

I lose track of time as the guys shift their focus to the band. Nikko seems particularly interested, raving about the swoon-worthy voice of the lead singer. It's nice to see him relaxed. I know out of all of us, he's struggling the most with our hiatus.

When I stand to go to the restroom, my legs protest the movement, the whiskey making my balance uncertain as I grip the edge of the table for support.

"I think it's time for me to go home," I say. The room tilts slightly before settling, confirming that switching to whiskey might not have been my wisest decision.

"I'll drive you," Mik offers, his tone casual but his eyes knowing. "Kay wants to go hiking to take photos for a school project. We'll never hear the end of it if we're too tired to keep up with her."

The drive passes in comfortable silence, broken only by the soft sound of Tyler humming along to whatever's playing on the radio. I press my forehead against the cool window, watching familiar landmarks slide past. Every turn brings me closer to home, closer to the decision I feel building in my chest.

"Whatever you decide," Mik says finally as we pull up to the farmhouse, "just be honest—with him and yourself."

I nod, not trusting my voice. Seven years of unfinished business weigh on my shoulders as I stand in the driveway, looking toward the path that leads to Taylen's house. The night air is cold enough to burn my lungs, but it does nothing to cool the heat building under my skin.

The house appears through bare branches, lit by the moon. I haven't been this close since the day I hugged my friend goodbye with the promise to come back in time for Christmas, even if for just a day. The memory makes me stumble slightly, or maybe that's the whiskey making the path swim beneath my feet.

My pulse sprints as I approach the porch steps. The porch light flickers on, the motion sensor catching my movement. My knock sounds too loud in the quiet night. Through the door's frosted glass, I see movement, hear footsteps approaching. My pulse races faster, anticipation and anxiety tangling in my chest until I can't tell them apart.

The door opens, and Taylen stands there like an apparition from my most complicated dreams. He's wearing sweatpants and a faded T-shirt that might have once been black, his hair slightly mussed from sleep, and I suddenly realize that Elvis will be up in just a few hours, and I'm no better than him.

"Bastian? What are you doing here?"

I don't answer immediately, can't find words past the surge of desire that rushes through me at the sight of him looking soft and uncertain in his doorway. Instead, I push past him into the house, needing to move, to act, before courage or recklessness abandons me.

The living room wraps around me like a time capsule. Same furniture, same photos on the walls. Taylen follows me in, his arms crossing over his chest in that defensive posture I know too well.

"We need to talk," I say, the words coming out rougher than intended.

He doesn't throw me out, which feels like victory and terror combined. Instead, he stands there studying me with those impossibly blue eyes. The space between us crackles with tension, with years of unfinished business, with everything we've left unsaid.

"You're drunk," he observes, but there's no judgment in his voice, just quiet certainty.

"Not drunk enough to forget this in the morning," I

counter, and his breath catches audibly. The sound goes straight to my core, making me sway slightly where I stand. Or maybe that's the whiskey finally catching up with me, making the room tilt like a ship in a storm.

"Why do you hate me so much?" The question bursts from me like a dam breaking, all the hurt and confusion of the past seven years pouring out at once. "What did I do that was so unforgivable?"

He moves closer still, close enough that I can smell sleep and mint on his breath, can see the slight stubble darkening his jaw. "You really don't know?" His voice drops lower, making me lean in to hear him. "You left before I could ask you to stay."

My heart pounds so hard I'm sure he must hear it, must feel it in the shrinking space between us. "Taylen," I breathe, his name feeling like a prayer and curse combined.

"You left," he continues, each word deliberate despite the slight slur of exhaustion or emotion, "and then you came back like nothing happened. Like years of pretending I don't exist can just be erased with smiles and plans and promises to stay this time. Like that night seven years ago never happened."

"I never meant to hurt you," I say, the words feeling inadequate against the weight of everything between us.

"But you did." His eyes lock with mine, holding me in place more effectively than any physical restraint. "You hurt me by leaving. You hurt me by ignoring me every time you came back, and you're hurting me now by coming back and making me feel things I spent years trying to forget."

The confession lands like lightning between us, charging the air around us. We stand there in his living room, breathing the same air. Every heartbeat is like a countdown to something inevitable, something years in the making.

"Tell me to leave," I challenge, my voice rough with need and fear. "Tell me to go, and I will."

His breath catches, his pupils dilating slightly as he processes my words. The moment stretches between us like taffy, sweet and dangerous, and threatening to snap at any second.

"You've always done exactly what you wanted."

The last thread of my control snaps. I surge forward, pressing Taylen against the wall as our lips meet in a kiss that feels like coming home and starting a war at the same time. His mouth opens under mine immediately, hot and demanding, years of frustrated desire compressed into this one moment.

My hands find his waist, fingers digging into the soft fabric of his T-shirt as I pull him closer. His body fits against mine perfectly, all lean muscle and barely contained energy. One of his hands tangles in my hair, the other gripping my shoulder like he's afraid I'll disappear again.

The kiss deepens, turns desperate. I trace his bottom lip with my tongue, drawing a soft sound from him that goes straight to my core. He tastes like whiskey, mint, and forbidden desire, like everything I've been denying myself since that night in Burlington.

His fingers tighten in my hair as I press closer, eliminating any space between us. The wall supports his weight as I explore his mouth, relearning the textures and tastes I've dreamed about only in the safety of my own space. Each point of contact between us feels electric. His chest against mine, his thigh between my legs, his heartbeat pounding in time with my own.

Time loses meaning as we kiss, the world narrowing to the points where our bodies connect. My hands slip under his shirt, finding warm skin and taut muscle. He arches into the touch, making a sound that's half growl, half whimper.

The noise shoots through me like lightning, making me press harder against him, wanting to draw more sounds from his throat.

Years of wanting crash over us like a wave, turning the kiss into something wild and desperate. His teeth catch my bottom lip, the slight pain making me groan. My hands roam his sides, his back, learning the geography of his body while I still can. His fingers flex against my scalp, the sensation sending shivers down my spine.

His response is just as fierce, just as hungry. He kisses me like he's trying to prove something, or maybe trying to break something. His body moves against mine with perfect rhythm, creating friction that makes my head spin more than any whiskey ever could.

When we finally break apart, we're both breathing hard. Our foreheads rest together as we gulp air. Taylen's hands have moved to my chest, fingers curled in my shirt like he's holding me in place. My own hands still span his back beneath his shirt, feeling the rapid rise and fall of his breathing.

"Tell me this isn't just the whiskey," Taylen whispers against my lips, vulnerability creeping into his voice. "Tell me you'll remember this in the morning."

The words are sobering and remind me of all the reasons this is complicated, all the ways it could go wrong. But with his body pressed against mine, his taste still on my tongue, I can't bring myself to care about anything else.

"I'll remember," I promise, my voice rough with emotion and desire. "God, Taylen, I'll remember every second of this."

"Then stay and prove it."

His eyes burn into mine as he waits for the inevitable, and I hate that I'm about to prove him right.

"Not tonight, Taylen."

14

TAYLEN

"YOU'RE AN IDIOT," I say aloud as I grip the steering wheel of my truck until my knuckles turn white.

The truck's heater struggles against the November cold, creating a small bubble of warmth that doesn't quite reach my feet. I flex my fingers on the wheel, trying to chase away the memory of how Bastian's skin felt under my hands.

"Stupid. Monumentally stupid." The words fog in the cold air, disappearing almost instantly like the rational thought process that abandoned me when Bastian showed up at my door last night.

Seven years of distance shattered by one kiss. One incredibly ill-advised, absolutely perfect, completely devastating kiss.

"Then stay and prove it," I say, repeating my words from last night. They taste sour in my mouth now.

What did I expect? For him to drag me to my bedroom and make up for all the years we should have been together with multiple rounds?

I run my hand through my messy curls. Yes, that was exactly what I had hoped would happen when he kissed me like that. People who kiss like that don't just walk away, right?

The proposed Christmas Festival site comes into view through gaps in the trees, and I force myself to tamp down my anger. I'll face Bastian by maintaining a professional facade while pretending last night never happened. Part of me hopes he was drunk enough to forget, although it's just my luck that he would keep *that* particular promise and remember every single second of that kiss.

Up ahead, vehicles cluster at the field's edge like dark birds on a wire. My heart slams heard in my chest as I spot Bastian's truck among them, flanked by an official-looking SUV that must belong to the town safety inspector and a white truck with the fire department's logo on the door. Stone's rental sits slightly apart, its pristine paint job already collecting a fine layer of mud splatter. Of course Bastian's already here. He probably didn't spend hours lying awake replaying every moment of last night, analyzing every touch, every sound, every breath shared between us.

My tires crunch over frozen grass as I approach the makeshift parking area. Through the windshield, I watch Bastian emerge from his truck, Gouta trotting at his heels like a loyal shadow. The sight sends fresh heat through my body.

I put the truck in park with deliberate slowness, buying precious seconds before I have to step into the cold morning air. Before I have to face the man who's spent twenty years complicating my life just by existing. The man who showed up at my door last night and shattered my whole being with one devastating kiss.

I step out of the truck, hoping to join the group of men gathered by the fence, but Bastian is already too close, moving with the determination that made him the successful musician he is. Gouta bleats a greeting, but her owner's expression holds something far less innocent. Intent and heat that make the morning air feel thin.

"Good morning," he says. Before I can respond, he's there, crowding me against the truck door with one hand on either side of my body. His body radiates heat even through layers of winter clothing, making my skin prickle with awareness.

I take a steady breath, but dammit, he smells like fresh pine and lemon, like lazy Sunday mornings and—fuck, I'm never going to pull unaffected off.

"We should talk," he continues, one hand coming up to tuck one of my stray curls behind my ear. The position mirrors how he pressed me against my living room wall last night, and my body responds before my brain can object, leaning toward his warmth like a flower tracking the sun.

I force myself to straighten, to remember all the reasons this is a terrible idea. "No thanks." I plant both hands on his chest, feeling solid muscle beneath his jacket, and push.

Gouta protests with an indignant bleat, like she's outraged by my behavior, but I'm already moving, putting distance between myself and temptation. My boots are steady on the frozen grass as I head toward where Nikko and Stone wait near the field's edge.

Stone looks irritatingly fresh. I've never met someone who looks perfect all the time. His designer boots somehow remain spotless despite the muddy ground, and his perfectly groomed appearance makes me suddenly aware of my simple care routine. I'm just a farmer. No time for expensive creams and regular haircuts. Beside him, Nikko huddles deeper into his coat, expensive sunglasses hiding what looks like an impressive hangover.

"Where's Fox?" Bastian asks as he catches up.

Stone's laugh carries a hint of worry beneath its usual easy tone. "Disappeared on us last night. Said he had to handle something and he'd catch a cab back to the house." He shrugs. "Haven't seen him since."

"He's not answering his phone," Nikko adds, like it's physically painful to talk. "Again."

The word "again" catches my attention, making me wonder what other disappearances I've missed. But it's not my business. Fox isn't my friend. I have enough complications in my life without adding someone else's mysterious behavior to the mix.

Instead, I focus on the field before us, trying to imagine it transformed into the Christmas festival Finn envisions. Anything to keep my mind off the man standing too close behind me, the man whose taste I can still remember with perfect clarity.

"He'll turn up," Stone says with forced confidence. "He always does."

The sound of approaching tires pulls my attention from the endless task of not watching Bastian. Finn's car appears through the morning haze like a herald of salvation, bringing with it not just my friend but Fox.

Nikko straightens as Fox emerges from the passenger seat, his sunglasses doing little to hide his concern. "Where have you been?"

Fox shrugs. "At the house," he says. "Slept late, saw Finn's car coming up the drive, jumped in."

Finn clears his throat. "Anyway. Let's get this show on the road." He gestures to a stocky man in his fifties with salt-and-pepper hair and wire-rimmed glasses. "This is Marcus Chen, our public works coordinator. He's been keeping our town's infrastructure running smoothly for the past twenty years."

Marcus nods at the assembled group, his handshake firm as he works his way through the introductions. "Pleasure to meet you all. Though I have to say, my daughter's going to lose her mind when I tell her who I met today." His smile is warm despite the professional clipboard tucked under his arm.

"And this is Chief Dan Morrison, our fire marshal," Finn continues. "He's the one who'll make sure we don't burn down half of Vermont with our holiday lights."

"Just making sure everyone stays safe," Dan says with a tone that suggests he's dealt with his share of ambitious holiday displays. He shakes hands with each band member. "Though I'll admit, this is probably the most high-profile safety inspection I've done in Winterberry."

Stone grins. "We promise to keep the pyrotechnics to a minimum."

"Please do," Dan replies, the corner of his mouth twitching. "My insurance paperwork is complicated enough as it is."

We begin our tour of the site, and for most of it, we just follow as the officials take measurements and make notes. The public works coordinator mutters about power lines and water access, while the fire marshal paces out distances between theoretical structures.

Throughout the inspection, I feel Bastian's gaze following my every move. Every time I glance his way, his eyes are already on me. Each accidental meeting of our gazes sends electricity through my system, making it harder to focus on Finn's excitement about vendor placement and crowd flow.

"The power supply shouldn't be an issue," the public works coordinator announces, making another note on his clipboard. "We can run lines from the main road, supplemented by generators if needed."

The fire marshal nods approval at the wide access paths Finn proposes, his initial skepticism warming into cautious optimism. "The natural curve of the land will make crowd control easier and help with emergency response times," he comments.

I try to focus on their discussion, but my attention keeps drifting to Bastian. He stands slightly apart from the group, Gouta pressed against his legs, his brow furrowed as he surveys the field. "What about the livestock?" he interrupts, his voice carrying an edge of concern. "We're talking thousands of people potentially wandering near active barns, disturbing and stressing the animals." His hand gestures toward the neighboring properties. "It's not just us. The Petersons share that fence line, and the Whitakers are right behind them. How do we keep festival crowds from spilling onto working farmland during one of the most critical seasons?"

Dan looks up from his notes, his expression shifting. "Good catch. We'll establish clear barriers with fencing and signage well before the livestock areas. Part of our preliminary safety assessment includes marking off-limits zones." He makes a note on his clipboard. "We can also coordinate with your neighbors to ensure their properties are clearly demarcated. Standard protocol for events on working land."

He tucks his notebook away. "With proper planning and adherence to safety protocols, this space could handle the expected crowd capacity."

Marcus nods his agreement, his clipboard full of measurements and calculations that will become permits and requisitions. "We'll need to start immediately on the power installation," he says, "but the infrastructure requirements are manageable."

Finn's excitement practically vibrates through the cold air as the officials complete their assessment. When they leave, he goes over to his car, returning with some paperwork. He hands us each a copy of what looks like a task list.

"The town's maintenance crew can handle most of the heavy lifting," Finn explains, his finger tracking down the list. "But we'll need you two to coordinate on-site logistics, power routing, and vendor placement." He looks between Bastian and me as though he's waiting for one of us to combust at the mere suggestion of collaboration.

"This is going to change everything," Bastian says quietly. His eyes scan the field, like he sees something beyond frozen grass and bare trees. "Once word gets out that Hall of Fame is hosting this…"

"We can keep it quiet," Finn offers, but Bastian's already shaking his head.

"No." The word carries weight and resignation, but they're mixed with something that might be determination. "We can't. And honestly?" He looks up, meeting first Finn's eyes, then mine. "If we're doing this, if we're really opening up the farms for the festival, then we should do it right."

Stone perks up at that, a slow grin spreading across his face. "Oh, I like where this is going."

"If Hall of Fame is known for anything, it's for putting on a hell of a show," Bastian continues, his voice gaining strength. "If Winterberry needs a Christmas festival, then let's give them the best damned one they've ever seen." He turns to Finn. "Add proper lighting design to that list. Professional sound systems. The works."

I stare at him, trying to reconcile this declaration with the man who'd been so resistant just yesterday.

"You're serious," I say, the words coming out more like an accusation than a question.

His eyes find mine, holding steady despite the chaos I know this decision will bring. "The farm's always been about community, about the land supporting the people who work it. Maybe it's time we remembered that includes more than just agriculture."

Nikko's already on his phone, no doubt pulling up contacts. "I can reach out to the lighting crew from our last tour. See who's available."

"And I know a dozen sound engineers who'd kill for a chance to work on something like this," Stone adds.

"One rule," Bastian says. "Hall of Fame is not performing. I don't want this to be about us."

The guys all nod their agreement.

The energy shifts around us, transforming from a simple site inspection into something bigger. Finn's fingers fly across his tablet, updating lists and timelines to accommodate this new scope.

I stand there with papers growing damp in my hands, watching Bastian commit fully to the very thing he fought against. His shoulders are set with that particular determination I recognize from our arguments, but directed now toward making this work rather than preventing it.

"This is insane," I mutter, but there's no heat in it. Just growing realization that my careful plans to avoid him are thinning like a whisper in the wind.

Bastian's eyes find mine again, and something passes between us. "Probably," he agrees. "But if we're going to do this, let's do it right."

Behind me, I hear Gouta's approving bleat, as though even she understands the significance of this moment. The distance to my truck suddenly feels less like salvation and more like cowardice. Whatever complications this brings, whatever chaos follows, I realize I want to be here for it.

"Okay if I review these and call you later?" I ask Finn, already turning toward my truck. "Need to check on the morning harvest crew." The excuse sounds weak even to my ears.

"Taylen." Bastian's voice follows me. "Can we talk? Please?"

I stop and turn around. "Later." Because I need to work out a plan to be around Bastian without losing my mind.

FROST AND FIRE

125

15

BASTIAN

THE BARN SMELLS LIKE WINTER. Hay dust and frost-tinged air mixing with the earthy warmth of sleeping animals. Most people would shy away from this, but for me, this is home. On stage, when I'm singing, I feel like I'm flying, but this place, the animals, they ground me.

Years ago, the band accepted the offer for a documentary to be made about us and our rise to being one of the most successful bands in the country. I had only one condition: there would be no filming on the farm. Winterberry was and still is our sanctuary.

We rented a farm in Pine Ridge, Colorado, and thankfully, the owner wanted to keep his anonymity. The NDA we had to sign was more ironclad than the one we had him sign.

In addition, he joined us when we donated the proceeds from the making of the documentary to a charity that helps young people gain the skills and knowledge to not only find employment in farming but also thrive by using sustainable farming methods.

Every day that I wake up before sunrise and walk to the

farmhouse to share an early cup of coffee with my parents, I know I made the right decision.

I make my way down the center aisle, pitchfork balanced against my shoulder. In the corner, Gouta watches with her usual regal disinterest. She seems to have taken issue with the cows and no longer wants to join them in the pasture.

My arms protest as I lift the first forkful of fresh hay, muscles reminding me that I'm not as young as I used to be. Or maybe it's just that I barely slept last night, too busy replaying moments I should probably try harder to forget.

"This is ridiculous," I announce to the empty barn. Gouta's ears twitch slightly—the only indication she's listening. "He can't just keep avoiding me." The pitchfork strikes the floor with more force than necessary as I gather another load.

The physical work should help clear my head, but each movement just seems to wind me tighter. "What did he expect?" The words echo off the wooden beams, coming back to me like accusations. "That we'd fall into bed straight away without talking about it first? Especially when I was half-drunk?"

I pause mid-motion, remembering how Taylen looked this morning. As if last night never happened. As if I hadn't crossed the space between our properties with my heart in my throat and whiskey burning in my blood. As if his lips hadn't met mine with seven years of pent-up want.

"And now he won't even look at me." The hay scatters wider than intended, my movements growing less steady as frustration builds.

Gouta bleats softly from her corner. I can't tell if it's sympathy or judgment. I lean against the pitchfork, letting its solid weight ground me in this moment instead of the ones I keep circling back to.

"You know what the worst part is?" I ask her, not

expecting or waiting for a response. "He kisses me back. Every time. In Burlington. Last night. He kisses me like he means it. Like he wants it as much as I do. Then he refuses to talk and acts like I'm the one who did something wrong."

Last night comes back to me with too much clarity considering the alcohol in my blood. Taylen's body pressed between mine and the wall, his fingers tangled in my hair, the soft sound he made when I deepened the kiss. More intense than that night in Burlington, more real somehow. No interruptions, no groups of paparazzi around the corner ready to snap their next paycheck. Just us and years of denied attraction finally breaking free.

"How long?" I say between gritted teeth. How long has he wanted me? Was that night in Burlington the start? Was it because he missed Jackson and, like me, wanted to connect with someone? Or did he feel it before?

I think back to when I turned thirty-two. Jackson fucking drove to a gig in Toronto and went as far as buying VIP tickets that included the meet and greet. When I'd gotten pissed off at him for spending the money when I could have gotten him in backstage for free, he said I could pay him back by coming home and having a good old birthday party at Joe's.

By the time we arrived back home the next day, there was a crowd at Joe's ready to celebrate my thirtieth, two years late. In the crowd was Taylen, who'd turned twenty a few days before my birthday.

For the first time in my life, I'd stopped seeing the little kid who grew up chasing us.

Stopped seeing the twelve-year age gap. Because Taylen was all the way grown up and looking at me like he knew exactly what to do with his grown-up body.

I'd taken a flight out of Vermont the day after the party to join the band in Montreal. My excuse was that we had a meeting with the producers of the new album. I definitely wasn't running away from the way my eyes had seemed to find Taylen everywhere at the party, or at how wrong it was that I was feeling this way for my best friend's younger brother.

If Jackson knew, he'd have kicked my ass because if there was one person he was protective of other than me, that was his younger brother.

I drive the pitchfork into a fresh bale with enough force to make the handle vibrate. "And now we're supposed to work together on this festival. Coordinate everything. Be professional." The last word comes out like a curse. "How exactly am I supposed to do that when he won't stay in one place long enough to have a conversation?"

The physical labor grows more aggressive as my frustration builds. The hay flies into stalls with increasing force, scattering wider with each toss. Part of me knows I'm just making more work for myself, but the satisfaction of the movement outweighs my concerns.

Sweat begins to gather at my collar despite the chill in the air, but I welcome the discomfort. It's better than the ache in my chest when I think about how Taylen looked at me this morning, chillier than the November frost.

"What was I thinking?" I continue. "Showing up drunk at his door and kissing him without warning?" The words taste bitter, like truth usually does. "Should have waited. Should have talked first. Should have done anything except what I actually did."

My hands throb from gripping the pitchfork so tight.

"God, I want him," I admit.

But his anger runs deeper than just one abandoned kiss in Burlington or one whiskey-soaked one. "What happened to you, Tay? When did you start carrying so much anger? And how much of it is really about me?"

The silence that answers makes me look up, scanning the barn's shadows for my usual audience. But Gouta has disappeared, probably bored with my romantic crisis or off seeking more interesting entertainment. "Great," I mutter, returning to my task with renewed determination. "Now even she can't stand me."

How do I get him to talk to me?

How do you fix what's broken when you're not even sure where the cracks started? The questions pile up like the hay I'm spreading, each one adding weight to an already heavy load.

"One thing at a time," I tell myself, putting down the pitchfork and grabbing the broom to brush off the hay dust. "Finish the stalls. Feed the animals. Figure out how to make him listen." The list grows as I work.

Gouta returns when I'm almost done, trotting through the barn door with her usual determination. She doesn't pause to inspect the quality of my work or sit on her throne. Instead, she makes a beeline straight for me.

She grabs my shirt sleeve between her teeth, her grip firm.

"What do you want?" I ask, but she just tugs harder, backing up with purposeful steps that clearly mean I'm supposed to follow.

I try to pull away, more interested in finishing my work than following whatever scheme she's involved in. But Gouta is nothing if not persistent. Her grip on my sleeve tightens, and she pulls me along like a child leading a reluctant parent.

"If you want treats, I'm not falling for it. I bet you've been in the house all this time getting fed by Mom," I tell her, though we both know it's a lie. I've never been able to resist her when she gets like this: determined, focused, and mischievous.

But even as I protest, my feet follow her guidance. The

broom leans forgotten against a stall as Gouta leads me toward the barn door.

We emerge into cold air that catches in my lungs, making each breath sharp and clear. Gouta pulls me toward Mom's small orchard, where her cherry and pear trees are ready to face the Vermont winter.

Her pace never falters, though she does glance back occasionally as if checking that I'm still following.

The orchard approaches slowly. Mom loves this place, tends it with the same care she gives to her family. The trees know her touch, respond to her gentle guidance year after year.

As we approach the orchard's center, Gouta slows down. And there, perfectly positioned between the trees, sit two wooden boxes that definitely weren't there yesterday.

My steps falter as recognition hits. The boxes are familiar in shape and size, and even from this distance, I can see the care that went into their placement. The perfect angle to catch the morning sun.

Beehives.

Gouta releases my sleeve, her job apparently complete. She moves to sit beneath the cherry tree, watching me with what looks suspiciously like satisfaction.

I approach the boxes slowly. As I draw closer, details become clearer: the smooth wood, the careful joints, the small entrance holes positioned exactly as they should be.

A small tag dangles from one of the boxes, its paper curling slightly at the edges. I reach for it to read the message clearly written in Taylen's handwriting.

These girls don't sting, unlike some people we know.

Even though I know this is meant to piss me off, I'm unable to stop the curl of my lips into a smile.

"Clever, Taylen," I say softly. "Very clever."

Gouta bleats from her spot beneath the cherry tree, sounding entirely too pleased with herself. I turn to find her watching me with what can only be described as smug satisfaction. "You knew about this all along, didn't you?" I ask, but she just settles more comfortably into her chosen spot.

I run my hand along one of the hive's edges. "Game on, Taylen." Because this forces me to make a choice. "Game. On."

I stare at the waiting hives, my decision forming with unexpected clarity. "If this is how you want to play it, I'm game." Because two can play this game. This dance of gestures and meanings, this way of saying things we're not ready to voice directly.

"Come on, Gouta," I call, turning back toward the barn. "We've got work to do." She rises with elegant grace, falling into step beside me as we leave the hives. Behind us, afternoon light will soon give way to dusk.

On the walk back, each step feels lighter, more purposeful, as plans form in my mind. Taylen wants to communicate through elaborate gestures? Fine. I can work with that. Can match him gesture for gesture, meaning for meaning, until we find our way to words that don't need translation.

Winter air fills my lungs with each breath. Somewhere across the property line, Taylen is probably wondering if I've found his gift yet, if I understand what he's trying to say. The thought makes my smile grow wider, more determined.

Because this is a language I'm finally starting to understand. And if this is how we need to start, how we bridge the distance between us, then I'm ready to become fluent.

16

———

TAYLEN

My boots drag against each porch step like they're coated in cement, muscles screaming from hours of work on top of supervising the move of the fences to make sure the festival doesn't encroach on land that it's not supposed to.

The only thing that makes it all better is that I've had two full days without having to see Bastian's face or deal with the electricity that crackles between us whenever we're forced to occupy the same space.

The satisfaction of avoidance dissolves instantly when I spot a small package propped against my door, wrapped in brown paper. No shipping label or return address. Just my name written in a familiar hand that makes my stomach clench.

"No," I mutter, fumbling with my keys. "Whatever game you're playing, I'm not interested." But my fingers betray me, already reaching for the package even as I push through the door.

Inside, I remove my mud-caked boots before I drop onto the couch. The paper crinkles as I turn the package over, studying it like it might detonate. Knowing Bastian, it might.

He's playing my game now, and I'm suddenly not sure I want to keep participating.

The wrapping comes apart easily, revealing a small box that still carries the faint scent of cedar. My heart kicks against my ribs as I lift the lid. Inside, nestled on a bed of soft fabric, lies a single key attached to a leather keychain stamped with *Property Manager* in elegant script.

A note rests beneath it.

Full access granted.
Make yourself at home.
B

Anger floods my system, hot and sharp as summer lightning. "Make yourself at home?" I spit the phrase like poison, surging to my feet. The box tumbles to the floor, but the key burns in my palm like a brand.

What exactly does he think this means? That he can walk away from a kiss, *twice*, then dangle sex like some kind of reward?

The leather keychain mocks me with its implications. Property manager. Like I'm some kind of employee he can summon at will.

I pace the living room, each step driving splinters of fury deeper under my skin. My gifts were meant to prove to him that staying in Vermont requires commitment. Time. Dedication. But this? This is different.

"Bastard," I call, the word echoing off the walls of my empty house.

I stand there in the middle of my living room, exhaustion weighing down every inch of my body, fury crackling under my skin.

My reflection catches in the darkened window. I look

wild-eyed, flushed, and half-feral. This is exactly what Bastian does to me. Reduces me to this churning mess of want and anger and confusion.

I need to wash this day off. All of it. The physical labor, the festival prep, and especially whatever game Bastian thinks he's playing.

The shower calls like salvation, promising to wash away both physical grime and emotional turmoil. I strip quickly, letting my work clothes fall where they land. Hot water pounds against sore muscles, but it does nothing to quiet the storm in my head.

What would happen if I used the key? Just walked into his space unannounced, demanded explanations for this latest move in our complicated game? The thought sends heat through my core, which makes me even angrier. Why does my body react to him like this?

It's not like I haven't been with other guys. I've even tried one or two relationships that never lasted longer than a few months. Their reason was that my farm life wasn't compatible with dining out or regular trips to Burlington to watch a show. Now I'm wondering if maybe my stupid body gave me away without consent. That they knew I wasn't as invested in making it work as I thought I'd been.

I shut off the shower with more force than necessary, reaching for a towel. My closet offers too few choices because every pair of jeans has fallen victim to a fence that needed to be urgently repaired.

I settle on dark jeans that I know fit well and a Henley that brings out my eyes. If I'm going to do this, I want to look good while doing it.

The key sits on my dresser where I tossed it. I study it while running fingers through my damp hair. I could still ignore it. Could leave it on his porch with a note of my own. Could pretend this latest escalation never happened.

But my feet carry me back to the dresser, my fingers closing around the cool metal. Because ignoring Bastian has never worked. Not in Burlington, not after his return, not now. The time for running has passed.

Time to end whatever dance we've been doing since that night in Burlington.

The sun hangs low as I step back onto my porch, casting everything in shades of gold and shadow. Across the property line, warm light spills from Bastian's cabin windows. My feet find the familiar path, each step carrying me closer to the moment that will either destroy us both or forge something neither of us can walk away from.

The key slides into the lock with embarrassing ease. Music drifts through the door, something low and intimate that makes my anger spike higher. The cabin's warmth wraps around me as I step inside, carrying scents of garlic and wine and deliberate seduction.

Bastian stands at the stove, sleeves rolled to expose forearms that flex as he stirs something that smells ridiculously good. He doesn't turn around, but he doesn't need to for me to know a smile plays at the corner of his mouth. "Oh good, you got my invitation."

The casual tone ignites something in my chest. I pull the key from my pocket. "What the hell do you think this means?" The words come out sharp enough to cut.

"Exactly what the tag says." He moves the pan off the heat, still not looking at me directly. "Property manager. Since you seem so invested in adding to my livestock."

"Your livestock?" The laugh that escapes me carries no humor. "You mean the goat that follows you around like a devoted puppy? The chickens you've probably already named and spoiled rotten?"

My point is proven when I see the chickens and Gouta

huddled together on top of a blanket in the corner of his living room.

He turns around. "Let me introduce you to Moira and Myrtle," he says mildly. "And since you've taken such an interest in their welfare, I thought you might appreciate official access to check on them."

"Bullshit." I take a step closer, anger making me bold. "This isn't about the animals. This is about you trying to manipulate the situation. Again."

His eyebrow rises slightly as he reaches for the wine bottle breathing on the counter. "Manipulate? That's an interesting accusation from someone who installed beehives in my mother's orchard without asking."

"That was different." The defense sounds weak even to my ears. "That was about the farm."

"Was it?" He pours wine into waiting glasses with elegant precision. "Had nothing to do with proving a point about commitment? About staying power?" His eyes meet mine over the rim of his glass. "About permanence?"

Heat crawls up my neck that has nothing to do with the cabin's warmth. "You're a manipulative bastard, you know that?"

"Takes one to know one." The words carry no heat, just quiet acknowledgment that makes something twist in my chest. "We're both playing games, Taylen. Have been since Burlington. Maybe it's time we stopped pretending otherwise."

I move closer, drawn by some force stronger than anger or pride. "Is that what this is? Another game?" My hand sweeps to indicate the intimate table setting, the wine, the music still playing softly in the background. "Another move in whatever chess match you think we're playing?"

"No games." He sets his glass down with deliberate care. "Not anymore. You gave me permanent residents for my farm. I'm giving you permanent access to my space. Seems like a fair trade."

"There's nothing fair about this." My voice drops lower as the distance between us shrinks. "You don't get to walk away from kissing me—*twice*—then act like giving me a key makes everything okay."

"I walked away because I was drunk," he counters, moving to meet me in the middle of his kitchen. "Because you were angry. Because we've spent seven years turning attraction into ammunition, and I wanted to do this right for once."

The admission lands like lightning, charging the air between us. "This?" I gesture between us, close enough now to see the flecks of silver in his hair, to smell cologne and wine and something uniquely him. "What exactly is this, Bastian?"

"You tell me." His voice carries challenge and invitation in equal measure. "You're the one who showed up at my door. Used the key I gave you. Walked into the trap you claim I set."

The laugh that escapes me sounds slightly wild. "Yeah, the trap. You knew exactly what you were doing when you left that key. It's all an elaborate setup to get under my skin."

"Get under your skin?" He moves closer until I can feel the heat radiating from his body. "That's rich coming from you. You've been driving me wild since the day I came back. The goat, the chickens, the beehive, and even going along with my brother's plan to host the Christmas Festival here. Every perfectly calculated move designed to prove I don't belong here."

"That's not—"

"Isn't it?" His eyes hold mine with dangerous intensity. "Baby, you've had me twisted up in knots for weeks. Hell, for years, if I'm being honest. Every look, every argument, every moment you let your guard down just enough to remind me what I'm missing. So the question is, what are you going to do about it?"

The endearment makes my breath catch. "Don't," I warn, but it comes out more like a plea than a protest. "Don't act like you know what I want."

"But I do know." I take another step closer, eliminating what little space remains between us. "Same thing you wanted in Burlington. Same thing you wanted the other night in your living room. Same thing you want right now."

His certainty should make me angry, should make me want to prove him wrong. Instead, it sends heat pooling low in my stomach, making my skin prickle with awareness. "You're awfully sure of yourself."

"No." He shakes his head slightly, close enough that I can see his pupils dilate. "I'm only sure of this thing that's been burning hotter than a wildfire in the summer. Of the way you look at me when you think no one's watching."

The words hang between us. "And how exactly do I look at you?"

His smile turns dangerous. "Like you want to fuck me or kill me. Sometimes both at once."

"Maybe I do," I say, like it's a dare. "Maybe that's the problem."

His breath catches slightly, the only indication that my words affect him. "The only problem," he says carefully, "is that we've spent years running from something we both want. And I'm tired of running."

The declaration lands like a challenge and a confession. We stand in his kitchen, breathing the same air, both of us swaying slightly with the gravity of what's building between us. Every heartbeat feels like a countdown to something inevitable, something years in the making.

"Prove it," I challenge, my voice rough with need and fear. "Prove you're done running."

His eyes darken at the words, pupils blown wide with want that matches my own. The moment stretches between us like a wire pulled too tight, threatening to snap at any second. When he speaks, his voice carries edges sharp enough to cut. "Make me."

The space between us vanishes as we move together, my hands finding his hair while he grips my hips with bruising force. Unlike the first two, this kiss is all teeth and tongue and years of wanting compressed into a single point of contact.

Bastian's mouth opens against mine immediately, hot and demanding as his hands slide beneath my shirt. The touch of skin on skin sends electricity through my system, making me arch closer.

I use the grip on his hair to adjust the angle of our kiss. He makes a low sound in his throat, a growled surrender that goes straight to my core. The vibration of it travels through every point where our bodies connect, turning want into desperate need.

"This what you wanted?" I manage between kisses, the words coming out more breathless than challenging. "This why you gave me that key?"

His answer comes in the form of teeth against my bottom lip, the slight pain shooting straight to my groin. Then his mouth travels lower, finding the sensitive spot below my ear that makes my knees threaten to buckle. "I've wanted you for so long," he murmurs against my skin.

The admission breaks something loose in my chest. My hands move to his shoulders, pushing him back until he hits the counter. The new position lets me press my thigh between his legs, drawing a groan that sounds like victory. "Show me," I demand, rolling my hips to create friction that makes us both gasp. "Prove it."

In one fluid motion, he reverses our positions, lifting me onto the counter with a strength that sends heat flooding through my system. My legs wrap around his waist instinctively as his mouth reclaims mine, the new angle allowing him to control the kiss completely.

Hands fumble with buttons, each new inch of exposed skin demanding immediate attention. My shirt lands somewhere behind us, followed quickly by his.

I gasp when I see the *J* tattooed on his chest, but I don't have a chance to ask about it before he's on me again.

"Bedroom," Bastian growls against my neck, but makes no move to release me. His hands map my back, my sides, my chest. Each point of contact is a brand against my skin, marking me as his in ways I've spent years pretending I haven't wanted but couldn't deny.

"Then move," I challenge, but my body betrays me by pulling him closer. My fingers trace the muscles of his shoulders, learning textures and patterns I've only admired from a distance. He feels better than any fantasy. Solid and warm and perfectly real against me.

The journey to his bedroom happens in stages, neither of us willing to break contact for long. Boots and socks disappear somewhere in the hallway. My back finds the wall beside his door as his mouth works its way down my throat, drawing sounds I barely recognize as my own. His hands settle on my hips again, thumbs stroking bare skin just above my waistband in maddening circles.

"Still think I'm running?" he asks against my collarbone, the words vibrating through my chest. Before I can answer, his teeth find sensitive flesh, marking me. The thought that I'll see the bruise there in the morning sends fresh heat through my system, making me arch into the contact.

"Shut up," I manage, pulling his mouth back to mine. The kiss turns deeper, slower, heavier. His hands slide lower, cupping my ass and pulling me tight against him. The increased contact draws moans from both our throats, the sounds mixing together like harmony.

We stumble through his doorway until the back of my knees hit his mattress, but before I can fall, he spins us around. My body covers his as we land together.

"God, look at you," he breathes, hands roaming my chest and tracing my tattoos with reverent attention. The praise makes me flush, but before I can deflect, he flips us again so I'm under him and his mouth is following the path of his fingers. My hands fist in his sheets as he works his way down my body.

His fingers find my zipper, the sound loud in the room's heated air. I lift my hips to help him remove the last barriers between us, then his mouth is on my cock, hot and perfect and exactly what I need.

"Bastian," I gasp, the name carrying years of desire compressed into those two syllables. His response is to take me deeper, drawing sounds from my throat that would embarrass me if I had any capacity for shame left. My fingers find his hair again, the silky strands tangling around my grip as pleasure builds like lightning in my blood.

17

BASTIAN

EVERY SOUND TAYLEN makes vibrates through me like guitar strings struck too hard, raw and perfect and slightly dangerous. His fingers tighten in my hair as I take him deeper until my mouth is full of him.

His hips buck slightly, but I hold him steady, savoring the way his muscles tremble under my palms. Each gasp, each plea of my name feeds something hungry inside me. Not just desire, but a darker need to prove something. To show him what we've been running from, what we could have had if he'd stopped pushing me away.

"God, Bastian," he moans, the words breaking on exhale. I hollow my cheeks in response, drawing another desperate sound from his throat. His soft skin tastes like salt and winter air.

I pull back slowly, letting him slide from my mouth. His protest dies as I begin moving up his body, mapping territory I've dreamed about since that birthday party years ago. My lips find the sharp curve of his hip, my tongue tracing the line where muscle meets bone. "You're perfect," I murmur against his skin. "Every inch of you."

His breath catches as I work higher, paying careful attention to the ridges of his abs, the definition years of physical labor have carved into his frame. A light sheen of sweat makes his skin gleam in the dim light, and I chase the salt taste with my tongue. "So beautiful," I tell him.

The flush spreading across his chest turns deeper at my words, but he doesn't look away. His eyes hold mine as I continue my exploration, marking my path with gentle bites and soothing kisses. When I reach his collarbone, I pause to admire the way color blooms beneath his skin where my teeth have been.

"What do you want?" I ask against his throat, letting my breath ghost over his sensitive flesh. His body shivers in response, but his mouth curves into that familiar sarcastic smile.

"World peace," he drawls, the words ending on a gasp as I bite down harder. "Maybe an end to hunger. You know, the usual."

Something dark and possessive rises in my chest. My hand finds his throat, not squeezing, just resting there with deliberate pressure. His pulse races against my palm as his eyes go wide, pupils blown with want. "Try again," I growl, watching his reaction closely. "What. Do. You. Want?"

The moan that escapes him sounds like surrender. His hips roll against mine, creating a delicious pressure that makes me gasp. "You," he admits finally, voice rough with need. "Inside me. Now."

I lean down to capture his mouth, savoring not only his taste but how his body hums with frustration because he needs more. "Do we need condoms?"

"You tell me. I'm not the one being followed around by roadies and groupies. Someone new in every city. I've read the headlines."

The implication that I fuck every willing body stings, but it's not like he'd know any different. The Hall of Fame band members aren't portrayed as saints for a reason. But for the last fifteen years, we've been hiding Kay. We were never the wild kids everyone thought we were, but as soon as Kay came along, it was as if we all had permission to not do the wild stuff we were expected to do. We were protecting Mik and his daughter. Headlines were carefully leaked by our manager, Daisy. But Taylen believes it, and that's not something I'm comfortable with.

"Stop." The word comes out harder than intended, making him blink. "How long do you think it's been since I've been with anyone?"

His expression shifts, caught between sarcasm and uncertainty. "I don't… That's not…"

"Eight years," I tell him, watching understanding dawn in his eyes. "Eight years since I've touched anyone like this. Since anyone has touched me."

The math isn't hard. His breath catches as he works it out. Eight years means before Burlington, means no one since that night we almost…since we were interrupted… since everything changed.

"I'm on PrEP," he says finally, voice smaller than before. "Get tested regularly. Always use protection with…" He trails off, like he's just realized what he's admitting. "We don't need…"

"Good." I cut him off before he can continue, not wanting to think about who else he's been with, about all the time we've wasted dancing around this thing between us. "Because I want to feel every inch of you. Want to make you feel every second of those seven years I've been waiting to do this with you."

His eyes go impossibly darker, surprise and arousal mixing in his expression. For once, he seems to be at a complete loss for words, his usual sharp wit abandoned in the face of my confession.

"I'm sorry," Taylen whispers, but I silence him with a kiss.

My hands frame his face, thumbs stroking over stubble as I pour everything I can't say into the contact. When I pull back, his eyes hold questions I'm finally ready to answer.

"I don't want your apologies," I tell him, my voice rough and needy. "I want you."

His response comes as movement rather than words, body arching into mine as his legs spread wider in clear invitation. "Then take me," he breathes against my mouth, the challenge in his tone softened by the way his hands clutch at my shoulders.

I reach for the bedside drawer, feeling for the bottle I keep there. The lube feels cold on my fingers, but I warm it carefully before touching him. His breath catches at the first press of my finger, his body tensing slightly before relaxing into the sensation.

"Okay?" I ask, watching his face for any signs of discomfort.

His expression holds only want, lips parted on quick breaths as I work him open, showing him what this really means to me. When I add a second finger, his back arches off the bed, a sound escaping him that shoots straight to my core.

"More," he demands, hips rolling to take my fingers deeper.

I comply, adding a third while my free hand strokes his thigh, soothing the tremors I feel building in his muscles. He's gorgeous like this. His curls untamed, his blue eyes dark as night, all that control stripped away, leaving just raw need and trust that makes my chest tight.

Time loses meaning as I prepare him, every gasp and

moan fueling my own desperation. When he starts riding my fingers in earnest, I know we're both ready. The loss of contact as I withdraw draws a protest from his throat, but it turns to approval as I slick myself and line up.

The first press inside feels like coming home. I freeze, overwhelmed by the sensation. By the realization that this is happening. His fingers dig into my shoulders hard enough to leave marks, and I welcome the slight pain, the proof that this is real, that we're finally here.

"Move," he growls, and I obey, starting a rhythm that draws sounds from both our throats.

Each thrust feels electric, pleasure building like storm clouds on summer evenings. My mouth finds his neck, alternating between gentle kisses and sharp bites that make him arch beneath me.

His legs wrap around my waist, changing the angle until we both gasp. One of my hands finds his hip, grip tight enough to bruise, while the other tangles in his hair.

We kiss deeply, messily, sharing every breath. His teeth catch my bottom lip as I thrust harder, the slight pain mixing with pleasure until I can't tell them apart. Every touch feels like a confession, every sound like prayer, every movement like something we should have done years ago.

When his release hits, it takes me by surprise. His body tightens around me as he cries out, his back arching perfectly, displaying his pleasure like a beautiful show that was made just for me. The sight and sensation push me over the edge, my own climax crashing through.

We collapse together, our hearts racing in sync as aftershocks ripple through us. The silence that follows feels weighted with things neither of us is ready to voice. After a moment, I press a kiss to his temple and slide carefully free, earning a soft sound of loss that makes my chest ache.

The bathroom seems too far, but I force myself to move.

The washcloth I bring back is warm, and I clean him with gentle thoroughness, paying attention to any signs of discomfort. His eyes never leave my face as I tend to him, expression unreadable in the room's dim light.

When I'm done, I throw the cloth on the floor and lie beside him, wrapping my arms around his body until he's pressed against my chest. The weight of his body feels both foreign and familiar, like a song I wrote so long ago I've forgotten the words but remember the melody. I trace idle patterns across his skin, mapping the art inked there with careful attention.

I'm afraid of saying the wrong thing, of breaking the spell.

He does it first.

"Tell me about this," he says, tracing the *J* on my chest. The only tattoo I have.

"I did it after he died. I couldn't come home, and…let's just say my behavior on the road made me unpopular with the band. Stone was the one who suggested doing something to focus my grief. Every time I look at it, I remember him, his words of support and encouragement. How he told me to chase my dreams."

He hums as his fingers move back and forth over my skin.

"Tell me about yours," I murmur, following a particular line that curves around his sides. He shifts slightly but doesn't pull away, his breath steady against my collar.

"They're for Jackson too. I get a new one every year," he says after a moment, his voice quiet in the room's stillness. "On the anniversary of his death."

The admission makes my hand still, but he continues before I can speak, "Each one means something different. Memories or inside jokes or things he loved." His fingers find mine, guiding them to various designs. "This one's for the constellation he always pointed out in the sky that he never got right. This is for the truck he was restoring. This is for the summer we all learned to swim in the lake."

My throat tightens as I recognize the memories he's preserved in ink and skin. Images I recognize from our shared past, and moments I wasn't there to commemorate with him. Twelve years of grief marked in permanent lines while I was away chasing the spotlight and trying to outrun my own loss.

I trace the palm of his hand with my fingers, noticing a tattoo for the first time.

"And this one?" I ask, touching the design on his wrist that looks like a worn leather band. He tenses slightly, but he doesn't pull away.

"That was the first one," he says, voice rougher now. "He had a leather bracelet he never took off. After the accident, I asked about it, but it was never found. The police said it probably got caught on something and snapped off."

I kiss his forehead and then turn slightly so I can reach the drawer in my bedside table to retrieve the most precious thing I own.

Taylen's breath catches as I unwrap it carefully, revealing the worn leather darkened with age and wear. The bracelet looks smaller than I remember, though the craftsmanship still shows in every careful stitch.

"How…?" Taylen's voice breaks on the word, his eyes fixed on the familiar band. "Is it really…?"

"He gave it to me," I admit quietly, watching emotion play across his features. "Last time I saw him. He joked that I didn't come home often enough, and one day, I'd forget about him. He didn't want that." The sound that comes out of my throat is like a weird guttural laugh that sounds foreign even to me. "Like I would forget my best friend who was like a brother to me."

Taylen's fingers hover over the leather, trembling slightly but not quite touching.

"He was everything," I continue, words spilling out. "The person who grew up with me, the one I came out to before anyone else. The one who encouraged my songwriting, told me singing was the coolest thing."

Tears gather in Taylen's eyes. My throat feels tight, and I'm hanging by a thread. I haven't spoken about Jackson since he died, and now I realize Taylen and I have both been grieving in our own way. When he finally touches the bracelet, his fingertips barely brush the worn surface, as though he's afraid it might disappear. Then, suddenly, he's kissing me, brief and hard, before turning away.

I watch him swing his legs over the bed's edge, his broad back like a wall between us. "Please stay...for dinner?" I offer, trying desperately to keep my voice steady. "I was cooking before you arrived..."

"Can't." The word comes out clipped, final. He stands and begins gathering his scattered clothing. I stay silent as he dresses, watching him rebuild his walls piece by piece, and hopeless to stop it from happening.

At the door, he pauses, glancing back with an expression I can't read. Then he's gone, footsteps fading down the hall. The bracelet sits heavy in my palm.

Losing my best friend broke me, but losing Taylen will obliterate me.

I put the bracelet back in its resting place as Gouta's head peeks through the open door to my room.

"Yeah, yeah, I know. I'll fix it," I say, hoping it's not another lie.

18

————

TAYLEN

THE BELLS above Noëlle's Bakery door chime as I shoulder my way inside, arms straining under stacked delivery boxes. As soon as I'm through, I'm met with the scent of Christmas spices: cinnamon, nutmeg, allspice, and orange.

"Taylen!" Noëlle's voice carries over the hiss of espresso machines and murmur of morning customers. "Can you drop those in the kitchen for me, honey?" She emerges from behind the counter, her floral-patterned apron dusted with flour. "Let me finish with this customer, and I'll give you a hand."

"I'll swap your help for a coffee," I say, moving around the counter toward the kitchen at the back.

"Sure thing, honey."

It takes three back-to-back trips to my truck to offload the boxes Noëlle has on a regular order. With every journey, my stomach reminds me it would be a good idea to have one of Noëlle's amazing pastries.

"You look terrible," she says, inspecting the delivery boxes. "When's the last time you slept properly?" Her eyes narrow as she studies my face, probably cataloging the dark circles and stubble I couldn't be bothered to deal with this morning.

I force a smile that feels more like a grimace. "Been busy with festival prep. Anyway, I got you the usual applesauce and preserves," I add quickly, gesturing to the boxes before she can press further. "Plus some of the experimental cider varieties you wanted to try."

"You are the bestest," she says, already lifting lids to inspect the contents. But her eyes keep darting to my face. "The Christmas Festival relocation must be keeping you running," she says carefully. "Such short notice, having to coordinate with the Hall property…everyone in town is talking about it."

My belly churns at her mention of the Hall name. "Something like that." The words come out clipped, earning another worried look from Noëlle.

"Sit," she commands suddenly, pointing to an empty table. "I'm making you coffee. And you're taking a spiced bun too." When I start to protest, she adds, "On the house. You look like you need it."

Before I can argue, the bell chimes again. My stomach drops as Finn enters, his usual energy somewhat subdued this morning. He spots me immediately. "Tay."

"Finn, your usual?" Noëlle asks. "Why don't you two sit over there by the window, and I'll get you both taken care of in no time."

I sink into the indicated chair, knowing resistance is futile when Noëlle gets that tone. Finn hesitates only briefly before claiming the seat across from me.

"You haven't been answering your phone," he says quietly. The accusation carries notes of hurt I'm not ready to deal with.

"Been busy." I study the scarred tabletop. "Festival stuff, you know how it is. After all, you made the list."

"About that…" He leans forward, voice dropping lower. "I know it's been chaotic. But I promise that as soon as the infrastructure is in place, we can handle most of it. I just want to make sure we don't accidentally take up more space than was agreed on."

"It's fine."

"Seriously, Tay. You don't need to—"

"Not everything is about the damn festival, okay?" The words explode out of me, harsher than intended, but thankfully, no one overhears my little outburst. "Maybe I have other problems that don't revolve around the fucking Christmas Festival."

Finn's expression shifts from concern to confusion. "Tay, what's going on?"

I scoff. "What? You're interested in being my best friend now?"

"Tay, that's not fair."

"Really? Because from where I'm standing, it seems you haven't made space or time for the person you call a best friend in weeks."

His face pales. "I'm—"

"Whatever." I'm on my feet now, chair scraping back with an ugly sound.

The bakery has gone quiet, every eye on our corner table. Noëlle stands frozen behind the counter, coffee pot in hand. Shame and anger war in my chest as I look at Finn's stricken expression.

"Sorry, Noëlle, I'll take your coffee another time. Just remembered I have another delivery to make this morning."

I move, shouldering past customers toward the door, taking a deep, cold breath when I'm outside again. I knew I should have gotten someone else to make the deliveries today.

My hands shake as I fumble with my truck keys, adrenaline making that simple task difficult. Behind me, I hear the bakery door open, but I'm already sliding behind the wheel. The engine turns over with a familiar growl, and I pull away from the curb.

In my rearview mirror, Finn stands on the sidewalk looking lost. The sight sends fresh guilt through my system, mixing with anger and confusion until I can't tell them apart. I press the accelerator harder. The sooner I'm back at the farm, the sooner I can take this energy out on work.

Minutes later, gravel sprays beneath my tires as I pull up to my farmhouse, and I'm out of the truck before the engine fully dies.

The axe feels too light in my hands as I approach the woodpile.

The first log splits with a satisfying crack, pieces falling to either side like my composure at Noëlle's. I set up another immediately, not allowing myself time to think. The axe bites deep, sending vibrations up my arms that feel like the punishment I deserve.

I know I was a dick to Finn, and I'll need to apologize. It's not his fault I'm all torn up inside over his brother. But he's not totally without fault. I would have talked to him if he'd been around. If he'd uttered any words to me that weren't about the Christmas Festival.

Probably.

Sweat begins to gather at my collar despite the cool air. Each swing carries more force than the last, the wood giving way beneath the steel of my axe. The pile of split logs grows as the morning turns into the afternoon.

My shoulders burn, but I welcome the sensation. Physical pain feels cleaner than the mess in my head, simpler than remembering Finn's hurt expression or Bastian's hands on my skin. The axe rises and falls with increasing speed, my breathing growing ragged as I push harder.

A particularly aggressive swing sends splinters flying, one catching my cheek with a sharp sting. Blood wells, warm against my wind-chilled skin.

Fuck.

I need to stop before I get seriously injured, but I can't just leave this mess, so I start hauling it into the barn.

The chicken coop needs cleaning. It always needs cleaning. An endless task like trying to sort out my own mess. When I'm done with the logs, I attack them with furious energy, scraping and scrubbing while Elvis watches from his perch. The rooster's occasional comments sound like criticism, but maybe that's just guilt talking.

By late afternoon, I'm physically exhausted and starving. My muscles tremble with effort at each simple movement, but my mind feels clearer, like manual labor has scraped away some of the confusion clouding my thoughts.

Dusk paints the world in shades of apology as I trudge toward my house, my muscles screaming with each step. Finn's silhouette on my porch stops me short. He's sitting on the bench I have on the porch, hunched against the evening chill. The sight sends a load of fresh guilt through my system.

"You look like hell," he announces as I approach, his voice carrying more concern than judgment. His eyes track over my disheveled appearance. Work-stained clothes, bleeding hands, the cut on my cheek I'd forgotten about until now.

"Yeah, well." Words fail me as I reach the steps, body suddenly too heavy to move farther. I sink down beside him. "About this morning—"

"No," he interrupts, turning to face me fully. "Let me go first." His shoulders square like he's preparing for something difficult. "I've been a terrible friend lately. You're right. I haven't been there when you needed me. And I'm sorry."

The simple admission catches me off guard. "Finn…"

"I've been dealing with…stuff," he continues carefully. "Things I'm not ready to talk about yet. But I let it affect our friendship, and that's not okay."

"You know you can tell me anything, right?"

His smile carries an edge of something I can't quite read. "I know. And I will, when I'm ready. But right now, I miss my best friend. Miss knowing what's going on in your life."

The words break something loose in my chest. "I hooked up with someone," I blurt out.

His eyebrows rise slightly, but he doesn't seem surprised. "And?"

"And I should regret it." My voice catches on the words. "But I don't. Even though it's complicated everything, even though it's probably a huge mistake, I can't make myself sorry it happened."

"Why would you want to regret good sex?"

"It's just…complicated." The word feels inadequate to describe the mess I've made, but it's all I have.

Finn has this knowing look that makes me wonder if he knows how I feel about Bastian. Whenever he's mentioned his brother in the past, I've always been so busy pretending I don't care, so he won't find out how I feel, that I've probably missed the fact that he's provided the information voluntarily.

His hand finds my shoulder, squeezing gently. The gesture breaks the last of my defenses, and suddenly, we're hugging properly.

"I love you, Tay."

"Love you too, Finn."

Movement catches my eye over his shoulder. Bastian stands at our property line, watching us with an expression I can't read from this distance. Our eyes lock across the space between us, and for a split second, I want him to be the one whose arms are around me, but he turns away immediately, retreating with long strides that carry him quickly out of sight.

My heart hammers in my chest as I pull back from Finn's embrace. The evening air feels suddenly colder. "Let's get drunk," I suggest impulsively. "Forget all the shit in our lives for one night."

"God, yes." He follows me inside, complaining dramatically about the house's temperature. "Do you not believe in heat? Are we practicing for winter survival scenarios?"

I shove him playfully toward the thermostat while heading for the cabinet that holds Dad's old liquor collection. The bottles clink together as I pull out likely candidates: whiskey for courage, vodka for honesty, rum for when things get really interesting.

"You're going to freeze to death in your sleep," Finn continues, fiddling with temperature controls. "They'll find you perfectly preserved like those mountain climbers, except surrounded by apple crates instead of snow drifts."

The familiar banter feels like coming home as I line up shot glasses on the counter. "You volunteering to keep me warm?" I tease, earning a snort of laughter.

"Not with you stinking like that. Besides, I'm pretty sure that job's taken," he returns without missing a beat. Before I can process that, he claims a bottle of whiskey and heads for the living room. "Come on, let's see what truths we can extract from each other."

"Let me grab a quick shower first. I wouldn't want to harm your sensitive nose."

"Honey, I love the smell of sweaty man like any other warm-blooded gay man, but I draw the line at chicken shit."

I grab the nearest pillow from the couch and throw it at

him. As I disappear to my room, I shout at him to order some food, which, depending on how lazy he's feeling, means a call to order takeout or a short walk to his parents'.

The night stretches ahead, promising honesty or oblivion. But as the hot water relaxes my muscles, I find myself ready for whatever truths might surface. Some things can't stay buried forever, no matter how deep we try to hide them.

19

BASTIAN

"THE REVERB IN HERE IS DIFFERENT," Stone announces, head tilted like he's listening to something only he can hear. "Must be the temperature change. We should adjust the—"

"If you touch one more setting," Fox warns from his corner, "I will personally ensure your next drum solo involves nothing but a cowbell."

The space feels smaller with all of us crammed in the small studio. Stone at his kit, Fox perched on an amp with his bass, while Nikko balances his tablet on his knee as he scrolls through what looks like concert dates, probably for the Christmas Festival. The only absence is Mik. They went back to Stillwater but promised to return for the festival once Kay is out of school for the holidays.

Sheet music litters every surface. I pick up my guitar and let muscle memory find the opening chords of the song we've been working on all morning.

"About the album timing. Daisy—" Nikko starts, but Stone cuts him off with a particularly aggressive cymbal hit.

"We're not rushing this one," he says, voice carrying the

tone that means he's prepared to die on this hill. "The last album felt forced. This one needs to breathe."

He's right. Every song we've written since our hiatus feels different, more grounded somehow. Like we're finally writing what we love instead of what we think people want to hear. "I agree. Besides, we're supposed to be on a break. Even without a tour, an album still needs promoting, and I'm not ready to leave Vermont."

"Speaking of not leaving Vermont," Stone says, rolling his sticks around his fingers. "Elm Street in town. What's it like to live on?"

I know the question is directed at me because the only person who knows Winterberry better than I do is my brother, and he's not here.

"It's a good area. Quiet family homes. Why?"

He puts his stick down. "A house went up for sale there, and I think I'd like to buy it."

Silence follows his words. To say I'm shocked is an understatement. Stone has always been a California guy, but I won't lie. This is excellent news.

"That's right next door to the hot vet," Fox says casually.

I laugh. "How do you know?"

He shrugs. "Overheard someone talk about it at Noëlle's the other day. Word on the street is that pet adoptions are on the rise in Winterberry because of him."

"That's ridiculous and irresponsible," Stone says, standing all of a sudden. "Pets aren't toys. They're a responsibility."

"Maybe you should tell him." Fox laughs.

We fall back into the practice, the music flowing beautifully because that's what we do. Twenty-five years of performing together means our bodies know the rhythms even when our minds are elsewhere. My fingers find the right chords while my thoughts drift from calving schedules and winter preparations to documents waiting for my signature in Dad's office to a certain orchard owner who still hasn't answered my texts.

We play until the natural light starts to fade. Something is happening to us, individually and as a band. I can feel the change, even if I can't exactly point out what it is. But it's bigger than the biggest band in the country announcing an indefinite hiatus.

I retreat to the cabin after the guys leave, but it feels too quiet, the silence broken only by the occasional pop from logs settling in the woodstove. Gouta has claimed her usual spot among the chicken brigade in the corner, all of them huddled together like conspirators plotting revolution. The sight sparks something in my mind. An idea reckless enough to work, or at least force the confrontation I've been craving.

My phone sits dark and silent on the counter, offering no distraction from all the thoughts that seem determined to surface. Three days of unanswered texts mock me from its screen.

It started with me trying to draw him out to talk about what happened.

BASTIAN:

Can we talk?

We need to talk about it.

It doesn't need to happen again.

Then I tried to appeal to his sense of responsibility.

BASTIAN:

About the festival setup...do you want to do the final fence inspection with me?

I don't know what I'm doing with this. I need your expertise.

Do I need to buy flowers for the bees, or will they go hunt on their own?

Yesterday I moved on to unashamed desperation.

BASTIAN:

You're going to have to talk to me at some point.

Taylen, please.

I scroll through timestamps, marking my increasing lack of dignity. But dignity seems less important than breaking this silence, than finding a way past the walls he's rebuilt between us.

Gouta bleats her encouragement from her corner.

"If this doesn't work, I'm blaming you."

My fingers hover over the phone screen, composing and deleting several versions before settling on:

BASTIAN:

Gouta's missing. Can't find her anywhere. Meet me at the lake by the oak tree?

I hit send before I can change my mind, then grab my heavy coat from its hook. Gouta watches with what looks suspiciously like amusement as I check my reflection, running my fingers through hair that refuses to behave. "Don't give me that look," I tell her. "Wish me luck."

After spending most of the day indoors since completing the morning chores, the night air makes my lungs ache with each breath. I get in my truck and drive to the lake. We used to run there when we were kids, but as my joints remind me every morning, I'm no longer a kid.

The tree appears slowly through the darkness lit by the

moonlight. This close to the water, the wind carries an extra bite, but I welcome the sting.

I pace near the shoreline while waiting, each step marked by the sound of ice cracking beneath my boots. The lake stretches dark and still beyond ancient oak, its surface reflecting the moon, which on a surprisingly clear night like tonight, makes everything brighter.

My breath creates steam clouds, and I breathe out my anxiety, each minute stretching longer than the last.

Headlights cut through the darkness, and anticipation turns to certainty. He's coming. Whatever happens next, at least the silence will be broken. We'll be face-to-face again, and close enough that I'll be able to read what's in his eyes.

I square my shoulders against the approaching confrontation. Time to see if my reckless plan leads to a resolution or just creates new complications.

Taylen jumps out as soon as the truck stops, the door slamming with a force that echoes across the lake.

"What happened? Where is she?" The questions come fast, concern making his voice rough. His cheeks are flushed from the cold, and something in my chest tightens at the sight.

"She's...fine," I admit, watching as realization dawns in his eyes. "She's at the cabin with the girls. I just...needed to talk to you."

The change in his expression would be fascinating if it weren't so dangerous. Concern for Gouta turns into fury. "You manipulative bastard," he spits, already turning back toward his truck.

"Wait." My hand catches his arm, and I pull him closer. "Please. You won't answer my calls, won't reply to my messages. What choice did I have?"

"What do you want?" he asks, stepping aside and walking toward the oak tree.

"I want to know what happened the other night."

He laughs. "Well, when a boy likes another boy, things happen," he says, voice carrying an edge as sharp as winter wind. "No need to make it complicated."

"So you do like me," I say, a smile tugging at the corners of my lips.

"Not really." His laugh holds no humor. "You were just there," he shrugs.

The lie hangs between us, visible in the way his eyes drop to my mouth before snapping back up. I take another step forward, backing him toward the oak tree without touching. "Just there?" My voice drops lower. "Like I was just there in Burlington? Like I was just there in your living room?"

His back hits the rough bark, but he lifts his chin in defiance. "Exactly. Convenient. Available. Nothing more."

My hands find his waist, and before he can dodge, my fingers slip beneath the layers of his clothes to find skin that burns against my cold touch. He tries to push away, but I follow, using my height advantage to crowd him against the tree.

"Liar," I breathe against his ear, feeling a shiver run through him. "Your body gives you away every time. The way you lean into my touch, the sounds you make when I kiss you, how hard you get just from me being close…"

"Bastian." My name comes out as a warning and a plea. His hands press against my chest, but don't actually push. "Don't."

"Don't what?" I let my teeth graze his earlobe, drawing a gasp that sends heat straight to my core. "Don't point out how much you want this? Don't remind you how perfectly we fit together? Don't—"

His mouth crashes into mine with a force that makes my head spin, anger and need mixing in a kiss that feels like we're redrawing battle lines. His fingers tangle in my hair, pulling hard enough to hurt as he takes control. I let him, welcoming the pain, the passion, the proof that he wants this as much as I do.

The kiss turns deeper, hungrier, all pretense of resistance abandoned. My hands roam under his clothes, mapping territory I've memorized but can't get enough of. His skin burns against my palms despite the cold, his muscles flexing as he arches into my touch.

When we break for air, his eyes are filled with desire and resignation. Before he can speak, I drop to my knees, my hands already working at his belt. His protest dies as I free him, replaced by a moan that travels across the frozen lake when I take his cock in my mouth.

I don't give two shits about the stones digging into my knees or the snow seeping through my jeans. It's completely worth it to hear the sounds he makes, to feel his fingers clenching in my hair, to taste him on my tongue.

I take my time, drawing it out until he's practically sobbing my name with lust and raw honesty. I won't stop until he can't pretend this means nothing, until he can't hide behind anger or sarcasm or distance.

When he comes, it's with a force that makes him slam his head back against a tree trunk. I swallow everything he offers, keeping his cock in my mouth until the aftershocks fade. Only then do I pull away, looking up to find him watching me with half-lidded eyes.

I rise slowly, letting him feel every inch of contact as our bodies align. "Tell me you don't live for this, Taylen."

"Just because I like it," he manages finally, his voice wrecked in a way that makes me want to drag him back to my cabin immediately, "doesn't mean it'll happen again."

"Keep telling yourself that," I murmur against his mouth, tasting a hint of blood where he's bitten his lip. "Maybe eventually one of us will believe it."

He pushes me away with shaking hands, tucking himself back together. But I catch him watching me as he walks to his truck, his gaze carrying heat that promises this isn't over.

The engine turns over with a familiar growl, and then he's gone, leaving me standing in the snow, hard as a goddam rock but with the biggest smile.

I touch my lips, still feeling the ghost of his kiss. The taste of him lingers on my tongue. Whatever he claims, whatever lies we tell ourselves, the truth lives in the way our bodies respond to each other. In how perfectly we fit together, the sounds we draw from each other's throats, and in the heat that builds whenever we're close.

"You can run away, Taylen, but I'll keep up with your pace until you realize we're as inevitable as snow, calving season, and maple syrup in March."

20

TAYLEN

THERE'S nothing like an honest day's work to keep unwanted thoughts at bay. Especially thoughts of a certain rockstar with talented hands and magical lips that are as addictive as the cider I'm bottling today.

So much for keeping those thoughts at bay.

It's a good thing I've done this process so many times that I know I'll catch myself before I miss a step.

The cider flows golden through layers of filtration, each pass removing more impurities until what remains runs clear as spring water. If only my emotions could be filtered so easily. But Bastian lingers in my system like unfermented sugar: sweet, volatile, and impossible to remove.

I absolutely love the science of making cider. Turning simple juice into something more complex is like my own brand of magic, and I must be doing something right because I have multiple clients competing for my brews.

Still, my traitorous brain keeps wandering to the frozen lake, to Bastian on his knees with his mouth on my skin. The taste of him lingered on my tongue as I drove away, pretending each encounter would be the last.

"Six point eight percent," I mutter to myself, so I can force my brain back to the task at hand. "Right where it should be." I record the alcohol content and then line up the bottles.

I place the Howard Orchard label perfectly on each bottle. There's no room for crooked applications or bubble flaws. Maybe one day I can expand the orchard and automate some of the process, but today, this is the therapy I need.

"This can only end badly, you know?" I tell the growing row of bottles. "He'll leave again, and then what? I go back to pining from afar, but this time knowing exactly what I'm missing?" The words taste bitter as overfermented fruit. "It'll be hell."

My phone buzzes against the metal work table, screen lighting up with a familiar name.

"Hey, Remy, what's up, man?"

"Taylen, my dude. How's it going?" After twelve years of working on my skin, Remy has become a friend. I'm sure we'd be closer if he didn't live and work all the way in Burlington.

"I'm good. Bottling a new batch of cider."

He groans. "Man, I'll never leave Burlington, but if I ever reconsider it, it'll be to live next door to you."

I laugh. "I don't love that you love my cider more than you love me."

"Why choose?" he asks with the flirty voice he uses on everyone. It stopped working on me when his husband told me I wasn't special. He does it for everyone. The man is a serial flirt. "Anyway, I'm calling to confirm your appointment. Same time as always?

"Yeah, same time." I swallow against the sudden thickness in my throat. "Still working on the design though."

"No rush, brother. We've got time to get it perfect."

Remy's tone is filled with understanding. "Twelve years now, right?"

"Twelve years," I confirm quietly. Twelve years of marking the loss of my brother in permanent lines on my skin. Of trying to keep Jackson's memory alive. "I'll bring you a few bottles."

"Dude, you should play harder to get. I'd totally divorce Jack for full access to your brews."

No, he wouldn't. I smile to myself. Those two are glued at the hip, and I'm sure their idea of foreplay is to ink each other.

I get back to work as soon as the call is over. The last thing I need right now is to spiral down a rabbit hole of missing my brother and wondering how he'd feel about what's happening with Bastian. Would anything even have happened if Jackson were still alive?

My phone buzzes again, but this time, with a message.

FINN:

Joe's Bar tonight. Not taking no for an answer.

I reply straight away. Maybe an evening out with my friend is just what I need. As long as he doesn't decide to press too hard to find out who I hooked up with.

While I don't exactly regret confiding in him, I've kept this secret for so long that I don't know how to handle anyone else knowing how I feel about my best friend's brother.

Hours later, after finishing the last of my orders and a quick shower, I find myself pulling into Joe's parking lot.

Warm air hits my face as I step inside, carrying scents of stale beer and old wood. It doesn't take long to spot Finn. Not when he's at the largest table surrounded by Bastian, Fox, Nikko, and Stone.

He stands when he sees me. "You made it!"

The only free chair is next to Finn and dead opposite Bastian. Because, of course, it would be.

"What's the occasion?" I ask. Clearly, this isn't one of our usual evenings. Not when the whole band is here.

I place my sole attention on Finn, but my eyes betray me, finding Bastian across the table like a compass finding north. He watches me over his beer, his expression unreadable in the bar's dim light.

"Things are about to get busy around here. Not just for me, but for all of you. I know running a small-town Christmas festival isn't what you signed up for, but I cannot thank you enough." Finn turns to me and then Bastian. "You two are the best brothers anyone could have."

"If only I knew all it would take to get that title was to give up a tiny bit of land," Bastian jokes.

"Joint best," I add. "And I don't see a beer in front of me anywhere."

Finn laughs. "No one told you to be late for round one. Anyway, from the land to ideas, running the music activities and coordinating schedules, you've all been amazing. So, for tonight, all food and drink is on me. Well, it's on the mayor, but I'm taking credit because I asked."

The declaration draws an immediate response from around the table. Stone raises his glass with characteristic enthusiasm, looking like he's calculating what "on me" means.

"Now that's what I like to hear," Stone says, grin spreading wide. "Finn Hall, enabler of fine drinking and finer company. Can we just clarify that this deal includes top-shelf whiskey?"

Called it.

"Sure does," Finn says, and I laugh. Joe's top-shelf is as low as it gets. This is beer and cider land.

Nikko raises his beer. "About time someone appreciated our work. Do you know how many spreadsheets I've created for this festival?"

"Spreadsheets don't count as work," Stone interjects, already signaling Joe for another round. "Real work involves actual sweat. Which reminds me—" He turns to Bastian with exaggerated seriousness. "Your brother here made me move fence posts. Plural. In freezing temperatures."

"You volunteered," Finn protests, but he's smiling. "Multiple times, actually. Something about 'getting authentic farm experience' so you can feel like a local."

Fox snorts. "He took seventeen photos of himself with the fence posts," he offers, deadpan. "For Instagram. Winterberry's social media scene is thriving."

The table erupts in laughter, even Stone joining in as he pulls out his phone to prove the artistic merit of said photos.

"Seriously, though," Finn continues once the laughter settles. "I couldn't have done this without you guys. The sound system alone—" He gestures helplessly, words failing to capture the scope of what they've accomplished.

"It was nothing," Nikko finishes firmly. "Compared to what this town's done for us over the years." His expression softens with something that might be nostalgia. "Every time we needed to disappear from the spotlight, Winterberry welcomed us home. No questions, no press leaks, just... acceptance. We'll move all the fence posts in the world for that kind of peace."

"Says he who moved exactly zero," Stone says.

"Not my fault that I'm good at delegating."

"More like being elsewhere when physical work is required," Bastian says, and Nikko replies with his middle finger.

Joe keeps us fed with his legendary wings, and the drinks

keep on coming. After a while, I almost stop noticing how often Bastian's eyes land on me. Almost.

"The opening ceremony is nearly ready," Finn continues, licking barbecue sauce from his fingers. "The sound system installation starts tomorrow, weather permitting."

"Weather better permit," Stone grumbles, fingers tapping against his glass. "Can't adjust acoustic balance in a snowstorm." His technical concerns launch a discussion that should hold my attention, but Bastian's presence across the table is way too distracting.

Our eyes meet between other people's words, and suddenly, I feel too hot under my sweater.

"I gotta take a leak," I announce abruptly, pushing back from the table. The guys are so engrossed in their discussion that they don't pay attention to me leaving.

The restroom is significantly cooler than the bar. I run cold water over my hands while I debate staying and playing it cool, or leaving so I can go home and figure out a way to exist in the same space as Bastian without combusting from wanting him, from wanting to give in and believe he's here to stay. Maybe stay with me.

The door creaks behind me, and my heart skips a beat, but it's just another guy, barely nodding as he passes. I dry my hands and step outside the restroom, only to find myself face-to-face with Bastian Hall.

"Come with me?"

Before I can respond, his hand wraps around my wrist, and he's pulling me toward the emergency exit. The bar's noise fades as the heavy door swings open, and I'm slapped with the cold night air.

My back hits brick before I fully register what's happening, the rough texture catching on my jacket. Bastian cages me in, his palms flat against the wall on either side of my head. He doesn't touch me, but his body radiates heat just inches away, close enough that I can smell his cologne mixed with the single beer he's been nursing.

"I'm having a weird sense of dejá vu," I say, hoping my voice comes out sounding unaffected by his closeness.

"This time there's no one to interrupt," he murmurs, fingers ghosting along my jaw. "No paparazzi, no reasons to stop." His thumb traces my bottom lip, drawing shaky breath from my throat.

"Bastian," I manage, but his name holds no warning, just a want that builds with every touch, every moment. His mouth covers mine before I can say more.

My body betrays me as I wrap my arms around his shoulders. The leather of his jacket feels cool under my palms, but his body burns against mine as he presses closer. His tongue traces the seam of my lips, and I open for him immediately. What's the point of pretending I don't want this?

One of his hands cups my face while the other grips my hip, holding me against the wall like he thinks I might try to escape. But escape is the last thing on my mind as his thigh slides between my legs, creating friction that draws embarrassing sounds from my throat.

"Come home with me," he breathes against my mouth. His lips trail kisses across my neck until his teeth find a sensitive spot below my ear, sending electricity through my system.

Want wars with fear in my chest, making it hard to think past the sensation of his body against mine. "I can't," I whisper, even though my hands clutch at his shoulders like I'm afraid he'll disappear. "This is… We shouldn't…"

"Why not?" He pulls back enough to meet my eyes, his pupils blown wide with a desire that matches my own. "Give me one good reason why we can't have this." His thumb strokes my cheek with gentleness that hurts worse than any roughness.

"Because you'll leave." The words escape before I can catch them, carrying more truth than I mean to reveal.

"What do I have to do?" His voice drops lower, rougher. "What do I have to do to make you believe I'm not going anywhere?" His hands frame my face, forcing me to meet his gaze. "Tell me what you need, Taylen. I'll do it."

But I can't find words to explain how this fear feels like a second skin, how twelve years of barely seeing the only person who would have understood my grief left scars. I can't voice how wanting him feels like falling without knowing where the ground is, like driving too fast on icy roads, like every reckless choice I've ever tried to stop making.

"I have to go," I manage, pushing against his chest with hands that shake slightly. He steps back immediately, giving me space I'm not sure I actually want. The cold rushes in where his warmth was, making me shiver.

I go back inside the bar, make a quick excuse to Finn, and grab my coat.

My lips burn from Bastian's touch all the way to the farm. It's not until I park in front of Bastian's cabin that I realize I have no control anymore. I'm not the one in charge. I'm not the one making the decisions here.

I stare at the front door, knowing I need to turn around and go home, but my feet make a different decision. Suddenly, I regret keeping that goddam key he made for me.

Gouta greets me at the door with enthusiasm. The chickens follow her lead, Moira and Myrtle investigating my boots with curiosity.

"What the hell am I doing here?" The question falls into empty air, drawing no response except Gouta's gentle head-butt against my leg.

I drop down on the couch and hold my head in my hands. Why am I running? Why am I so afraid that he'll run?

And why the fuck am I here if I'm running? Am I running toward him or away from him?

The photos on the walls catch my attention when I look up. The band throughout the years and family moments. Jackson appears in several, his smile preserved forever. He looks exactly like I remember, forever young while the rest of us keep aging without him. This is the Bastian no one sees.

The eager paparazzi, the press, the fans. They get rockstar Bastian. Out here, we get real Bastian. The farmer. The local boy who grew up to achieve amazing things.

"He'll leave again," I tell Gouta, but I'm pretty sure I'm just trying to convince myself. Because everything Bastian is doing indicates otherwise.

In the end, my fear rules as I stand and leave.

21

BASTIAN

I⊤'s funny how a place that used to bring excitement now just makes me feel suffocated.

The record label's conference room is all glass and chrome and filled with expectations.

Here, from this fortieth-floor Manhattan view, Vermont seems impossibly far, like some dream I had about simple things like dairy cows and farm work.

Beside me, Stone's jaw works like he's chewing on words he can't quite swallow. His fingers tap nervous rhythms against his thigh. On my other side, Mik maintains his professional mask, but I can see tension in how straight he's holding himself.

"Q3 is our optimal release window," the exec—Bradley or Braden—leans forward with practiced aggression. "The market analysis supports—"

"We need time to get the songs right," I interrupt, keeping my voice level despite the frustration building in my chest.

Bradley-or-Braden's face reddens slightly, but before he

can respond, his colleague, a younger, hungrier version of him, jumps in. "The numbers don't lie, Mr. Hall. Summer touring season is crucial for maximizing—"

"We understand that. But as we discussed at length, the band is on hiatus." Maybe I need to pull out the definition of the word for him. "We're still writing songs, but we reserve the right to decide when we're ready to release." After twenty-five years of loyalty to the label, we've earned every second of time off.

The air feels thick with unspoken tension as Bradley-or-Braden leans back, his chair creaking slightly. Behind him, Manhattan's skyline stretches endlessly, glass and steel monuments to commerce that make me ache for Vermont's gentle hills.

"Perhaps," Daisy interjects smoothly, "we should take a brief break. Give everyone a chance to review the proposals more thoroughly."

The executives file out with poorly concealed irritation. As soon as the door closes behind them, the tension breaks like a summer storm.

"Corporate vultures," Stone mutters. "Did you see them? Like sharks circling bloody water." His hands spread wide, mimicking the exec's aggressive posture. "Fuck the market analysis. We've earned a fucking break."

I move to the window, pressing my palm against the cool glass. Forty stories below, people move like insects, oblivious to the deals being brokered in the buildings that surround them. "Remember when making music was about music?"

"Still is," Fox says quietly. He's been his usual quiet self, watching everything with that kind of focus that always makes me wonder what he's really thinking. "At least, it should be."

Stone leans back, running his hand through his long,

wavy hair. "As much as I hate to say it, a new album would help us with the winter coat drive, the music education initiative, and the food bank contributions we've always done. Not to mention we've been looking at all those Vermont-based charities with Finn."

The mention of home sends a fresh ache through my chest. Three days in Manhattan, and I'm already desperate for Vermont air, for the smell of hay and earth instead of designer perfume and corporate ambition.

"Why are we still playing?" Fox's question cuts through the growing discussion. We all turn to face him, surprised by the direct challenge from our quietest member.

Before anyone can respond, he adds an equally simple follow-up: "Who's doing it for the money?"

I look around our small circle, seeing the same realization dawn on each face. No hands rise for the money question. There's no hesitation in our unanimous response about why we play. Music runs in our blood.

"Well then," Fox says softly, satisfaction clear in his slight smile. "Seems like we have our answer."

The simplicity of it hits like truth usually does. We're not here for market windows or profit margins. We're here because music demands to be made.

Stone's grin grows wider. "Fuck their timeline," he announces with considerable satisfaction. "We do this right or not at all. Let's push back."

Nikko clears his throat and shifts in his chair like he's about to deliver bad news. "You're forgetting you're under contract."

"Actually." Daisy's grin transforms her entire face. Ever the firecracker, her eyes spark with familiar mischief as she leans forward, voice dropping like she's sharing a conspiracy theory instead of a business strategy. "Your first agent was a shrewd man, and he must have loved you because there's a clause in your contract that states that after twenty-five years or ten albums, whichever comes first, the band can break the contract without penalty. The only caveat is that if you are in the middle of a tour, you must finish the tour."

"Not a tour in sight," Nikko says, stating the obvious.

"Gentlemen," she drawls, drawing out the word until Stone growls with impatience. "Have you considered the 'Taylor Swift' model?" Her fingers form air quotes around the name, but her expression remains deadly serious.

"You want us to date celebrities and write songs about them?" Stone asks, but his drumming fingers have slowed, interest replacing nervous energy. "Because I volunteer as tribute for that market research."

Daisy's eye roll could power small cities. "Independence, you musical heathen. Complete creative control. No more suits telling you when to breathe." Her grin turns sharper as understanding dawns across our faces. "You're Hall of Fame. In case you've forgotten while you've been playing Santa's elves in Vermont."

We must look like those dolls that shake their heads as we look at each other, taking in the idea that, for the first time in our careers, we can do anything we want.

"You can cut out the fat cats," Daisy continues, winking as she glances toward the door. "Though I suppose I am one of those fat cats."

"As if we'd let you go," Stone declares immediately. "You're family."

The simple statement draws nods from all of us, appreciation for how she's guided us through the last decade of industry changes and ever-growing success.

Something softens in Daisy's expression. "About that," she says quietly, hands moving to rest against her stomach. "Family's about to get a bit bigger."

The room erupts in chaos, Stone actually jumping from his chair while Fox and Nikko roll theirs to squish the poor woman.

"I'm three months along," Daisy admits as we crowd closer, her smile filled with so much joy it makes my chest tight. "Wasn't exactly planned, but…" She trails off.

"The father?" Mik asks carefully, voicing a question we're all considering. We've watched Daisy's on-again-off-again relationship drama for years, seen her struggle to balance personal life with her professional demands.

"Well, when a mommy and daddy love each other very much," she starts, deflecting with humor that doesn't quite hide vulnerability, then, softer, "Ryan. It's Ryan. Again. Still. Always. Probably." Her laugh carries notes of wonder and resignation combined. "Amazing how impending parenthood clarifies a relationship status."

"Dibs on godfather and naming rights," Stone announces immediately, setting off a chain reaction of competing claims that fills the room with familiar banter. "I'm clearly the most responsible choice."

"You set your own drums on fire," Nikko points out dryly. "Twice."

"Artistic expression!"

The playful argument continues, but I notice how Daisy's hands never leave her stomach. The timing feels significant. A new life, new direction, and new possibilities opening before us.

"I could expand the studio," I say suddenly, drawing attention back to practical matters. "Start building toward independence now."

Fox nods slowly. "The acoustics are already better than half the professional studios we've used," he says. "With proper equipment upgrades…"

The conversation shifts to technical details until Daisy

declares that she's informed the execs waiting outside the room, like vultures, that we would like to postpone the meeting until the new year.

"How about a celebration dinner?" she asks, standing, which for her means she's barely taller than us sitting down.

"To family," Stone proposes, raising his water glass in a toast that feels more significant than any champagne celebration. "Both blood and chosen."

"To independence," Fox adds.

"To new beginnings," Daisy finishes.

Outside the building, Manhattan continues its endless dance of commerce and ambition. But in here, we've found a different rhythm. One measured in heartbeats and hope rather than market projections and profit margins.

"Now," Daisy says, reaching for her phone, "who's ready to make dinner reservations that will give the label's accounting department absolute fits?"

Stone grins. "I know just the place," he announces, already dialing. "Time to remind them exactly who they're dealing with."

Hours later, after a celebratory dinner that will indeed give accounting heart problems, we find ourselves at Stone's recommended nightclub, his idea of continuing the celebration into the early morning hours.

After the relative peace of dinner, this assault of sound and motion feels like a punishment.

Stone and Nikko disappear almost immediately, their practiced scanning of the crowd suggesting tonight won't end in solitary hotel rooms. I follow Mik and Fox to a corner table, grateful for the relative shelter of the shadows and distance from the dancefloor's chaotic energy.

I don't miss the not-quite-hidden attempts at photos from strangers. The attention is different here than in Vermont, where people know us as neighbors first, musicians second. Here we're commodities, content for social media feeds and gossip channels.

Thank fuck for VIP areas. If we can't stop them from taking photos, at least we can have a conversation without being interrupted for multiple selfies. The server brings our drinks over, and as soon as he's gone, Mik leans back in his chair and takes a swig of his beer.

"So," he drawls, "how's it going?"

I shake my head, unable to hide the frustration that's been building since the first time we gave in and kissed. Every encounter follows a pattern of heat and retreat, Taylen's body speaking truth while his words maintain a distance.

Fox leans forward slightly, his amber eyes sharp despite the club's dim lighting. "I'm clearly missing something here," he says

Mik glances between us, giving me an apologetic look. We don't keep secrets between band brothers, but Taylen is close to all of us, and the last thing I want is for him to feel like he's the focus of my brothers' well-intentioned gossip and cupid-aspirations.

I run a hand through my hair, buying time to organize my thoughts. "It's complicated," I start, but Fox's raised eyebrow tells me that won't be enough. "Taylen and I...we keep...connecting. Physically. But every time we get close to something real, he pulls away."

"And you let him," Fox observes, not unkindly.

The truth of it stings. "Yeah," I admit. "I do."

The bass pounds through my chest while I consider how much to reveal. These men are my brothers in everything but blood. They know me better than family in some ways. But admitting the depth of what I feel for Taylen means acknowledging the complications I've been avoiding.

"I think I'm in love with him," I say, finally uttering the words that have been playing in my head for weeks, maybe even years. Before they can respond, I add a quieter confession. "Not sure it can go anywhere. There are too many walls between us."

"What's the biggest obstacle?" Mik asks.

The truth rises like a tide I can't fight anymore. "Taylen is Jackson's younger brother. Seven years ago, we kissed in a club. I'm not sure either of us was in the right place then, emotionally. It was the fifth anniversary of Jackson's death, and I was a wreck. After that, I started avoiding Taylen whenever I went home. Jackson was very protective of his baby brother, and the last thing I want is to end up hurting him and feel like I've let my best friend down."

Mik's face transforms with understanding, while Fox maintains his usual stillness when he's taking in important information.

"Have you tried being in the same place at the same time?" Mik asks pointedly. "Actually talking instead of whatever dance you've been doing?"

My expression must answer for me because he continues without waiting for a response. "Physical connection is easy," he says, gentler now. "Emotional honesty? That's the hard part."

Fox remains unusually quiet, his focus fixed on the drink he's barely touched. Something about his silence feels weighted, like he's holding something back. But before I can question it, Mik continues, "Love is worth fighting for," he says simply, words carrying the authority of someone who's fought his own battles and won. "Show him you're ready for battle."

"He's definitely worth fighting for," I say finally. "Worth whatever it takes to prove this isn't just a convenient release or temporary comfort."

It's time to show Taylen exactly how important he is to me, what we could be if we both stop running.

In the city that never sleeps, Vermont feels a million years away, but for the first time since Burlington, since that first kiss that changed everything, I feel something like hope building beneath uncertainty. Because some things are worth fighting for, worth risking everything to prove possible.

22

TAYLEN

"Everything's going to be fine," I tell Finn as he checks his phone for what must be the hundredth time today.

Instead of replying, Finn makes a sound that might be agreement or maybe the beginning of a panic attack. His town logo pin sits slightly crooked on his lapel. I resist the urge to fix it for him.

The Christmas market stalls stretch behind us, vendors arranging their products with excitement. The stage crew's equipment check sends occasional bursts of static through speakers that will later carry the sounds of Christmas carols.

"Look around you. Everyone's doing what they're supposed to do, and even the weather is cooperating."

"Why did you have to jinx—" Finn starts, then stops mid-sentence as Mayor Caldwell appears at the far end of the market area.

"Oh god," Finn mutters, his clipboard creaking under a suddenly tighter grip. "I need to catch him. Do you mind—" He's already moving before finishing the sentence, weaving between vendors with surprising agility for someone who looks ready to faint.

I take in the calm before the proverbial storm.

The transformation of mine and the Halls' combined properties into a winter wonderland still catches me off guard. Strings of white lights are draped between lampposts, each bulb wrapped in frost that makes them sparkle even in daylight. Red and green garlands twist around every available surface, their pine scent mixing with cinnamon from nearby vendor stalls to create that quintessential Christmas smell that hits you right in the childhood memories.

The Christmas tree stands at the market's heart, easily twenty feet tall, decorated with ornaments that are ready to shine once the lights are turned on in just a few hours. Finn has arranged music stands for carolers near its base, their sheet music already clipped and ready for the opening ceremony.

The vendor stalls look like something from a Hallmark movie. Each booth sports its own wreath, some simple pine circles with red bows, others elaborate creations featuring dried orange slices, cinnamon sticks, and silver bells.

Welcoming visitors into the festival is a giant banner that stretches between two poles, with *Winterberry Christmas Festival* in letters that must be three feet tall, flanked by painted snowflakes and candy canes. It's almost too much, except it's not. It's exactly right. It's the kind of scene that makes even cynical hearts soften a little.

Joe's pop-up bar is already drawing attention at the far end, his handwritten sign promising *Holiday Spirits for Holiday Spirits*.

I check my watch, confirming there's still time. Soon, these paths will fill with locals and tourists alike.

But for now, I'm going to thank my mother's friend, Eleanor, for accepting the job of managing the stall for me for the duration of the festival. With the work on the farm and having to meet orders at the busiest time of the year, it would be impossible to manage the stall myself, no matter how much fun it always is.

Eleanor arranges jars of apple butter because they have to be just so. I can already hear her say the words before I reach the stall.

"Everything's perfect, Eleanor," I say, watching her adjust a jar that's barely a millimeter out of alignment. The familiar scent of Sylvie's cinnamon bread draws me closer, and I can't resist snagging a slice from the sample plate. Sylvie is a superstar for supplying me with the perfect foundation for my samples.

She swats my hand playfully. "You haven't changed a bit," she says, though we both know that's not true. "Still sneaking tastes when you think no one's looking."

"Stolen bits taste better," I say, giving her a kiss on the cheek.

I leave her to walk the market that fills steadily as the afternoon progresses. Vendors call greetings across aisles, share thermoses of coffee and snippets of gossip, and adjust displays.

A new stall I've never seen at the festival before catches my eye.

Dr. Hunter Cross, also known as the hot vet—although he probably doesn't know that—kneels beside his outreach stall, his movements careful as he lets an older woman's terrier investigate his hand.

He has a photo display of seniors with their pets next to pamphlets that read *Keeping Families Together: All Members Welcome.*

"We provide basic care for pets belonging to elderly community members," Hunter explains to the growing crowd. "Everything from routine checkups to dog walking services."

The terrier has progressed from investigating Hunter's hand to attempting to climb into his lap, making its owner apologize profusely. But Hunter just smiles. "This is exactly why we do this work," he says, scratching behind the dog's ears. "Every pet deserves care, and every owner deserves peace of mind."

I can see why he's so popular.

With his vivid red hair and bright-green eyes, the man is objectively hot, and who's not a sucker for a guy who loves animals?

Stone appears through the crowd, looking like he's stepped directly from a fashion magazine photo shoot into our small-town festival.

"Dr. Cross," he says, extending his hand and turning his smile to maximum wattage. "Stone Murphy. I've heard wonderful things about your work with animals."

Hunter accepts the handshake. "Nice to meet you, Mr. Murphy. And thank you. It's easy to do wonderful things when you love what you do."

"Please, call me Stone," he says, moving to maintain position in Hunter's line of sight. "I'm very interested in learning more about your program. How could I do that?"

The suggestion hangs in the air, but it seems the hot vet isn't catching Stone's drift. "Our website has comprehensive information about volunteer opportunities," he says. "All program details are available there."

"That's great, but I would love the opportunity to discuss the recent increase in pet adoptions. As they say, pets are for life, not just for Christmas."

Hunter's face remains neutral, but the flush rising above his collar tells a different story. He's a good few inches shorter than Stone, but he's clearly not easily intimidated.

The touch on my sleeve comes with no warning, but I know it's him before I turn. Bastian stands closer than strictly necessary, smelling like Christmas morning. His eyes carry that particular brightness that always means trouble for me, my resolve, and my careful plans to keep a distance between us.

Without a word, he pulls me toward the back of the main stage, where the equipment storage boxes create a convenient hiding spot.

"How was your little trip?" I ask, leaning against the support beam in a way I hope looks casual, unbothered.

Bastian's smile grows wider as he steps closer, eliminating what little space I'd managed to maintain between us. "Awww," he teases, voice dropping to a register that sends heat through my system despite the winter chill. "You missed me."

I roll my eyes. "Like a drought in summer," I say, but my heart betrays me by racing when he moves even closer. His cologne makes my head spin slightly.

"Well, I missed you," he admits quietly. "Thought about you every day I was gone."

I should step away now, but instead, I sway slightly closer, drawn by the heat of his body and the memory of how perfectly we fit together.

Before I can push him away, his lips find mine. Of course my hands betray me by finding his shoulders, pulling him closer despite all my resolutions.

He tastes like coffee and cinnamon. One of his hands cups my face while the other braces against the wall, boxing me in.

When he pulls back, his eyes are filled with a tenderness that makes my chest ache. "Have dinner with me," he says. "A real date. Please."

"I can't," I manage, though even I hear the lack of conviction in my voice. My hands still rest on his shoulders, contradicting words with actions in a way that's becoming a familiar pattern between us.

"Why not?" His thumb traces my bottom lip, a gesture so intimate it makes my breath catch. "Give me one good reason why we can't explore this properly, other than your silly idea that I'm somehow going to go somewhere."

But good reasons seem to evaporate when he's this close, when I can feel the heat of his body and remember exactly how well we fit together. "Because..." I trail off, distracted by the way his fingers are tracing my jaw.

"Because you're trying to protect yourself," he finishes for me, his voice gentler now. "Because you're scared this is real." His forehead rests against mine, creating a pocket of shared air between us. "I'm scared too, Tay. But I'm more scared of letting this slip away without trying."

I close my eyes. My hands grip his coat tighter, ready to give in and say yes to everything he wants.

"I'm not going anywhere," he says, reading my silence correctly. "Not this time. Not ever again if you'll let me stay." His hands frame my face, forcing me to meet his gaze. "Just give me a chance to prove it."

Part of me wants to believe him, but a larger part remembers that he left for tour buses, packed venues, and a life that exists beyond our small town's boundaries. "You can't promise that," I whisper, though my body betrays me by leaning into his touch.

"Watch me," he challenges, then kisses me again before I can argue further. This kiss carries a different energy. Less gentle exploration, more determined claiming. His body presses mine against the support beam while his hands tangle in my hair, drawing a sound from my throat that would embarrass me if I had any capacity left for shame.

When we break apart this time, we're both breathing harder.

"Think about it," he says finally.

"I'll think about it," I concede, knowing it's the best I can offer right now.

He brushes a final kiss across my lips before stepping fully away. "That's all I'm asking," he says, though we both know he's asking for much more than a simple dinner date. "Now come with me. I want to win a plushy for you."

I laugh. "How fantastically cliché."

The carnival section of the festival is all flashing lights and barker calls designed to draw people in. I follow Bastian past the game booths. He stops so suddenly that I almost run into him, his attention caught by the ring toss booth that looks like every other tourist trap along our path.

Bastian hands over the cash and grins at me with the confidence of someone who's been winning these games for a long time.

"Three rings for the gentleman," the attendant announces.

Bastian weighs the first ring in his hand. I want to tell him it's rigged, that no one actually wins these games, that he's wasting time and money on an impossible task.

But his first throw lands perfectly, the ring settling around the bottle neck. The second follows the same path, and I realize I'm holding my breath. His movements carry the same determination he brings to everything: guitar playing, farming, or kissing me senseless in places we shouldn't.

The third ring hangs suspended in the air for a moment and then drops into place with its predecessors. The attendant's professional smile slips slightly. "Well, we have a winner!" he announces.

"Told you I'd win you a plushy."

Bastian studies the available prize options. When he

points to a stuffed goat with ridiculous eyelashes, my heart skips more than a few beats.

"For you," he says, presenting me with the toy. "Since you don't have your own pet goat, this one will do."

Our fingers brush as I accept the offering. The plush toy's exaggerated features somehow look endearing rather than tacky. I tuck it under my arm, fighting a smile.

Sebastian Hall won a plushy for me. Today, this is a cliché I'm on board with.

"Thank you. You didn't have to, but I love it."

"I know," he replies. "But I wanted to." His hand finds the small of my back as we move away from the booth. "Like I want a lot of things involving you."

The admission hangs between us as I clutch the stuffed goat closer. "Bastian…"

"I know," he says again, gentler now. "You need time. Space. Proof that this is real." His smile is filled with patience and determination that makes my chest tight. "I can wait. Just don't make me wait too long, okay?"

Around us, the festival continues. The carnival music competes with holiday songs and the scents of varied foods mixing in the winter air. But in this moment, everything narrows to the space between us. His eyes hold mine with perfect focus, and I can't help the smile that spreads across my face. He mirrors it, that devastating grin that makes my stomach flip, and for a moment we're just standing here like idiots, beaming at each other in the middle of the crowd.

The festival noise increases around us. Then I hear it: "Ten! Nine! Eight!" The countdown ripples through the crowd. "Seven! Six! Five!" Bastian's hand finds mine, our fingers tangling as anticipation builds. "Four! Three! Two! One!"

The world explodes into light. Thousands of bulbs ignite simultaneously, transforming the festival grounds into a winter wonderland of twinkling white and warm gold. The crowd erupts in cheers and applause, but I'm watching the lights reflect in Bastian's eyes. His thumb strokes across my knuckles as we stand together, bathed in the glow of a thousand tiny stars.

"Yes," I say suddenly, the decision forming before conscious thought. "I'll have dinner with you."

"Yeah?" He steps closer. "You're sure?"

I nod, and his smile could put the Christmas tree lights to shame.

"I should get back," I say finally, though leaving feels increasingly difficult lately. "It's the first day, so I want to make sure Eleanor is okay."

"I'll see you soon," he says, squeezing my hand before letting it go.

As I walk away, clutching the ridiculous stuffed goat like a lifeline, I don't even try to erase the smile from my face.

23

BASTIAN

"How are you doing, girl?" The sunlight streams into the barn from the top windows as I check Martha's water bucket for the third time in an hour. Her heavy breathing fills the space, each exhale carrying the weight of the impending birth. I've seen hundreds of calvings, but anticipation still runs through my veins as I watch her shift restlessly in the fresh straw.

I move around her stall, noting each sign that suggests her labor's approaching. Her tail raises periodically, and her muscles ripple beneath the black-and-white hide as early contractions build.

"Easy girl," I murmur, running my hands along her swollen sides. The calf shifts beneath my touch, a strong movement that suggests a healthy life waiting to begin. Martha turns her head to watch me with those liquid brown eyes. "You're doing great, Momma. Just a little bit longer now."

The barn door's hinges announce an arrival, so both Martha and I turn our heads to the door.

"Bastian?" Taylen calls out, his expression changing when

he takes in the scene. His eyes move from me to Martha, understanding dawning as she shifts again with clear discomfort.

"She's close," I explain, gesturing to the visible signs of impending birth. "Started showing real progress about an hour ago. Did you need something?"

He moves closer. "I was looking for you to give you this. One of my regulars makes these cranberry and walnut loaves that taste amazing." The way he bites his lip as he tries to conceal his smile makes me want to kiss him so bad. "Thought you might enjoy it."

The simple gesture feels like a tiny break in the wall between us. Because he's showing that he cares. To anyone else, it's a loaf, but to me, it means so much more than a food offering.

"Join me?" I ask, nodding toward the hay bale I've claimed as my observation post. "She'll probably be a while yet, but I could use the company." I wash my hands in the sink before joining Taylen by Martha's stall.

He settles beside me, handing me the still-warm loaf. The bread's aroma fills my senses as I unwrap it and then pull out a piece, handing some to Taylen.

The bread melts in my mouth. The balance of cranberries and walnuts is perfect.

"I get at least one of these every holiday season," he explains as I pull out two more pieces. "But usually I don't have anyone to share it with."

Another little crack in the wall.

We eat in comfortable silence broken only by Martha's occasional movements.

"Tell me about her," Taylen says finally, gesturing toward our patient.

"Martha's one of our steadiest producers," I explain.

"Fourth pregnancy, all healthy deliveries. She's got a sweet temperament, and passes it to her calves too."

When Martha shifts again, he leans forward automatically, probably as anxious as I am to see the big moment.

"Maybe not Cupcake though. Cupcake has a temper and likes to escape, so she's definitely not like her mom. Did you know I had to fit her with an AirTag to stop Dad from wandering around the land looking for a cow who loves to play hide and seek?"

Our shoulders brush as he laughs, but he doesn't pull away.

"I missed this," he admits quietly, his words barely louder than Martha's breathing. "Hanging out with you." His hands twist slightly in his lap. "The last time this happened, I must have been a teenager." He laughs then. "Totally crushing on the local rock star."

I resist the urge to reach for him. Instead, I offer a truth that's been building since my return. "I missed this too. Staying in Vermont isn't just about the farm or facilitating my dad's retirement for me. I missed this…when the world outside stops because a new life is on its way."

"It's pretty magical, isn't it?" he asks, and I nod, glancing at Martha.

"I don't really mind if you have a crush on your local rockstar though," I tease.

"Who? Stone?"

I poke his side, and his laugh carries a genuine warmth that makes my heart stumble.

Martha's sudden movement draws our attention back to the main event. Her tail rises as a contraction ripples visibly across her side, a sign that her labor is steadily progressing toward its inevitable conclusion. Taylen's breath catches slightly.

"How long?" he asks, showing the same mix of excitement and concern I had the first time I witnessed the birth of a calf.

"Could be hours yet," I admit, shifting slightly on the hay bale that's growing less comfortable the longer we sit. "The first stage can take a while. But she's doing everything right so far."

Silence settles between us again, comfortable now rather than the charged energy we've experienced since I came back. The bread disappears slowly as we continue our vigil. Outside, the afternoon turns into evening.

When Martha shifts again, more forcefully this time, Taylen's hand finds my knee. The touch burns through denim, and I have to force myself to remember I'm here for Martha, not to think about the beautiful tattoos under Taylen's clothes or the sounds he makes when he comes.

"Thank you," he says suddenly, fingers still resting against my leg like he's forgotten they're there. "For sharing this with me."

I cover his hand with mine, giving it a squeeze that says all the things he's not ready to hear yet. Because this moment feels too precious for words that might break the spell.

Martha's persistent movement keeps us focused even as something shifts between us. The barn lights cast a gentle glow over this ordinary and extraordinary scene—two people waiting for a new life to happen.

As midnight approaches, Martha's contractions grow stronger, each wave drawing soft sounds from her throat that echo in the barn. Taylen leans forward every time she moves as though he can speed up the process with the power of his mind.

"The contractions are getting closer together," I explain, watching Martha's sides heave with increasing frequency.

Taylen nods, completely focused on the process unfolding before us. His hand still rests on my knee, a touch so natural now that moving feels impossible. When Martha shifts again, more forcefully this time, his fingers tighten slightly. "Is that normal?" he asks as she paws at her bedding with increasing agitation.

"She's perfect," I assure him. "She's trying to make a nest to get everything just right before the main event."

"I didn't have watching a calf being born on my Bingo card for today," he jokes.

"There," I say quietly as clear fluid appears, signaling the transition to active labor. Taylen's sharp intake of breath matches Martha's as another contraction ripples across her body. "Water's broken. Things will move faster now."

We move closer to observe while maintaining a safe distance from the increasingly restless mother.

"The calf is moving into position."

When the first hoof appears, Taylen covers his mouth with his hands. The second leg follows, the tiny hooves still wrapped in the translucent membrane. Martha keeps on pushing, her animal instincts guiding her.

"Should we help?" Taylen asks as a nose appears

"Not unless she shows signs of distress," I assure him. "She's doing all the work. We're just here to witness and help if needed. I gave Hunter the heads-up in case I need to call him after hours, but it looks like our girl is going to do it all on her own."

Martha pushes again. A powerful contraction brings the calf's head fully into view.

"Almost there," I encourage as Martha gives a mighty heave that delivers the calf's shoulders. The rest of the birth happens in a rush of fluid and movement, nature's perfect timing bringing a new life onto the fresh straw. I move forward immediately, taking over as I clear mucus from the small nose and mouth.

The calf's first breath puts my mind at ease, the tiny chest expanding as the lungs fill properly. I check quickly for the gender while Martha begins cleaning her baby with her rough tongue to stimulate circulation.

"We have a girl," I announce, unable to keep a smile from my voice. "A healthy heifer." Pride fills my chest as I watch Martha encourage her daughter toward her first tentative movements. Behind me, Taylen makes a sound that could be a laugh or a sob.

I turn toward him, seeing the wonder on his face. His eyes shine with emotion too pure for words, making him look younger and somehow more real than I've ever seen him.

Kissing him is inevitable. We're tired and overwhelmed. The adrenaline of the moment takes over. I wrap my arms around him while his fingers clutch at my shoulders.

"Come home with me," I beg.

His eyes search mine for what feels like an eternity. Then a simple, "Yes," falls from his lips.

Behind us, the heifer has found her feet properly now, all gangly limbs and cuteness overload. I will check on mother and daughter in the morning, but for now, I need something else.

The path from the barn to my cabin feels like it's a mile long, each step stretching impossibly as anticipation coils tighter in my chest. My heart pounds against my ribs with enough force that I'm sure Taylen must hear it in the quiet night air between us.

The cabin's dark shape grows larger ahead, but never seems close enough. I want to break into a run, to close the distance that suddenly feels unbearable, but I force myself to match Taylen's measured pace even as every single one of my nerve endings screams for the promise waiting just beyond that door.

Inside, I lead him directly to the bathroom without bothering with the main lights. The moonlight through the windows provides enough illumination to navigate the familiar space, creating an intimate atmosphere. The shower starts with a familiar hiss, steam filling the small space as the water heats.

We turn toward each other. I lower the zipper of his jacket slowly, feeling the rise and fall of his chest under my touch. He mirrors my action, quietly revealing layers of clothing until I see the beautiful tribute to his brother.

"I will never get tired of looking at these." My fingers trace the lines I can see through the moonlight.

Steam fills the space between us as our remaining clothes fall away. Water hits my back as I draw him under the spray. Every touch feels urgent but careful, like handling something precious yet unbreakable.

My mouth finds his neck, tasting water and salt and the essence that's uniquely him. His hands tangle in my hair, his grip tightening when I find a particularly sensitive spot below his ear. Each reaction feeds the growing need between us, but tonight feels different from the desperate encounters we've shared before.

"I need to taste you," I whisper against his ear.

"Please, Bastian," he moans.

I sink to my knees on the shower floor, looking up to find his eyes dark with want. I take him in my mouth, loving the weight of his cock on my tongue, the unique taste of his essence. Every sound he makes goes straight to my cock, and it takes everything in me to not touch myself.

This is all for him. My pleasure will come, but I want to take my time with Taylen. I want to burn into my memory every moan, every orgasm I draw out of him.

He screams his release with my name on his lips and his cock between mine. I swallow every drop until his body shudders under my hands. I hold him steady through aftershocks, feeling the tremors run through his legs as water continues its steady fall around us.

When I stand, he wraps his arms around me, holding me close as our lips meet and we share the taste of his cum.

"I'm not done with you yet, baby," I whisper against his temple.

"Good, because I believe I owe you at least two orgasms. Not that I'm keeping count, but—"

I kiss him until his cock rallies for another round, pressing hard and eager against mine.

"Bedroom," I growl.

24

TAYLEN

"Come here," Bastian growls, his hands finding my waist as he pulls me from beneath the spray.

Water streams from our bodies, puddling on the tiled floor as he reaches for a towel with one hand while the other keeps me pressed against him. He moves the towel over my skin in quick, impatient strokes.

"Bastian—" His name becomes a gasp as his mouth finds my neck, his teeth scraping against my sensitive skin before he sucks hard enough to mark me. The sensation shoots straight to my dick, making my knees threaten to buckle.

"Want everyone to see," he mutters against my throat, moving to a new spot. "Want them to know you're mine."

Heat floods through me at the possessiveness in his voice, at the evidence he's leaving on my skin. My fingers dig into his shoulders as he works his way across my collarbone, each mark burning like a brand I never want to fade.

"We're dry enough," he declares suddenly, tossing the barely-used towel aside.

I laugh breathlessly, water still dripping from my hair down my back. "We're not even close to dry enough."

"Don't care." His hands find mine, pulling me toward the bedroom with a single-minded determination that makes my pulse race. "Need you. Now."

I follow, almost slipping on the wet floor. When he stops all of a sudden, I almost bump into him.

"What the—" The sight in front of us makes me laugh harder.

Gouta sprawls across his pillows like a queen on her throne, while Myrtle and Moira have claimed opposite corners of the mattress with impressive territorial determination.

"Well," Bastian says with resignation, "I see my bed has been commandeered."

"It seems your security team has strong opinions about your nocturnal activities."

"We could try to move them," Bastian suggests, but his tone indicates he knows exactly how well that would go over.

Instead of responding, I turn toward the nightstand, retrieving the bottle of lube. "Or," I say, letting a smile curl the edges of my mouth as I face him again, "we could find somewhere else to continue this."

I take his hand, leading him toward the living room. The couch is lit softly by the moonlight, thanks to his uncovered windows. I guide Bastian onto the middle cushion, enjoying the way his breath catches as I drop to my knees between his spread legs.

His skin still carries traces of moisture from the shower, droplets catching the light as they trail down his chest. I lean forward, following one particularly tempting rivulet with my tongue. The taste of his clean skin and rising arousal fills my mouth as I work my way lower, maintaining eye contact.

"Tay," he breathes as I reach his cock. My hands find his thighs, and I grip firmly enough to leave temporary marks as I take him into my mouth.

The weight of his cock feels perfect against my tongue as I set a slow rhythm. My first orgasm took the edge off, so I can enjoy watching the reactions of what I'm doing play across his face.

His fingers thread through my damp hair. "You're a fucking tease, Taylen Howard."

I hollow my cheeks on the upstroke, pulling a sound from his throat. Each gasp and shiver tells me exactly what he needs, how to build this until he's cursing my name.

"Tay," he warns again, his hips beginning to move despite his obvious attempt at control. "I'm getting close." The words come between harsh breaths that fill the cabin's quiet space. But that's not what I want.

I pull off slowly, letting him slide from my mouth. His cock stands fully hard now. "Not yet," I tell him, as I straddle his thighs. "I have a better idea about how this should end."

"Yeah?" he asks, his hands grabbing my hips and pulling me flush against him. "Tell me about this idea."

Showing works better than telling, so even as I drag my hard cock against the length of his, I reach for the lube and place it in his hand.

"Not too much prep," I ask. "I want to feel this...you tomorrow."

The words make Bastian's pupils dilate, but his movements remain carefully controlled as he takes over and begins working me open. The first finger slides in with a familiar burn that makes my breath catch.

Why did I ever resist this?

His free hand grips my hip, steadying me as I rock back against the intrusion. "You're so impatient, aren't you, baby? You're dying to have me inside you again," he says, but I hear the strain in his voice that betrays his own urgency.

A second finger joins the first, the stretch becoming more

pronounced as he scissors them with the kind of slow, tender care that makes me want to scream.

"Yes," I admit, grinding against his hand while my own fingers dig into his shoulders for balance. A third finger pushes in before I'm quite ready, drawing a sound from my throat that's half pain and half desperate need. "Bastian," I manage as he works me steadily open. "That's enough. I'm ready."

I don't like the absence of his fingers when he removes them to cover his cock with lube.

When I finally lift up, positioning myself over his cock, time seems to suspend between one breath and the next. His hands return to my hips, steadying but not controlling as I begin a slow descent. The first breach burns exactly like I wanted, the stretch just this side of too much as I take him in inch by careful inch.

"Fuck," he breathes against my collarbone. "You feel so fucking good."

His thumbs stroke my hipbones so gently that I'm wondering if there's a "calm under pressure" award for sex.

I pause when he's fully seated, letting my body adjust to the fullness that feels new every time. Our skin slides slightly where we're pressed together.

"Move," he pleads, and I love that he sounds wrecked when we've barely started. "Please, Tay. Need you to move."

The nickname pulls a response from my throat as I lift slightly, testing the angle that makes both of us gasp when I drop back down.

I find our rhythm, each rise and fall drawing gasps and moans that fill the cabin's quiet space, mixing with the subtle creak of the couch beneath us. His hands guide more than control, letting me set a pace that quickly builds from careful to desperate.

Sweat replaces the shower's moisture on our skin as our

movement becomes more intense. My thighs burn, but I couldn't stop if the world ended right now—not with the way he's looking at me like I'm something miraculous, like he can't quite believe this is real. His cock hits the perfect spot on every thrust, sending sparks through my nervous system that build toward inevitable explosion.

"Close," I warn as pressure builds low in my core, the familiar tingling at the base of my spine suggesting imminent release. One of his hands wraps around my cock with a perfect grip. "So close, Bastian. Please."

His hips snap up to meet my downward motion, finally letting control slip as we race toward the finish line together.

"Come for me," he commands, his voice carrying an authority that sends me right over the edge.

My release hits me with force, and I cry out, my body clenching around him as pleasure whites out everything else.

He follows immediately, his grip on my hip turning bruising as he pulses inside me. The sensation prolongs my own orgasm, aftershocks running through both of us as we gradually come down together. My forehead finds his shoulder, my breathing begins returning to normal, and he wraps his arms around me, holding me close.

"You are so fucking perfect, Taylen. Just so you know, it's never been like this with anyone else." I almost can't tell what he's saying because his mouth is once again mapping all the free areas on my skin.

"You make it so hard to resist you."

"Then don't, Taylen. Don't."

"I can't believe you didn't have sex for seven years." It's not that I don't believe him, but seven years is a long time.

He laughs. "I didn't say I didn't have sex for seven years. I had plenty of sex. It just never involved anyone else."

His mouth on my skin turns my brain into mush. "And

you're very good at it. Clearly, the lack of practice with another person didn't affect your skills."

"Or maybe when you're with the right person, everything fits perfectly. My body has known for seven years that no one else would ever come close to how you make me feel."

His words draw a shiver from me, or maybe it's the cooling sweat. His dick slips out, and I feel way too empty, but I'm happy that I'll definitely feel this tomorrow.

He reaches over to the box of tissues on the table and cleans us both up. I'm certain I can't move a single inch, so when he pulls the blanket from the back of the couch over us and adjusts until we're lying face-to-face on the couch, I burrow deeper into his chest, seeking his warmth.

"So," he says after a comfortable silence stretches between us, "does this count as our first date?" His arms tighten around me as I start laughing.

"Hell no," I manage when I stop laughing. "First"—I poke his chest with a finger—"I've not agreed to a date. Just dinner. And second"—I poke again—"you'll have to do a lot better than that to woo me."

"Taylen Howard wants to be wooed." His smile presses against my shoulder, his lips curved in a way I can feel against my skin. "Noted. I can woo."

Movement from the bedroom doorway draws our attention. Gouta peers around the corner from the small hallway frame with an expression that clearly questions our life choices. Myrtle and Moira flank her like tiny feathered bodyguards.

She comes closer and sniffs us, giving a *very* disapproving bleat before heading to her bed in the corner.

"How very judgmental," I say with a chuckle.

"I should probably install a lock on the bedroom door before this becomes a regular occurrence. My couch is okay, but we're not twenty anymore."

The casual mention that this will happen again sends warmth through my chest. Because he says it like a certainty. Not *if* this becomes regular, but *when*. Like he's already planning for more nights like this, more time together.

"Let's not do age math because when you were twenty, I was—"

He shuts me up with a kiss that'll have me agreeing to anything.

"Stay," he whispers against my mouth.

My answer comes in the way I burrow deeper into his embrace, in how my fingers tangle in his hair, pulling him closer.

Something has shifted between us, like the first thaw changing frozen ground. Whatever comes next, proper dates, morning awkwardness, or judgmental farm animals, it feels less like fear and more like my new reality.

When Bastian drags me out of the living room to his bed and snuggles against me, I don't *think* I'm in trouble. I know for sure that I am. Because my puppy love, my teenage crush, the love that I thought I felt for him before, is nothing compared to how I feel right now.

Sebastian Hall better be here to stay because I've never in my life wanted to be proven wrong more than now.

25

BASTIAN

THE NOTE in my hand feels both light and heavy, its crisp folds shaking with my trembling fingers. I watch his front door, wondering if elaborate gestures mean more or less when you've already seen someone naked.

I pull out my phone and send a simple message asking him to come outside. The whoosh as it sends sounds louder than it should in the truck's quiet cab, and I watch three dots appear, then vanish, then reappear before a simple *Coming* appears on screen, making my belly flip.

For the love of cinnamon loaf, I've performed in front of thousands of people, and here I am. Nervous like a school boy asking his crush if he wants to go to prom.

Taylen's door opens, and he emerges wearing his coat, smiling but shaking his head a little because, yeah, this is weird.

"You know," he says as he reaches the passenger door, "normal people just knock on the door." But his smile betrays him as he climbs in, bringing a rush of cold air and his usual scent of apples and earth.

I hold out the folded note. "Normal is boring," I tell

him, watching as his fingers brush mine when he accepts the paper. "Besides, proper wooing requires proper invitations."

His laugh carries warmth that makes my chest tight as he unfolds the note with exaggerated care. "*You are cordially invited to be wooed*," he reads aloud with amusement. "A bit formal for someone who had his tongue—"

"Ah-ah," I interrupt quickly, heat rising in my cheeks despite my best efforts. "This is different. This is…" I gesture vaguely, searching for words that won't sound ridiculous. "This is doing things right."

"This is a dinner," he corrects, but his eyes hold warmth that contradicts his words. "I agreed to dinner. Not a date. Not wooing. Just dinner." The words carry no real conviction, especially given the way his hand has found my knee.

"If you say so," I agree easily, letting a smile fall from my lips. "Though aren't you curious what sort of wooing I'm capable of?"

"Maybe," he admits after a moment. His thumb traces idle patterns against my leg through the denim, making me want to reevaluate my plans in exchange for taking him back to his place. "I've always wondered if you ever had to put effort into your dates or if it came easy, given who you are."

I glance at him as I pull away from his drive. "All the best ones have made me work for it, but no one like you."

Winterberry slides past our windows as we drive. Despite the location change of the festival, the town is still dressed in its holiday finest. Christmas lights twinkle from every storefront despite daylight, people wrapped in coats, holding cups of hot drinks in one hand and Christmas shopping in the other.

"Where are we going?" Taylen finally asks. His hand still rests on my knee, his fingers occasionally squeezing my leg, making it hard to focus on the road.

"It's a surprise," I tell him, covering his hand with mine.

He turns his hand over, giving me the chance to link our fingers. I want to continue circling the town until I get tired of holding his hand, but I think my old truck won't survive it because I'm nowhere near ready to let go of Taylen Howard's hand.

The community center appears ahead of us, its parking lot already filling with cars. I find a spot for us and kill the engine, but I make no move to exit the truck immediately.

"Ready?" My eyes drift to his lips, but I'm not sure kissing him now is the right thing to do. We're in public. Sort of. What if he's not ready for people to know about us? Is there an us?

Before my thoughts spiral further, he leans over, his hand finding my jaw. The kiss starts gentle, almost tentative. His lips are warm against mine, tasting faintly of mint. I cup the back of his neck, pulling him closer despite the awkward angle, deepening the kiss.

When we part, his eyes meet mine. "Okay," he whispers. "Now I'm ready."

The community center's double doors open into a wall of warmth and Christmas music. Volunteers in red Santa hats weave between tables, carrying trays of food for people with limited mobility and clearing tables.

Paper snowflakes dance from ceiling strings, and a Christmas tree dominates one corner, its lights bringing seasonal cheer into the space. The smell of turkey and fresh rolls fills the space, reminding my stomach that nervous anticipation is a poor substitute for actual food.

"What is this?" Taylen asks quietly as I guide him toward the volunteer check-in table with a gentle hand against the small of his back.

"Weekly Christmas lunch for people who might be alone or struggling during the holidays."

A volunteer with tinsel woven through her gray hair

hands us clipboards without breaking the stride in her conversation with someone about checking the gravy temperature.

"Tyler runs a similar program in Stillwater," I continue as we return the clipboards. "When he visited over Thanksgiving, he connected with Finn about setting this up here."

Taylen's expression softens as he watches the young family enter through the main doors, three children bouncing with excitement while their mother tries to maintain order with exhausted patience. "How long has this been happening?" he asks.

"This is the first week," I tell him, accepting aprons from another volunteer who appears beside us with uncanny timing. "Word's still spreading, but turnout's been great."

The hall fills steadily as we receive our assignments: me on the main dishes while Taylen handles the vegetables and rolls. An older man approaches his station, and I watch as my...as Taylen leans in to listen, giving the gentleman his complete attention while the man tells everyone who'll listen about his late mother's famous stuffing recipe that his wife was never able to replicate.

The way Taylen naturally connects with people, drawing out their stories with patient interest, makes me forget to serve my own line until someone clears their throat.

I force myself to focus on my job, but my eyes keep finding him across the space between us, drawn like a compass to true north.

Tables fill with people from all walks of life, some clearly struggling with the weight of poverty and the ever-growing cost of living, others bearing the burden of loneliness that seems heavier during the holiday season. But here, in this space, everyone receives the same welcome, same food, same chance to feel part of something bigger.

"This is amazing," Taylen says during a brief lull in serving. "How many volunteers are here in total?"

"About thirty between all the servings on each day," I explain, ladling gravy over sliced turkey. "Plus, whoever can make it each week. Fox, Nikko, and Stone also volunteer, but we've devised a schedule where we don't cross over. We don't want this to be about us. Here we're just helping."

An older woman approaches the serving line, her walker decorated with small bells that chime softly with each step. Taylen hands her roll with a smile that makes her whole face light up. "Just like my grandson," she tells him, patting his hand with arthritis-curved fingers. "Such kind eyes."

I watch him blush slightly at the compliment, color rising in his cheeks. Our eyes meet across the serving table as the woman moves along the line, and then a man who looks to be just a little older than me approaches. His eyes hold a mix of grief and gratitude that makes my chest tight as he begins sharing a story. "Twenty-seven years," he tells us, his voice shaky. "Twenty-seven years, and I got let go before the holidays when I'd just put all my savings into paying my mortgage. It's nice not worrying about that, but finding a new job at this time isn't easy."

I watch as Taylen has a conversation with the guy about his job in a factory a few miles away from here. I could be wrong, but I have a feeling the guy won't be unemployed for long if Taylen has something to say about it.

We take a small break while the kitchen volunteers bring out more food. Taylen excuses himself to the restroom with a look that tells me I'm meant to follow him.

As soon as we're away from the bustle of the main hall, barely past the kitchen, he backs me against the wall, wrapping his arms around my waist.

"This is quite an elaborate plan," he says. "Bringing me to

a charity lunch, showing off how selfless and amazing you are."

"Is it working?" I manage, my voice rough as his hand finds its way under my sweater. His answer comes as a kiss that steals all the air from my lungs.

My hands tangle in his hair automatically, pulling him closer as the kiss deepens into something that probably isn't appropriate for a community center.

Taylen pulls back slightly, but his hands remain on my back while he catches his breath. "It's working," he whispers against my mouth.

We take a moment to compose ourselves before returning to the dining room for the next serving slot.

The rhythm of the afternoon continues. More plates filled, more smiles exchanged, more stories shared. Time blurs into a comfortable pattern of service as the crowd gradually thins, children growing sleepy in their parents' arms, and elderly guests lingering over coffee and conversation.

Before I realize it, we've moved from serving to cleanup. Taylen wipes down tables while I stack chairs. The volunteer in charge approaches us as we're collecting the last of the serving utensils. Her arms cradle two boxed portions of food.

"Thank you so much for your help this afternoon," she says, her smile carrying genuine gratitude that makes my chest warm. "We've got plenty of volunteers to finish the cleanup. You two have done more than enough today, but I hope to see you again next week."

"Absolutely," we reply in tandem.

"The children's choir will be here singing Christmas carols tomorrow," she adds, her eyes twinkling. "You should come if you can. It's always magical."

Taylen carries the lunch boxes to my truck. The winter air feels harsh after the community center's warmth, making us both inhale sharply as we step outside.

"Where to now?" he asks as we climb into the truck.

I hadn't planned this next part, but as I see the sun slowly lowering on the horizon and the steaming boxes between us, I know just what to do.

"Dinner with a view," I say as I drive us back to the farm, past my parents' farmhouse and my cabin, toward the frozen lake.

I park near the water's edge by the oak tree, reversing in. Taylen grabs the food and steps out of the truck. I grab the blanket I always keep in the cab and drape it over the lowered tailgate.

We sit side by side, taking a box each.

"Bastian Hall," Taylen says, "a romantic soul. Who'd have thought it?"

I chuckle. "Sometimes all you need is someone to be romantic for. Besides, who do you think wrote half of the love songs for the band?"

He takes a piece of turkey and puts it in his mouth. I could write songs about that mouth.

The food tastes better somehow in the open air, even though we have to eat it quickly before it cools completely.

"Thank you," he says, closing his almost-empty box. "It was a really fun day."

His head finds my shoulder as the last light fades completely from the sky. I wrap my arm around his waist automatically, holding him close against the winter chill that grows sharper with each passing minute.

"Still not a date though," he murmurs against my jacket, his words carrying a smile I can hear without seeing. "Just dinner, remember? Or more accurately, a late lunch with a sunset." But his body remains pressed against mine, betraying how little he means to protest.

"Of course not," I agree easily, letting my cheek rest

against his hair. "Just food, community service, and stargazing. Totally casual. Not a date."

The darkening sky deepens around us while we sit together, watching the stars become brighter in the sky. Neither of us seems inclined to move despite the growing cold.

Taylen's fingers find mine in the darkness. "You know how this non-date would end perfectly?" he asks.

"How?"

"Take me home and kiss me on the porch."

I chuckle. "Trust me, I have full intentions of doing that."

"Good. Because I might invite you in. For coffee, you know?"

"Coffee is good. I love coffee."

26

TAYLEN

THE MORNING AIR bites at my cheeks, but it's not just December's chill that makes my steps slow and hesitant as I approach the familiar single headstone where Jackson rests.

I've walked this path hundreds of times over the past twelve years, every single time wondering what it would be like if my big brother were still here. We were always best friends, but there are so many life milestones we've missed, so many celebrations and day-to-day stuff.

Would he have made the same decisions I've made for the farm? Or would they be different? Would we disagree on the direction of the business? I'll never know.

The shock of seeing someone at Jackson's grave stops me mid-stride. I recognize Bastian's broad shoulders and his silver-streaked hair immediately. He's crouched beside the headstone, one hand resting on the smooth granite while the other moves through the air like he's telling a story.

I'm torn between the desire to approach him and the need to preserve the privacy of the moment I'm witnessing. Bastian's voice carries faintly, but it's still too quiet to make out the words. The tone, however, is clear enough. Conversational, warm, like he's catching up with an old friend over coffee rather than speaking to a cold stone that marks the absence we both still feel.

I shift my weight slightly, trying to decide whether to retreat and return later, but the frozen grass betrays me with a sharp crack.

Bastian turns at the sound, and as soon as his eyes meet mine, I see his are red-rimmed and bright with tears. For a moment, we just stare at each other.

"I'm sorry," he says quickly, wiping the tears with the back of his hand. "I didn't... I mean, I should go. Give you privacy."

"Stay," I manage, my voice surprisingly steady. "Please. You don't have to leave." My feet finally remember how to move, carrying me closer to the grave that's drawn us both to this particular spot on my property on this frost-bright morning.

Bastian watches my approach with an expression I can't quite read, although the tension in his shoulders eases slightly. "I wasn't sure," he admits quietly as I reach him. "If you'd want me here."

I lay the flowers beside the headstone, my fingers lingering on the cold granite. "Have you...?" I start, then pause, gathering courage to ask the question I'm not sure I want the answer to. "Have you been here before? Other times?"

His expression is filled with so much raw honesty that it makes my chest ache. "Every time I'm home," he says, his gaze fixed on Jackson's name carved in the stone. "I've been doing it for years. Keeping him updated on everything: band stuff, touring stories, awards we've won..." His voice catches slightly. "Stupid things, really. Like he's just away on a trip and needs catching up."

The admission hits me hard. Because this is a piece of

Bastian I never considered, that while I've been guarding my grief like a precious thing, he's been here sharing his with a silent stone and morning air.

"It helps," he continues softly, "talking to him. Makes it feel less…" He gestures vaguely, searching for the word that might capture the magnitude of loss we both still carry. "Less final, maybe. Like he's still part of things, you know?"

I nod, unable to speak past the sudden thickness in my throat. Because I do know. I understand perfectly this need to maintain the connection that death tried to sever. My own visits are no different, but I've always kept my conversations with Jackson inside my head, where they can't be witnessed.

"I'm sorry," Bastian says again, but this time the apology feels different. "Not sure what for, exactly. Everything. Nothing. Just…" He trails off, sticking his hands in the pockets of his jeans. "For his loss, for my absence, for you."

"I know." It's all I can manage before the knot in my throat grows tighter. I'm starting to understand Bastian now. Why he stayed away but always returned. He was never the flaky rockstar I accused him of being.

Bastian settles onto the damp grass beside Jackson's headstone, and I wonder how many conversations I've missed, how many stories have been shared in this quiet space while I was elsewhere on this land.

The grass feels cold and wet as I lower myself beside him, close enough that our shoulders brush. My fingers find a blade of grass, needing something to do with hands that want to reach for him.

"Do you…?" I start, then pause, gathering courage to ask a question that's been building since his revelation. "When you talk to him, do you ever mention me?" The words come out smaller than intended, carrying a vulnerability I usually try harder to hide.

Bastian's laugh holds genuine warmth that makes my skin

prickle with awareness. "All the time," he admits, turning slightly so our eyes meet. "I tell him about the orchard, how you've expanded everything. How you're basically running this whole town's agricultural future." His smile carries so much pride that it catches me off guard. "I think he'd be impressed. Probably not surprised, though, because he always said you'd do amazing things."

"I miss him," I say quietly, the words feeling inadequate against the weight of absence that still presses against my chest some mornings. "Miss his stupid jokes and terrible advice and the way he could make anything feel possible." My voice catches slightly. "Miss having someone who knew exactly who I was trying to be."

Bastian's hand finds mine in the grass, tangling our fingers. "He knew who you already were," he corrects gently. "The rest of us just needed time to catch up."

"Do you know," Bastian continues, "if he was seeing someone? Before…" He trails off, letting the unspoken words hang in the air between us. His thumb traces patterns against my palm, the touch grounding me as I process the question.

"He wasn't dating anyone," I say, a smile tugging at the corners of my mouth despite the heaviness in my chest. "But he had a massive crush on a girl who worked at that hair salon in town.

"Seriously?" Bastian's eyebrows rise slightly. "He never mentioned her to me." Something like hurt crosses his face briefly before being replaced by curiosity. "What was she like?"

I shift slightly, turning more fully toward him while maintaining a connection through our linked hands. "Smart. Kind of quiet but funny when you get her talking. She's married now. Jackson would find excuses to walk past the salon, try to time it for when she was on a break."

"That sounds exactly like him," Bastian says, affection clear in his voice. "Too nervous to just ask her out?"

"He was working up to it," I explain, words coming slower now. "Had this whole plan about asking her to the Christmas Festival. She's a single mom, so he wanted to make sure she knew he was in it for the long haul, not just some fun." My free hand finds the headstone. "The accident happened the week before he was going to do it. I think he was really ready to settle down. Be a dad, have kids of his own with someone he loved."

"That's why he never wanted to join the band," Bastian continues. "He couldn't imagine being away from home that much, you and your parents. And he loved working on the farm."

His thumb continues to trace patterns on the back of my hand, unaware that he's revealing new information.

"Wait," I say. "Jackson was offered a spot in the band? Your band?"

Bastian's expression shifts to surprise. "I thought you knew," he says quietly, grip tightening slightly on my hand like he's afraid I'll pull away completely. "I wasn't discovered playing at Joe's. *We* were discovered playing at Joe's."

"Tell me. Tell me everything."

His thumb resumes tracing patterns against my palm as he gathers his thoughts. "Individually, we were good," he starts, smile touching his voice. "Together, we were very good. You must remember that."

I nod. "I do. I used to hide outside his room when you two were practicing."

"This guy kept watching us from the corner," Bastian continues. "I thought he was going to complain about the noise level, honestly. But after the set, he came up with a business card and started talking about forming a rock band.

He said we had perfect stage presence and natural charisma that couldn't be taught."

"He wasn't wrong. Jackson always had this way of making everyone feel like the most important person in the room," I say.

"Jackson just laughed," he continues quickly. "Said he wasn't made for that life and joked about not being suitable for the 'Hall of Fame' or whatever you want to call it," he says, imitating Jackson's voice. "The scout loved the name, and when he found out my last name is Hall, he said it was fate and a sure sign we were going to be the biggest band in the country."

"And you are. You did it, Bastian."

I look back at the stone. If Jackson had said yes, he wouldn't have been on the road that day. Would have been in a studio or on tour or somewhere that didn't end with the cold stone beneath my fingers. The thought burns in my chest like whiskey taken too fast, making it hard to breathe properly.

"Don't," Bastian says quietly, reading the direction of my thoughts with uncomfortable accuracy. "We can't change the past, Tay. Can't know what might have happened differently." His hand finds my face, his thumb brushing away moisture I hadn't realized was there. "Jackson made his choices based on who he was, what he wanted from life."

He's right. Jackson had a chance to leave, to be part of something bigger than small-town life. But he chose to stay, chose familiar roads and quiet moments over bright lights and screaming crowds.

Bastian's touch sends electricity through my system despite the heavy conversation, making me increasingly aware of how close we're sitting. "I know," I manage. "Just… a lot to process."

"I should have told you sooner," he admits, his fingers

still gentle against my cheek. "Should have shared so many things instead of letting distance grow between us." The words carry so much weight beyond a simple apology.

I'm not sure who moves first. Maybe we both lean in simultaneously, drawn together like magnets. Our lips find each other in a kiss that feels different from any we've had before. This one is less about passion and more about the gentle exploration of something we're both still learning to trust.

His hand slides into my hair while the other maintains connection with mine. My free hand finds his jacket, clutching the material like I'm afraid he'll disappear if I let go. Everything narrows to the sensation of his mouth moving against mine, to the way our breaths mix in the cold air between us.

Reality crashes back as a particularly loud bird call breaks the spell we've fallen under. I pull back slightly, feeling heat rise in my cheeks as I remember where we are. "Not in front of my brother," I manage, trying for a light tone that probably fails completely. "It's weird."

Bastian laughs. "Come home with me," he says, leaning in for another—briefer—kiss. "We can continue this conversation somewhere more private."

It would be so easy to say yes, but… "It's probably best if I don't," I tell him. "I'm all over the place right now." The excuse sounds weak even to my ears, but he accepts it with a grace I'm not sure I deserve.

Bastian's hand squeezes mine once more before releasing, his acceptance clear in the way he begins gathering himself to leave.

This is all about me, not him, so before I turn back toward my house, I wrap my arms around Bastian and kiss him again.

"Thank you," I whisper against his lips, feeling the way his tension evaporates.

"Any time, baby."

BASTIAN

"TAY?" I call again.

The food box burns against my palms as I stare at Taylen's empty driveway, his truck conspicuously absent from its usual spot beside the barn. Mom's lasagna still radiates heat through the box, the small opening on top allowing for steam to rise into the freezing air.

My knuckles rap against the wooden door. No response, no footsteps, no call of acknowledgment, just emptiness that worries me with each passing second. I try again, louder this time, but the house remains stubbornly silent.

The porch boards creak beneath my feet as I shift my weight, anxiety building in my chest. I set the food on the porch chair and pull out my phone. The call goes straight to voicemail.

"Hey," I say after the tone, trying to keep worry from bleeding into my words. "Just stopped by with some food from Mom. Call me when you get this?" The message sounds casual enough, but my heart pounds harder as I end the call, memories of our conversation at Jackson's grave coming back to me.

The wind picks up, sending dead leaves skittering across the porch.

I try texting next, my thumbs moving quickly.

BASTIAN:

Where are you? Mom sent food.

The message shows as undelivered, suggesting his phone is completely off rather than Taylen just ignoring me. Something twists in my stomach. Taylen would never have his phone off. There are a bunch of workers on our farms at any given time. We need to be available all the time, especially in case of an emergency.

Another call goes straight to voicemail. Another text fails to deliver. The steam coming out of the box dwindles as the food cools, but giving Taylen cold food is the least of my worries.

Is he avoiding me? The thought burns like acid in my throat. Did sharing those memories about Jackson push him too far, break the fragile trust that was building between us?

The orchard stretches away from the house, bare branches reaching as far as the eye can see. No movement, no workers checking trees, no equipment being moved, no signs of life at all.

"Come on, Tay," I mutter, dialing his number again, although I know it's futile. "Where are you?"

The voicemail greeting feels like mockery now, his recorded voice cheerful against the growing knot of worry in my stomach. I hang up without leaving a message this time.

One more circuit of the porch brings me back to the front door, where I try knocking again, although I know it's pointless. My watch shows that nearly an hour has passed since I arrived. The food is cold now, and wherever Taylen went, he hasn't returned.

"Fuck this," I decide finally, grabbing the box and

turning back toward my truck. The food box lands on the passenger seat with less care than Mom's cooking deserves, but my hands are already moving to a different task. Finding Finn's number in my phone contacts.

Finn is Taylen's best friend, so I can only hope that he offers some answers before I start calling hospitals and the police department.

The ring sounds impossibly loud in my truck's quiet cab as I wait for a response. Just as I'm about to hang up, the line connects with a familiar click that makes my heart skip a beat.

"Hey, big brother."

Finn's voice comes through the speaker with a warmth that usually calms me instantly. But today my nerves are too raw, my fingers drumming against the steering wheel as I try to keep anxiety from bleeding into my voice.

"You busy?"

"Never too busy for you," Finn responds, though the sound of rustling papers suggests he's in the middle of work. "What's up? You sound weird."

"Have you heard from Taylen?" I aim for a casual tone but probably miss by a mile, given the way Finn's silence stretches for a moment too long. "Mom sent a box with lasagna for him, but he's not home."

"Ah," Finn says finally, a single syllable that makes my chest tight. "Yeah, he's in Burlington. It's a trip he does every year."

The information makes me sit straighter in the driver's seat.

"Burlington?" My voice comes out sharper than intended. "What's in Burlington?" Besides bars and clubs and people who aren't me, my brain helpfully supplies. The steering wheel creaks slightly under my tightening grip.

Finn's sigh carries a clear note of exasperation that would

normally make me defensive. "Bastian," he starts, using a tone that suggests he's choosing words carefully. "What exactly are you worried about here?"

"I'm not worried," I lie automatically. "Just…curious. About why he'd suddenly disappear without telling anyone." The words sound pathetic even to my own ears.

"Right." Finn draws the word out like he's trying not to laugh. "You're definitely not sitting somewhere having completely rational thoughts about why Taylen might be in Burlington." The accuracy of his assessment makes me wince slightly.

"He could be hooking up with someone," I blurt before I can stop myself, voicing the fear that's been building since learning his location. "Trying to sabotage…because he's scared or uncertain or—never mind."

"Oh my god," Finn interrupts, laughter finally breaking free. "You're actually being serious right now. You genuinely think Taylen drove to Burlington for a random hookup?" The question makes heat rise in my cheeks despite being alone in the truck.

"Well, what else would he be doing there?" I demand, anxiety making my voice rougher than intended. "He's not answering his phone, didn't tell anyone where he was going—"

"First of all, I know where he is, so someone knows where he is. And second, since when are you so worried about someone you can barely stand?"

The question hits hard. "We don't…" I start, then stop, because what am I even trying to say? That we hate each other? That would be easier if it were true. "Something's happening between us," I admit quietly, the words feeling heavy in my mouth. "I don't know…but it's not nothing. And it sure as hell isn't us barely standing each other."

"He's getting a tattoo," Finn cuts in, his words clear and

certain enough to stop my spiral mid-sentence. "He does it every year around this time for Jackson. He stays overnight, so he's not on the road when he's feeling upset. Turns his phone off for those two days. I don't like it, but it's the way he processes the anniversary of Jackson's death. He just needs some time alone away from home and all the memories, you know?"

The information takes a moment to process, relief washing through my system so strongly it makes my hands shake slightly. "The tattoo," I repeat stupidly. Of course it's the tattoo. Jackson's anniversary was last week. "That's...? That's all?"

"That's all," Finn confirms, voice gentler now. "Though the fact that you immediately jumped to 'he must be hooking up with a stranger' suggests you two need to have an actual conversation about feelings at some point."

The observation hits uncomfortably close to home, making me shift in my seat as memories of our talk at Jackson's grave surface again. "We're working on it," I mutter, though the truth is we've been avoiding any real discussion of what's building between us.

"Work faster," Finn suggests dryly. "Because this whole assuming worst-case scenario thing isn't healthy for either of you. And he's as guilty," he says. "If you're serious about him—"

"I am," I interrupt quickly, surprised that I said it aloud. "I'm completely serious about this. About him." The admission feels terrifying and freeing at the same time, like jumping into a lake without knowing its depth.

Silence stretches between us for a moment, broken only by the soft sound of Finn shuffling papers again. "Then tell him that," he says finally, his voice carrying a mix of exasperation and affection. "Stop dancing around the edges and actually say words aloud."

"I've got to go," I tell Finn, already checking the mirrors to back out of Taylen's driveway. "I need to stop by the cabin for a few things before heading to Burlington." The statement draws a fresh laugh from my brother, though this one holds no mockery.

"Of course you do," he agrees easily. "Because driving three hours to deliver cold lasagna is a completely normal response to learning someone's getting a tattoo." But I hear his approval under the teasing tone, encouragement that makes me happy.

"Shut up," I mutter without heat, making him laugh again. "And…thanks. For talking me down from the ledge. Can you send me the address of wherever he's staying?"

"Anytime," Finn says simply. "Just…be careful, okay? Not just with driving. I'm sending you the address."

I end the call with a promise to update him later. My hands are now steadier on the wheel as I point the truck toward home. The anxiety that gripped me earlier has transformed into determination and hope.

Because Finn's right, we need to have a real conversation about what we're doing. And if that means driving three hours to deliver cold lasagna and finally say the words aloud, then that's exactly what I'm going to do.

The hotel hallway stretches endlessly before me, each step toward Taylen's door feeling too slow. The food box remains clutched in my hands like a shield or a poor excuse, although the lasagna inside has long since gone cold. My pulse slams my chest when I finally spot the correct room, hunting for courage I lost somewhere between Winterberry and Burlington.

My knuckles rap against the door before I can talk myself out of it. Time stops between one breath and the next as I wait, my ears straining for any movement from the other side. Just as I'm considering whether to knock again, the lock clicks and the door swings open.

Taylen stands in the doorway like an apparition from my dreams, hair slightly damp like he's recently showered. His eyes widen as they find mine, his mouth opening slightly in a surprised expression that transforms his whole face. "Bastian? What are you doing here?"

I hold up the food box awkwardly, the gesture feeling increasingly ridiculous as the moment stretches between us. "Mom sent food," I explain lamely, my words inadequate against the reason I'm actually here for. "For you."

His laugh carries genuine warmth that makes the tension in my shoulders ease slightly. He leans against the doorframe. "Are you for real?" he asks, a smile playing around the edges of his mouth. "You drove all the way here to give me your mom's food when I don't even have a way to heat it up?"

Heat rises in my cheeks, but I maintain eye contact. "May I come in?" The question comes out quieter than intended. "Please?"

He steps back to let me in. I follow him, letting the door close behind me with a soft click.

"So," he says after a moment of charged silence, watching as I set the food box on a small table near the window. "You drove three hours to deliver cold lasagna. Want to tell me what's really going on?" His voice carries a mix of amusement and something softer that makes my hands shake slightly.

"You don't have to do this alone," I tell him, my words coming out in a rush before I can second-guess them. "The annual tattoo, the grief, any of it. You don't have to carry everything by yourself anymore." The admission hangs between us like a breath in winter air, visible and fragile.

His eyes find mine across the room's limited space, connection crackling between us like lightning before a storm. "Bastian," he starts, but I step closer before he can continue, needing to finish what I've come to say.

"I mean it," I insist, close enough now to see flecks of green in his blue eyes. "This thing between us isn't just a convenient release or temporary comfort. At least not for me." My heart pounds so hard I'm sure he must hear it, blood rushing in my ears like ocean waves. "I love you, Taylen. If you don't feel the same—"

I have to take a step back when Taylen jumps into my arms, wraps his legs around my waist, and claims my mouth like a starved man. He tastes like coffee and toothpaste. His fingers cling to my hair so tightly it hurts, but it's everything I need. I hold him up with my hands under his thighs and walk us to the bed, sitting on the mattress and taking him down with me.

"Fuck, Tay." I gasp as I attempt to take a breath.

"Shut up and kiss me, Sebastian. I fucking love you too."

His fingers trail down my chest before he removes his T-shirt and then opens my shirt so hard that buttons fly all over the room before it joins the growing pile on the floor. I'm glad I grabbed a spare change of clothes.

"Wait," I manage as he starts working on my belt, my words catching in a throat that feels too tight. "I want… I mean, could we…" The request sticks somewhere between my brain and my mouth, vulnerability making it hard to voice my desire properly.

Taylen's hands still, his eyes finding mine, waiting patiently. "Tell me what you want."

"I want you inside me," I finally manage, words barely louder than the shared breaths between us. "Want to feel you. All of you." The admission makes heat rise in my cheeks, but I maintain eye contact, needing him to understand the depth of trust I'm offering.

His pupils dilate noticeably at my request, his hands

tightening slightly where they rest against my skin. "You're sure?" he asks, voice rougher now. "We don't have to—"

I silence him with a kiss. His response is immediate and intense, his mouth moving against mine with a passion that makes me shake.

His mouth leaves a trail of fire down my chest as he works his way lower, each kiss feeling like a brand against skin that's become hypersensitive to his touch. When he reaches the waistband of my jeans, his eyes find mine again, seeking final permission before continuing his exploration.

The first touch of his tongue against my cock draws sounds from my throat I barely recognize as mine, pleasure short-circuiting all of the higher brain functions. His hands hold my hips steady as he takes me deeper.

But it's when he moves lower still, opening my legs and settling his tongue flat against my hole, that I truly lose the ability to think coherently. Each lick sends electricity through my nervous system, building pressure that feels like a timer counting down to an explosion. My hands fist in the sheets as he works me open with his tongue.

"Please," I manage finally, my words coming out broken and desperate as his tongue continues its sweet torture. "Tay, please. I need you. Need more." My body trembles on the edge of something big, something that feels like flying and falling all at the same time.

His response is to press deeper, adding a finger alongside his tongue in a way that makes me arch off the bed with a desperate sound. Everything narrows to that single point of contact between us, to the way he's slowly taking me apart.

The pleasure builds higher, threatening to overwhelm the careful control I'm trying to maintain. But just as I'm about to beg for more, for anything, for everything he's willing to give me, he pulls back, leaving me gasping and desperate on sheets that feel too hot against oversensitive skin.

28

TAYLEN

BASTIAN'S BODY trembles beneath my hands as I reach for my wallet, my fingers fumbling to get to the packet of lube I've had in there since god knows when. The air in the hotel room feels thick with anticipation as Bastian watches me with his eyes gone dark and hungry.

My hands shake slightly as I add some lube to his hole and then use the rest to lather my cock.

"Please," he whispers again, with an edge of desperation that sends fresh heat through my system. His body arches slightly as I position myself. "Tay, please. Need you."

The initial push draws out a groan from both of us. "You're so fucking tight, Bastian."

"I can handle it."

"I have no doubt you can. It's me I'm worried about. I'm about to blow. Embarrassingly fast."

He laughs, which has the effect of helping me ease farther into him.

"It's a good thing you're younger than me. How's your refractory period, baby?"

I groan. "Keep doing that squeezy thing with your butt and you'll find out soon enough."

I pause when I'm fully seated, giving us both a moment to adjust. His hands find my biceps, gripping tight.

"Move," he commands. "Please, Tay. Need to feel you."

"Such a bossy bottom," I say between gritted teeth.

I pull out a little and then my hips snap forward with more force than intended, but his responding moan suggests he doesn't mind the intensity. Finding our rhythm takes no time at all. Each thrust draws fresh sounds from his throat, noises I want to record and keep forever.

He wraps his legs around my waist, changing the angle and making me go deeper.

"Fuck, Bastian. You feel so fucking good." I pull one of his legs over my shoulder and speed up my thrusts. His cock is hard between us, leaking beads of precum onto his tight stomach.

"Hmm, Tay, fuck…" He snaps his head back, closing his eyes. I lower myself onto him, letting go of his leg and latching onto the skin of his neck.

"You're mine," I growl, sucking his skin. Each word is punched out of me by my deep thrusts. "You're mine, Bastian. All mine."

He shudders as I keep sucking and thrusting until I'm no longer in charge of anything. My body has taken over and will tell me when it's over.

"I'm yours, Taylen." His words come between harsh breaths and broken moans. "Have been for a long time. Always will be."

The admission hits me hard, making my rhythm falter briefly before I pick up with renewed intensity. Sweat makes our skin slide together as our movements become more urgent, more desperate. His hands clutch at my shoulders while mine maintain a bruising grip on his hips.

"I'm so close," he warns. "Almost there, Tay. Please." His cock is trapped between our bodies and is leaking steadily, providing evidence of how much this affects him. I release my hand from his hip to wrap around his length, wanting to feel him fall apart completely.

He cries out my name, his body clenching around me and throwing me over the precipice. If this is what it's like to fall with Bastian, I never want to get up.

His arms wrap around my shoulders as we come down together, holding me close as aftershocks run through both our systems.

We stay joined for long minutes until my cock slips out of him, soft and spent. He strokes my back in gentle patterns with so much tenderness that it makes my throat tight.

We stand together and grab the quickest shower in the world before coming back to bed and snuggling under the blankets. I love that Bastian loves to do this. Even our first time, if I hadn't run, we'd have had a moment like this, when the rest of the world ceases to exist and it's just us.

"I really do love you," he says, his words clear and certain. "I know you've said it, but you don't have to just because I did," he continues quickly, his hands never stopping their gentle movement across my skin. "I just needed you to know. Needed to finally say it aloud."

I laugh. "You're such an idiot saying that after mind-blowing sex when my brain isn't working properly. And I do love you too. When I said it earlier, it wasn't because I felt obliged to."

His laugh rumbles through his chest, vibrating against my ear. "My timing might not be perfect," he admits, his fingers finding a particularly sensitive spot behind my ear. "But I can't take it back. I think I've loved you for longer than I probably should admit. I stayed away because I was afraid of it."

The confession draws a reluctant smile from my lips, though I maintain my position that lets me hide my expression against his skin. "Yeah, well," I mutter, my words muffled slightly by his chest, "likewise. Even if you are ridiculous and dramatic and way too good at making me feel things."

"Say it again," he requests quietly.

I lift my head enough to meet his eyes. "I love you," I tell him. "I've loved you for a long time."

"Do you remember when Jackson threw my surprise birthday party when I turned thirty-two?"

I nod.

"That's when everything changed for me. The moment I saw you, I *saw* you. You were Jackson's little brother, but that night..." He shakes his head.

I chuckle. "Does our age gap bother you?"

He shakes his head. "Not now. You?"

"Sebastian, I've just had sex with my teenage crush. You could be sixty for all I care."

He wraps his arms around me and flips us around so he's on top of me. "Sixty, my ass. You have fifteen years of putting up with my old ass before we get there."

The weight of his heavier body on me wakes up my cock. "What did you say about testing that refractory period?" I tease.

He gives me the sexiest wink known to humankind and then kisses his way down my body.

When I scream his name as I come into his mouth minutes later, I am more than thankful for being twelve years younger.

I will never get tired of sleeping with Bastian. He's like a cozy blanket that keeps me warm all night. He doesn't snore, and when he talks in his sleep, it's to tell me that he loves me again and again.

Bastian's eyes flutter open gradually, a smile spreading across his face when he sees me watching him. "Morning," he mumbles, his voice rough with sleep.

"Morning," I reply. "You snore."

"I do not."

"And you talk in your sleep."

He narrows his eyes and then opens them wide when he realizes I'm not lying. "But I do not snore."

"Hmm, it's these tiny cute snores. Usually followed by 'Oh, Taylen, you're so beautiful and smart. Definitely the best farmer I've ever met, not to mention amazing in be—' Oof." I find myself under his body again, which seems like a win-win situation for me.

"What time is your appointment?" he asks, and all of a sudden, the reminder of what I'm in Burlington to do takes the air out of my lungs.

"Ten," I manage.

"Hey, baby. It's okay. I asked only to see if we have time for a shower together."

I nod, and he kisses me gently. "Come on, let me wash you. If you're lucky, I'll blow you too."

One long shower and a rushed breakfast later, we're walking toward Church Street. Remy looks exactly like he has every year since I started this tradition. Heavily tattooed arms visible beneath rolled sleeves, gray beard neatly trimmed, eyes carrying warmth that makes everyone feel welcome. His smile widens when he spots me, and then his mouth falls open when he sees Bastian.

"Fuck me. Jack will die when I tell him."

I laugh. "Don't. Bastian already has a big head as it is.

Just treat him like you would the guys who play at your local bar."

"What? With disdain? They really aren't that good. It's like a car crash every Friday night, but you can't help watching it happen."

I laugh. "Anyway, this is Bastian," I say. "He's…" I trail off, suddenly unsure how to categorize what we are, at least in public.

"I'm his," Bastian supplies simply, reaching his hand out to shake Remy's. The declaration makes something warm bloom in my chest. Remy's smile grows.

"About time someone took you off the market," he says. "Shall we get started? What do you have in mind?"

I look at Bastian, knowing that the moment I get it out, I can't undo it. "Actually," I manage, "thought we'd do something different this time." I take the paper from my bag and unfold it. "This is traced from the initials that were carved in a tree between our farms."

I was going to take a photo, but I liked the pattern of the bark and wanted the initials to look exactly like how we carved them. Remy looks at the paper. "I can certainly do this for you if you give me a moment to trace it onto the transfer paper. Can I get you a drink while you wait?"

"I'm good. Thanks," I say, and Bastian shakes his head.

I turn to him. "Do you mind?"

"Do I mind you tattooing my initials onto your skin? Baby, short of us getting married, this is the most significant thing you could do."

Could I blush any harder? Fuck my life.

"I want to get it too," Bastian says suddenly. "If that's okay," he adds quickly, reading the shock in my expression. "I know it's your tradition, but…"

"You want…?" I trail off. Bastian is offering to share something I've kept private for years. He wants to carry the same marks on his skin that I use to remember what we've lost. "You'd do that?"

His hand cups my face, thumb brushing away a stray tear from my eye. "Of course I would," he says simply, like it's the most natural thing in the world. "I want to share everything with you, even the hard stuff. Especially the hard stuff."

Remy clears his throat gently, reminding us we're not alone in the room. "I can do both if you want," he offers. "I don't have any bookings until this afternoon."

The familiar buzz of the tattoo gun fills the air as Remy prepares the equipment.

"You first," I tell him, needing to watch him go through this before I can handle my own turn.

Watching the initials take shape on his bicep feels so perfectly right, like something I never knew I needed until this exact moment. His hand maintains a grip on mine throughout the process.

When it's my turn, his presence beside my chair feels like an anchor against the tide of emotions threatening to overwhelm me. The familiar sting of the needle carries a different weight this time. Less lonely somehow.

"You okay?" he asks quietly as Remy does his amazing work.

"Better than okay," I tell him, squeezing his hand gently.

Remy works with efficiency, completing both pieces fairly quickly.

When we leave the shop, everything feels lighter, brighter, even as the air bites at my skin.

Church Street spreads before us like a picture from a holiday card, every storefront dressed in its holiday finest. Bastian's hand remains steady in mine as we walk.

We've managed maybe a block of peaceful wandering before the first recognition hits.

"Oh my god," the woman says, a phone already

appearing in her hand like a magic trick. "You're Sebastian Hall. From Hall of Fame." The words come out slightly breathless, making her sound younger than she probably is. "Could I…? Would it be okay if…?"

"Of course," Bastian says before she can finish the request, his smile transforming his face into the public persona I sometimes forget he maintains.

My hand slips from his as he steps toward her, giving them space for a selfie that will probably be on social media within minutes. More phones appear as the word spreads, each new fan handled with the same grace as the first.

When the fans are finally gone, he makes his way back to me with an apologetic smile that I wave away before he can voice it. "Don't," I tell him quietly as we resume walking toward the hotel. "Never apologize for making your fans happy."

"Does it bother you?" he asks suddenly, sounding vulnerable. "The attention, the fans, the public side of things?"

The question makes me pause, and I consider my answer carefully.

"No," I tell him in earnest. "How could it? It's part of who you are, what you've built. Besides, I'm proud of you. Of everything you've accomplished, of how you treat your fans, of the way you balance both worlds."

His kiss catches me slightly off guard, though I respond automatically to the gentle pressure of his lips against mine. The contact remains brief, conscious of the public setting, but it's no less impactful.

"I want to go home," he says when we break apart. "Hide out in my cabin for the rest of the day. Just us."

"Yes."

We walk the final blocks to the hotel holding hands, neither caring if anyone notices or photographs a simple gesture of affection. Because some things matter more than public opinion, like the way his thumb rubs softly against the back of my hand.

"I didn't think this through," he says, looking at both our vehicles and pouting. "Race you there?"

My answer comes as a quick kiss before heading toward my truck, with the certainty that whatever speed we travel, we're both finally heading toward the same destination.

29

BASTIAN

TAYLEN'S "THIS ISN'T A DATE" protest died quickly when I turned up at his doorstep with a bunch of flowers to take him out to the festival. One very hot make-out session later, and we walk our private path to the festival—perks of having it so close.

The way he leans into my touch when I rest my hand on his lower back suggests he's not even trying very hard to maintain the pretense anymore.

"Hot cocoa?" I ask. His eyes light up despite the obvious attempt to maintain a neutral expression.

"If you insist," he says with affected indifference that makes me want to laugh. "Though this still isn't—"

"A date," I finish for him. "Just two friends enjoying the festival together. Completely platonic hot beverage sharing."

My fingers find a sensitive spot just above his waistband, drawing a slight shiver that contradicts his attempted stoicism. "I thought you said you love me."

"I lied," he lies.

The vendor adds extra marshmallows to Taylen's cup

without being asked, the kind of small-town knowledge that makes my heart ache with the rightness of being here.

"Cinnamon?" I ask, though I already know the answer.

Taylen nods. The way his eyes close at the first sip makes my cock a little less comfortable in my jeans, especially since my boyfriend told me we weren't allowed to come earlier. We had to save it for later.

"Stop watching me drink," he mutters, color rising in his cheeks. "It's weird." But he doesn't move away when I step closer, using the crowd as an excuse to press against his side.

"Can't help it," I tell him honestly. "You make everything look sexual."

The words draw a fresh blush to his face.

"Keep it in your pants," he says.

"I'm trying, but you're not helping."

Before he can formulate a cutting response, something catches my eye that makes a smile spread across my face.

"No," he says immediately, following my gaze to Santa's booth decorated with oversized candy canes and twinkling lights. "Absolutely not."

"Is that Tommy Matthews?" I ask, though I'm certain it is. "Didn't you two have chemistry together senior year?"

The question makes him groan, but he doesn't resist when I begin steering him toward the booth with a gentle pressure against his back.

"He copied all my lab notes," Taylen says. "Then asked me to tutor him because he 'couldn't read his own handwriting.' Now he's got five kids and teaches second grade. How do you know?"

I raise a brow. "Did you meet your brother? You couldn't jump without him proudly announcing to the world how high."

Tommy spots us approaching, recognizing us immediately. "Ho, ho, ho!" he booms with an enthusiasm that manages to sound both practiced and sincere. "Have you been a good boy this year?"

"Kill me now," Taylen starts, but I'm already reaching for my wallet to pay the booth fee. His protests die as I guide him toward the elaborately decorated chair. "I hate you," he mutters, but the way he settles onto Tommy's lap suggests he's accepted his fate.

"No, you don't," I tell him cheerfully, positioning myself for the perfect photo angle.

Tommy plays his role with admirable dedication, asking about Christmas wishes while Taylen maintains an expression of dignified suffering that makes the whole situation even funnier.

"Smile," I say before snapping a photo.

"I'm never forgiving you for this," he declares as we walk away, but his hand still finds mine.

"Yes, you will," I tell him confidently, pulling him close enough to press a quick kiss to his temple. "Because you love me." The words still feel new enough to send a thrill through my system, though we've been saying them more frequently since our hotel room confessions.

His response is to lean into my contact briefly before pulling away. "Jury's still out," he mutters.

Taylen tastes like chocolate and cinnamon when I steal a quick kiss behind the wreath vendor's display, his hands clutching my jacket as if he's torn between pulling me closer and pushing me away. The festival swirls around us in happy chaos, but all I can focus on is the way his breath catches when my fingers find the gap between his coat and scarf.

"Behave," he mutters against my mouth, though he was the one who initiated this particular hidden moment. "We're in public."

"You started it," I remind him. "I was being perfectly innocent until you dragged me behind these wreaths."

We make our way through the festival grounds slowly, stopping frequently to greet people who want to discuss everything from apple crops to Hall of Fame's last album.

The veterinary charity booth appears ahead, and Dr. Hunter Cross's short frame almost looks taller as he talks passionately about animals.

"Dr. Cross," I call when a family moves away, drawing his attention.

"Sebastian," he greets, then nods to Taylen. "How's our newest arrival doing?" The question draws a proud smile to my face as I think about Martha's heifer.

"Thriving," I report happily, squeezing Taylen's hand as I remember the night we spent watching the birth. "Though Gouta's appointed herself the unofficial guardian. Won't let anyone near the baby without her approval first."

Hunter's laugh holds genuine amusement. "That goat has more personality than most people I know," he observes, shaking his head slightly. "Should I be concerned about her adopting all your newborns?"

"Probably," I admit, thinking about the way Gouta herds the calf around the barn like an anxious mother. "My cabin's already turning into an impromptu animal sanctuary. Wouldn't be surprised to come home and find them both asleep on my bed one of these days."

My attention is suddenly drawn to Stone approaching the booth with the determination that suggests a man on a mission. His perfectly styled hair and usual designer clothes look almost out of place among the festival's casual atmosphere, yet somehow, he manages to make even winter wear seem effortlessly fashionable.

"Dr. Cross," Stone purrs. "How nice to see you again." His smile holds a practiced charm that's worked on countless admirers over the years, but Hunter's polite response suggests immunity to such tactics.

"Mr. Murphy," Hunter acknowledges professionally. "Are you interested in supporting our local animal rescue efforts?"

Stone's laugh carries a hint of frustration beneath the surface charm. "Always happy to support good causes," he says smoothly. "Especially when they're championed by such dedicated professionals."

Taylen's thumb continues tracing patterns against my palm as we watch Stone make a few more attempts at engagement before accepting temporary defeat.

"Poor Stone," I murmur against Taylen's ear, using the crowd as an excuse to pull him closer. "He's not used to having his charm fail so completely."

"Should we be concerned?" he asks quietly, watching Stone's perfectly styled hair disappear into the festival crowd. "About him buying a house so close to Hunter?"

I shake my head slightly, using my hold on his hand to guide him away from the booth. "Stone rarely pursues anyone he's likely to see regularly," I explain. "Besides, there's no indication Hunter's even interested in men."

We weave between clusters of festival-goers, past the mulled cider stand, and around a group of carolers warming up for their next performance, until we find ourselves in a quiet corner where the vendor stalls back up against the temporary fencing.

Taylen's back meets the rough wood with a soft sound that sends heat through my core as I cage him between my arms.

"You really think Stone will give up that easily?" he asks, though his attention seems more focused on the way my body brackets his against the stall's wall. His fingers find my waist, slipping beneath my jacket to trace patterns that make it hard to concentrate on the conversation.

"Stone's not used to rejection," I manage, trying to maintain coherent thoughts despite the way Taylen's touch sends electricity through my system. "But he's also careful about not creating awkward situations. If he actually buys that house…" I trail off as his hands slide higher under my jacket.

"Living that close to Hunter would definitely be awkward," Taylen finishes for me, but the smile playing around his mouth suggests he's enjoying the effect he's having on my ability to focus. "Especially if Hunter's straight."

I lean closer, using my position to trap his wandering hands between us. "Stone will figure that out," I assure him, my voice dropping lower as the festival sounds fade into background noise. "He's smarter than he lets people think. More careful with his heart too."

"Unlike some people?" Taylen asks, the challenge clear in his tone.

"Unlike me," I agree easily, letting one hand cup his face while the other maintains our position against the wall. "I gave you my heart years ago, even when I was pretending I hadn't."

His eyes search mine for an endless minute. "You're ridiculous," he mutters. "Always saying things like that when I can't properly respond."

"Why can't you?" I ask, my thumb tracing a line across his jaw. "Nothing ever stopped you from saying whatever you want, especially when it comes to me."

His response is to surge forward, closing the distance between us with a kiss that steals all the air from my lungs. His hands escape the jacket prison to tangle in my hair.

"I love you," he whispers against my lips when we break for air. "Even when you're being dramatic."

Laugh bubbles up from my chest, my joy too big to contain. "Especially then?"

"Especially then," he agrees, tilting his head to capture my mouth again.

The festival noise gradually filters back into my awareness as the kiss ends.

"We should probably rejoin civilization," he suggests. His fingers are playing with the buttons on my jacket.

"Or we could go back to my cabin. It's closer. I declare this date over. Time to ravish my boyfriend in the relative safety of my own home."

He shakes his head. "Not a date."

I sigh.

"Come on," he says finally. "Let's go see what other trouble we can find at this festival." The words carry a teasing note that makes my heart stumble with joy.

I take his hand as we emerge from between stalls.

The Christmas lights seem brighter somehow as we rejoin the main flow of celebration, although maybe that's just the effect of happiness making everything shine more intensely. Taylen's grip remains steady in mine as we weave between booths and crowds.

Even though I would give anything to have Taylen naked in my bed, I can't deny loving this carefree, teasing Taylen.

30

TAYLEN

THE FESTIVAL LIGHTS pierce the darkness like stars. It's a particularly cold night, but this is Winterberry. We don't have winter in the name for nothing.

As the temperatures go down, our spirits go up, especially in the face of such an important event.

In the twenty-five years of the band's history, Hall of Fame has never played in Winterberry because they haven't wanted to attract attention to the place they've called home, even for those in the band who aren't actually from here.

"I still can't believe they're actually doing this," a woman says beside me, clutching her husband's arm with barely contained excitement. "Twenty-five years of following them to Boston, New York, even that time we drove all the way to Montreal, and now they're playing right here at home."

"And at Christmas," her husband adds. "It's like a gift to the whole town."

Mrs. Stanton from the general store appears at my other side, practically bouncing on her toes. "Did you hear it's just going to be a short set? Five, maybe six songs? They're opening for our local boys." Her eyes shine with pride.

"That's what makes them special, you know? They could headline anywhere in the world, but they're here supporting local musicians."

"That's what I've been saying," Old Jim chimes in from behind us. "Must be something in the water around here to grow all this amazing talent. And they're so generous too."

"Sebastian helped me fix my fence last week," someone else adds. "Didn't even mention it. Just showed up with tools and got to work."

"And Stone overheard my Bonnie talk about her college application at Noëlle's and spent an hour talking to her about how to make it stand out," another voice joins in. "Wouldn't even accept a pastry for it either."

The crowd presses closer as show time approaches.

I maintain my position near the sound booth, far enough from the stage to watch the show while keeping an eye on Eleanor. With the crowds today, she might need my help, although she threatened to kick me out, saying she'd recruited her grandson to help.

Nikko moves between monitors, checking everything but touching nothing. As the band's tour manager, he must know the jobs of the supporting crew inside out.

When Bastian steps onto the stage, the audience's response is immediate and electric. His presence fills the space with his easy confidence and natural charisma that draws every eye.

That's my man, right there on the stage. Pride swells in my chest with the knowledge that the voice about to sing the songs that have made them famous, that have served as soundtrack to so many lives, is the voice that will talk into my ear until I'm asleep tonight.

Fuck, I'm way too sappy in love.

"Evening, Winterberry," he says into the microphone.

The crowd responds with an enthusiasm that makes me

wonder how many are locals versus tourists drawn in by the news that Hall of Fame would perform tonight. "Thanks for letting us crash your festival."

The crowd laughs, but I know exactly how hard Finn worked to convince them to play this small set.

As if conjured, my best friend shows up beside me. "I believe the words used were blackmail, old school photos, and the video recording of a song he wrote when he was ten."

I laugh. "Nothing like a little encouragement."

"They would have done it anyway, but it was fun seeing Bastian squirm and then sit back as he convinced the rest of the band."

The first notes of their opening song get the crowd screaming. Bastian's voice carries the rough warmth of aged whiskey, deepened by years of singing and shouting over stadium crowds.

I fall for him a little more as I watch him work the crowd, pointing at familiar faces and making eye contact with fans who probably haven't slept since hearing Hall of Fame would perform. This is his element, the place where Sebastian Hall becomes more than just a dairy farmer's son who got a lucky break.

The next song shifts into darker territory. One of their newer pieces that explores themes of leaving and returning, of trying to balance opposing forces in one life. They wrote the song for their last album, before Mik announced he wanted to settle down with Kay in Stillwater, but the irony of the lyrics isn't lost on me as I watch Bastian pour himself into the performance. His hands move over the guitar strings with the same grace they showed when touching my skin earlier today.

When they launch into their biggest hit, the audience's response drowns out the first few notes completely.

I lean into Finn so he can hear me. "Hey, I'm going to

grab a hot drink and then check in on Eleanor. Be back in a bit."

The excuse sounds as I intended it, but the truth sits heavy in my stomach as I claim an empty space near Joe's counter. I need time to process what loving Bastian really means, what sacrifices might be required from both of us.

Because watching him perform tonight has reminded me of a fundamental truth I've been trying to ignore: Sebastian Hall belongs to more than just me, more than just this town. And loving him means accepting that his heart will always be divided between worlds that sometimes feel impossibly far apart.

"Taylen, you look like you need some hot cider, am I right?" Joe says.

"You are. Bring it on," I say, using the smile I've practiced over the last twelve years whenever people ask me how I am but don't really want to know that I'm dying inside.

It's always easier for everyone if I look happy.

The cider burns my tongue as I take a too-large sip, desperate for the warmth that might chase away the chill.

"Careful there," Joe warns as he slides a fresh napkin across the counter. "Just made that batch. Still pretty hot." His attention shifts to new customers before I can respond, leaving me alone with a scalded mouth and racing thoughts.

A flash of an expensive coat catches my eye, and I recognize its owner immediately. Daisy, the band's agent, stands partially turned away from the crowd, her perfectly manicured hand pressing her phone closer to her ear.

"No, listen," she says, voice carrying barely contained excitement. "The timing is perfect. We've got momentum from the Christmas show. You should see the crowd here tonight." Her free hand gestures despite the fact that the person she's talking to can't see the movement. "Nikko has worked his magic on them."

My fingers tighten around the paper cup, heat seeping through the cardboard. But the cider doesn't burn as much as her next words do. "You know how it is, he could never be idle. Six months max before we start recording." She laughs at whatever response comes through the phone. "Trust me, I know my boys."

The cider turns bitter on my tongue as implications sink in. Six months. Recording. Words that carry promises about to be broken. A future I've barely allowed myself to imagine is crumbling before it can fully form. Because Bastian swore he was staying this time. He promised me the farm and his family come first now.

"The label will be thrilled," Daisy continues, oblivious to the way her casual conversation is shattering my world into sharp-edged pieces. "Nikko's already got a preliminary tour schedule worked out."

Of course he does. Nikko's efficiency is legendary. After all, his efforts combined with Finn's have made this year's Christmas Festival a success. But the knowledge that he's been plotting this while we've all believed Bastian's promises about staying burns like acid in my throat.

"No, they're all on board," Daisy assures whoever she's talking to, the confidence clear in her tone.

The festival continues around me as I stand frozen with my cooling cider. Laughter and music mix with the scent of pine and cinnamon, creating a holiday atmosphere that feels like a joke now.

Because I know the truth now. I understand with a clarity that burns like winter wind against exposed skin. No matter what promises Bastian's made, no matter how sincere his intentions might be, Sebastian Hall will always choose performing over everything else. Over farm, over family.

Over me.

I don't know how much time has passed while I'm deep

in my thoughts, but I notice a shift in the music. Hall of Fame has a particular sound they've honed over the years. I'd recognize it anywhere.

"Hey, you disappeared," Bastian says as he slides into the space beside me. His face glows with post-performance energy, a slight sheen of sweat still visible at his temples. When his hand brushes mine, his touch feels like a brand against skin that's suddenly too sensitive.

"I needed a drink," I manage, my words coming out steadier than I feel.

His smile shows no sign of guilt or hesitation, no indication that he's planning to shatter everything he's promised. The realization makes something twist sharply inside me.

"Come on," he says, his fingers lacing with mine. "Let's watch from a better spot. These guys are incredible live."

His enthusiasm appears genuine. How does he manage to compartmentalize so effectively?

The crowd shifts to accommodate us as he guides me closer to the stage, his hand steady against my lower back in a way that used to feel comforting, but now it makes me want to curl up and disappear. We end up near the sound booth where I was before. Finn is no longer here.

"Watch their drummer," Bastian says, leaning close enough that his breath stirs the hair near my ear. "She's amazing."

When the song ends, the lead singer launches into a speech about the importance of community and connection, but all I can focus on is the weight of Bastian's presence beside me. The way his body moves unconsciously to the music in a rhythm he probably doesn't even realize he's matching. Because music is his natural habitat, not quiet mornings in a barn or stolen moments between farm chores.

My head begins pounding in earnest as minutes stretch endlessly before me. Each song blends into the next, creating a soundtrack to thoughts that won't stop circling—six months, recording, tour plans already being made. The pressure builds behind my eyes until the lights blur into meaningless patterns.

"You okay?" Bastian asks suddenly, concern clear in his voice as he studies my face. His hand finds my cheek. "You look pale."

"Just a headache," I tell him. "I think I'm going to head home."

"I'll come with you," he offers immediately because, of course, he does. Because he's still playing the role of devoted partner perfectly, even while planning his escape from promises he's made. "I can have Nikko handle—"

"No," I cut him off sharper than intended, drawing a slight frown that I force myself to ignore. "Stay. Enjoy the show." My voice softens slightly as I add, "Spend time with your friends."

"You sure?" His concern appears genuine, making everything hurt worse somehow. Because he probably does care, probably means every sweet word and gentle touch. Just not enough to choose this life over the call of the spotlight that's already drawing him away.

"I'm sure," I manage, already pulling away. "Just need some sleep." The excuse sounds weak even to my ears, but he accepts it with a nod.

"Text me when you get home safe?" he asks, hand reaching for mine one last time. I let him capture my fingers briefly, then I pull away, turning toward the exit before he can see the truth written across my face.

The crowd parts around me as I move with a single-minded determination toward the festival's edge, the music following me home. My vision blurs slightly as I finally cross the threshold into my house, allowing the first tears to fall.

31

BASTIAN

NIKKO PRACTICALLY GLOWS as he directs the crew in breaking down the equipment. Most of it is stored away overnight for tomorrow's events, but our instruments are stored in my studio.

Stone and Fox have already left for the farmhouse, and Finn is around somewhere. I swear my brother hasn't slept a single night since the start of this festival.

"You good here?" I ask, catching Nikko's attention.

"Of course. Go get some rest. I've got this handled."

The walk to the barn feels longer than usual. I put it down to the post-gig adrenaline crash, but something's gnawing at the back of my mind. I look at my phone. It's past one in the morning. Way too late to slip into Taylen's bed, especially since Elvis seems to ramp up his wake-up calls as revenge for the nights Taylen spends with me and gets a full night's sleep.

That rooster is a dick, and I take full responsibility for every single dark shadow under Taylen's eyes.

Before I head to the cabin, I check in on the cows.

Martha and her daughter have been doing great, and something tells me we've got a few more impending births.

My suspicions prove correct as soon as I push open the heavy barn door. Miss Maple's distressed lowing carries unmistakable pain. I find her in her stall, her sides heaving unnaturally as she struggles with what's clearly a difficult labor. Next to Miss Maple's stall is Poppy, also showing signs of early labor.

"Easy girl," I murmur to Miss Maple, approaching slowly to avoid startling her. My hands find her flanks, feeling the unnatural positioning of the calf within. The way she shifts uncomfortably under my touch confirms what I already suspect—this birth will require intervention.

I pull out my phone and call Hunter.

"Sebastian?" Hunter's voice is alert despite the late hour. "What's wrong?"

"Miss Maple and Poppy," I explain quickly, watching as Miss Maple's legs tremble with another contraction. "Both in labor, but Miss Maple's calf feels wrong. Positioned badly, I think. And Poppy's not far behind."

"On my way," he responds immediately, and I hear rustling that suggests he's already moving. "Keep them calm, try to get Miss Maple lying down if you can. I'll be there in fifteen."

The minutes crawl by like hours as I divide my attention between the two cows. Miss Maple allows me to guide her down, though each movement clearly causes discomfort. The familiar smells of hay and livestock surround me as I kneel beside her, murmuring reassurance while monitoring Poppy's progress.

Hunter's arrival brings immediate relief. His calm demeanor as he assesses the situation helps steady my own nerves.

"You made the right call," he confirms after a careful

internal examination of Miss Maple, which drew a pained sound from her. "Calf's turned wrong. We'll need to reposition before she can deliver safely." His eyes find mine. "You good assisting? I can call my tech."

"I'm good."

What follows next tests the limits of both my physical and emotional endurance. Hunter's arms disappear inside Miss Maple as he works to turn the calf, while calmly telling me what to do from the outside. Sweat soaks through my shirt, my muscles burning from maintaining an awkward position to give Hunter the best access.

Miss Maple's increasing distress puts me on edge, but Hunter maintains a steady calm throughout, his movements never growing rushed despite the urgency of the situation.

"There," he says finally, satisfaction clear in his voice as something shifts within Miss Maple. "Calf's turned properly now. She should be able to deliver with just a little help." His prediction proves accurate as Miss Maple's next push produces hooves, positioned correctly this time.

But nature rarely follows convenient timing. Poppy's water breaks just as we're guiding Miss Maple's calf into the world, adding fresh urgency to an already intense situation. Hunter and I exchange glances. This night is far from over.

Miss Maple's bull calf emerges in a rush of fluid and effort, his wet coat glistening under the barn lights as he takes his first shaky breaths. But we barely have time to ensure he's breathing properly before Poppy's increasingly distressed sounds demand our attention.

The next couple of hours blur together. Poppy's labor proves slightly easier than Miss Maple's

Finally, Poppy's heifer joins her new barn mate, her arrival drawing exhausted but satisfied sighs from both Hunter and me. We watch as both mothers fuss over their calves.

"Good work," Hunter says quietly as he washes his hands in the barn sink. "They're all healthy, and that's what matters."

"Sometimes I think I'm too old for this, and then I see miracles happen." I shake my head, looking at the new mommas and their babies.

"You should get some rest," Hunter says as he packs his bag. "They'll all be fine now, but you look dead on your feet."

I manage a tired nod, knowing he's right but feeling reluctant to leave the new arrivals so soon. "Thank you," I tell him. "For coming out so late, and for stopping me from spiraling into full-blown panic."

"It's what I do," he says simply. "Call if you need anything else." The barn door closes behind him with a gentle thud.

I take a few more minutes to ensure both pairs are settled properly, checking their water and bedding one final time. The sight of new lives reminds me of why I love this life despite its demands and irregular hours.

But exhaustion pulls at every muscle as I finally force myself to leave, each step toward the cabin feeling heavier than the last.

My shower calls like a siren song, promising relief from the night's work. As the water pounds against my shoulders, I think of Taylen and his strange mood shift last night.

Maybe he picked up a bug or something, but my gut tells me there's more to his sudden headache.

Pre-dawn air bites through my jacket as I make way to the farmhouse, the sky showing the first hints of the approaching sunrise. Lights already glow from my mom's kitchen windows because she exists in a time zone that operates independently of normal human schedules.

When I open the door, I'm welcomed by warmth and the smell of coffee.

"You look terrible," Mom says by way of greeting, already moving toward the coffee pot. Her own cup sits half-empty on the counter, suggesting she's been up for a while already. "What happened?"

"Two new calves," I tell her, accepting the mug she presses into my hands with a grateful smile. "Miss Maple and Poppy decided to go into labor simultaneously. Hunter had to help with Miss Maple's. Her calf was positioned wrong."

Her face lights up at the news. "Both healthy?" she asks, moving to pull fresh bread from the oven. The familiar scent fills the kitchen, reminding me that the last time I ate was more than a few hours ago.

"Perfect," I assure her. "Bull from Miss Maple, heifer from Poppy. Both already on their feet." The pride in my voice draws a smile to her face.

"But something else is bothering you," she observes, sliding the bread she just wrapped across the counter toward me.

"Taylen left the festival early," I admit finally. "Said he had a headache, but something felt off."

"Did something happen?"

"No," I tell her, even though I'm not entirely sure. "Everything seemed fine until after the performance. Then he just…left."

Her hand finds mine across the table. "You're exhausted. Maybe wait until you've both had some sleep before assuming the worst?"

The suggestion carries wisdom I know I should listen to, but anxiety continues to churn beneath the surface of my bone-deep fatigue. "What if I've messed everything up?" The question comes out smaller than intended. "What if he's realized this is too complicated or—"

"Sebastian James Hall," Mom interrupts, using my full name, making me feel about five years old. "That boy has been in love with you since he grew his first chin hair. Whatever's bothering him, running away isn't his style. Now," she continues practically, pushing the wrapped bread closer to me. "Take this home, get some real sleep, then go talk to him."

I manage a tired smile as I stand. "Thanks, Mom," I tell her quietly.

"That's what mothers are for."

Despite her advice, my feet carry me across the path toward next door.

The sight of Taylen heading toward his barn stops me in my tracks. His steps falter slightly when he spots me, surprise flickering across his face.

"What happened?" he asks as I approach, his eyes taking in my tired look.

"Two calves," I explain. "Miss Maple and Poppy decided synchronized birthing was the way to go. Hunter had to help with Miss Maple's."

His expression softens slightly as he processes this information. "Both okay?"

"Perfect," I assure him, managing a tired smile. "Boy and girl. I've already told the other cows they need to schedule future births during daylight hours so we can all sleep like regular people."

The joke draws a reluctant laugh that makes something ease in my chest. For a moment, the tension between us feels less acute. My hands still clutch Mom's wrapped bread, a reminder of the purpose that brought me here.

"Mom sent fresh bread," I tell him, holding up the

bundle like a peace offering. "Thought you might want some if you haven't had breakfast yet."

"Just had coffee," he admits. "But I will never say no to real breakfast."

When we get inside, Taylen goes straight to the coffee maker.

We fall into a comfortable silence as he slices the bread and cooks some eggs and bacon.

"You should sleep," he says finally, watching as I struggle to keep my eyes open between bites. "Real sleep, not just dozing in a chair or on the couch."

"Could I...?" I pause. "Could I stay here? Just for a little while?" The request hangs between us.

His expression does a complicated thing before he smiles. "Come on," he says, standing up. "My bed's more comfortable than the couch."

I remove my clothes until I'm just in my boxer shorts and T-shirt and sit on his bed. "Stay?" I ask as he helps me settle onto a bed that smells like him. "Just until I fall asleep?"

He toes off his boots and removes his clothes, his body radiating warmth as he lies beside me.

"Sleep," he says quietly, his hand finding mine in the space between us.

When I wake up, the first thing I notice is that Taylen's gone. Sunlight streams through the curtains. My body protests as I push myself into a sitting position. The clock on the bedside table shows early afternoon.

I use the bathroom and then get dressed. I want to check on Miss Maple, Poppy, and the babies before I do anything else.

But it's the door across the hall that draws my attention as I prepare to leave. Somehow, while I've been falling for Taylen, the pain of returning to this house fell into the back of my consciousness. But now, standing at the threshold of my best friend's bedroom, it's all coming back. The pain. The regret.

The air feels different inside the room. Posters still cling to the walls, their edges curling slightly with age, but the images are as vibrant as the day Jackson put them up. Books line the shelves in an order only he understood, their spines carrying titles that speak of dreams and plans never realized.

Clothes still hang in his closet, visible through the crooked door.

The photo on the bedside table calls to me. Jackson and me with Taylen smiling wide between us.

My fingers shake slightly as I lift the frame, tracing Jackson's features with a gentle touch that carries years of accumulated grief and guilt. The glass is cool against my skin as I study the three faces frozen in time, none of us aware of how precious those moments really were.

"I love him so much," I whisper. "I wish I'd come home more instead of panicking about what you'd think if I told you I liked your little brother. I missed out on precious time with you."

The silence that follows feels different after my confession.

"I can promise that will not happen with Taylen," I tell the photo. "I won't waste time being afraid anymore. Won't let anything, my career or fear or my own stupidity, keep me from being here for him the way I should have been for you."

My hands shake slightly as I return the photo to its place of honor, careful to position the frame exactly as I found it.

As the door closes behind me with a gentle click, I feel like I've just written the period at the end of a sentence I've been trying to write for years.

TAYLEN

WHEN SYLVIE ASKED me to deliver a basket of apples to her this afternoon, I thought maybe it was divine intervention. Or maternal intervention, which amounts to the same thing when it comes to Sylvie Hall. A chance to talk to someone who might help me sort through the mess in my head about Bastian and the future I'm too afraid to believe in.

But as the hours crawled by, doubt crept up. Maybe I'm spiraling over nothing. Maybe I'm looking for reasons to run before I can get hurt, sabotaging something good because I'm too scared to trust it's real.

Sylvie opens the door before I can knock, like she's been waiting for me. Her smile carries that particular warmth of mothers who've spent decades making everyone feel welcome. "There's my favorite apple supplier," she says, gesturing me inside.

"These are the last of the winter keepers," I explain, following her into the kitchen. "Thought you might want extra for baking."

"You have perfect timing," she says, taking the basket and starting to move the apples into her own box. "Coffee's just brewed. Sit, sit." She makes a shooing motion toward the table with her hands. "Fresh cinnamon bread too if you're interested."

The chair creaks a familiar welcome as I settle into it.

"Sugar?" she asks, even though she's already reaching for the container she keeps specifically because I like it in my coffee.

The gesture makes something catch in my throat. Sylvie is the reason I don't miss my parents more. Sure, I miss them, but on a day-to-day level, I still get the warm hugs, the conversations, the knowing looks, and the love only a mother can give.

"Thank you," I manage, watching as she pours coffee into mismatched cups.

She settles across from me, her own mug cradled between her hands.

"How did you do it?" The question comes out before I can properly frame it, carrying an edge of desperation I'd hoped to hide better. "When Bastian left for the band, when he was gone for months at a time. How did you cope?" My fingers clutch my mug too tightly.

Her smile carries a trace of sadness that makes my chest ache. "Oh, honey," she says softly, reaching across the table to cover my hand with hers. "It was never easy. But Vermont is where his heart is. He will always come home." The certainty in her voice settles something inside me.

"But he was so young," I persist, needing to understand how she managed what feels impossible to me now. "Barely more than a kid himself. Didn't you worry about…everything?" The last word carries the weight of all my current fears—overeager fans, accidents on stage or on the road.

"Every single day," she admits, even if her smile never leaves her face. "But worrying doesn't change anything except how much joy you can find in the moments you do have together." She traces a gentle pattern against my knuckles, her touch carrying comfort I didn't realize I needed. "So I learned to make every return special."

She rises suddenly. "Did I ever tell you about his first singing competition?" The question feels rhetorical as she crosses to a cabinet I've never seen opened. "He was barely six. A tiny thing with the biggest voice you've ever heard."

The cabinet doors open with a slight protest, revealing a collection of items I've never seen before. Trophies line the shelves. Sylvie's hands move with reverent care as she lifts the first one with its silver slightly tarnished.

"Elementary school talent show," she explains, setting the trophy before me. "Sang 'You Are My Sunshine' because it was the only song he knew all the words to." Her laugh carries pure joy. "Brought the whole audience to tears. Not because he was particularly good yet, but because he put his whole heart into every note."

More trophies appear on the table between us, each matched with a story. "This one was from the county fair. He was eight and insisted on wearing cowboy boots despite the fact that he was singing a classical piece. And this..." Her hands lift a slightly larger award. "State competition when he was twelve. That was the first time we realized he might have a real future in music."

My fingers trace the engravings that mark achievements from before I was born or when I was just a baby, evidence of the path that would eventually lead him away from Vermont but always bring him back.

"He used to practice in the barn," Sylvie continues. "Said the animals were the best audience because they never cared if he hit the wrong note." Her smile grows softer. "Would spend hours up in the hayloft, singing to whoever would listen."

"That has to be the most adorable thing I've ever heard."

"Some people are born with gifts too big for small towns to hold. It doesn't mean they love those towns any less. It just means they have to share that gift with the wider world."

Her hand finds mine again as she continues, "But Vermont is in his blood, same as his music. He might fly away, but his roots are here. In this land, in this family." Her eyes meet mine with an intensity that makes my skin prickle. "In the people who love him enough to let him go when he needs to, knowing he'll always find his way back."

The words hit me harder than I expected, making me blink against the sudden heat behind my eyes. Because this is the truth I've been avoiding—loving Bastian means accepting all the parts of who he is, including his need to share his gift with the world beyond our small corner.

"Besides," Sylvie adds with a smile that carries a hint of mischief, "absence makes the heart grow fonder. Or, in our case, makes celebrations better because we never knew exactly when they'd happen." Her expression grows more serious as she continues, "We had Christmas in July once because the European tour schedule meant he missed the actual holiday. Thanksgiving in September, and I'm sure we did Easter in the summer once."

"Wasn't that hard though? Never knowing for sure when he'd be home?" And this is one of my biggest fears. That I will still be on my own for all the moments that count.

"Of course it was hard," she acknowledges, squeezing my hand gently. "But joy isn't about having perfect timing. It's about making moments count when you have them."

"Thank you," I tell Sylvie quietly as she begins returning trophies to their cabinet home. The words feel inadequate against the weight of what she's shared, but her smile suggests she understands everything I can't quite voice.

"Anytime, honey," she says. "Now, how about some of

that cinnamon bread? Can't solve life's big questions on an empty stomach."

I laugh. "Thought you'd never ask."

The bread tastes like comfort as we settle into lighter conversation about the festival and my parents' plans to visit over Christmas.

Eventually, I stand to leave, thanking Sylvie with a hug that lingers a moment longer than usual.

Her words about Bastian replay in my head as I skip the path that leads to my house and instead stay on Hall land.

The barn's weathered red boards come into sight. Somewhere inside those walls, the man I love has no idea I'm approaching with a heart that feels too full and words that feel too empty.

"I love you, Bastian. I love you enough to let you go sometimes." I try the words on for size. The declaration feels closer to the truth I'm trying to express, while anxiety still churns beneath the surface.

My fingers shake slightly as I reach for the barn door, my rehearsed speech vanishing like dew at first light. Because this is the moment when practice meets reality, when my carefully planned words will probably desert me completely.

The barn smells of fresh hay and new life. Bastian stands between stalls, his attention focused on the latest additions to the growing family while Gouta prances between spaces like a self-appointed supervisor. The sight makes something catch in my throat. This man who belongs to the world somehow looks perfectly at home among barn animals.

He spots me before I can properly gather my thoughts, his whole face lighting up with a smile that still makes my stomach flip. "Hey, you," he says, already moving toward me. "Was just thinking about you."

His kiss lands gentle against my lips as his hands find familiar places on my waist.

"Gouta's appointed herself official calf instructor," he tells me, gesturing to the goat who's currently standing on her hind legs to peer into the nearest stall. "Pretty sure she's giving lectures on proper feeding techniques."

"She's always been bossy," I manage, watching as Gouta shifts her attention to the other stall, clearly taking her duties seriously.

Bastian's hands remain steady on my waist as he studies my face, concern growing in his expression. "What's wrong?" he asks quietly, reading the tension I'm trying to hide. "You look like you're carrying the weight of the world on your shoulders."

"Are we for real?" The words come out in a rush. "I mean, is this…? Are we…?" I trail off, suddenly unsure how to voice everything I need to know.

His response comes without hesitation, certainty in his voice making something ease slightly in my chest. "Are we for real?" he repeats after me, like the question surprises him. "I sure hope so." He hooks his finger in the belt loop of my jeans, pulling me closer as he adds, "Because I can't see myself loving anyone else for the rest of my life."

I take a deep breath, resting my hands on his chest, hoping that whatever comes out of my mouth next makes sense. "It'll be hard," I tell him, forcing words past the tightness in my throat. "When you aren't around. Especially now that I've gotten used to being pulled into dark corners to be ravished." The attempt at lightness probably fails completely, but I push forward anyway. "But I'll be fine. You'll just have to promise to make up for your absence every time you come back."

His whole body goes still against mine, confusion clear in his eyes, but I keep going. "I do reserve the right to sleep at your place whenever Elvis is being a dick and I want to know what cologne you use so I can spray it on all the bedsheets and pretend you're not really gone."

I bite my lip, hoping he won't laugh at the next one. "And I want a mold of your cock because…well, you can guess why. So anyway, those are my conditions."

He laughs. "A mold of my cock, huh?"

I shrug. "It's only fair. I'm only thirty-three and a guy has needs."

He kisses me hard, wrapping his arms around my waist until my body is flush with his. I feel his growing cock between us, showing me exactly why having a mold of it is not a requirement but a necessity.

"Baby?" he asks once I'm kiss-drunk and trying to remember my name.

"Hmm…"

"What the fuck are you talking about?"

33

BASTIAN

"WHAT DO YOU MEAN?" Taylen asks, his confusion evident in the way his brow furrows.

I cup his face gently, forcing him to meet my eyes. "Baby, as endearing as that little speech was—down to your request for a mold of my dick, which we can absolutely discuss later —it makes no sense." My thumbs stroke his cheekbones as I study his expression. "Not unless… Do you think I'm going somewhere?"

His body tenses against mine, answering the question before his mouth does. "I overheard Daisy," he admits quietly, "at the festival. She was on the phone talking about recording schedules, tours, saying you'd be back in the studio within six months."

Understanding crashes over me like a wave. "And you assumed I was leaving," I finish for him, watching as guilt and fear war across his features.

"What else was I supposed to think?" The words carry years of accumulated hurt. "You kept saying you were staying, but then I hear your agent making plans—"

"Plans that aren't happening the way you think they are," I interrupt gently. "Sit with me?"

I guide him to a hay bale, settling beside him while Gouta investigates our legs with her usual nosiness. The new calves shuffle in their stalls, providing a gentle soundtrack to what I need to say.

"There are two things I need to tell you, and I should have mentioned them earlier. That conversation you overheard? Daisy wasn't talking about us."

His eyes go wide. "What?"

"She was talking about the local band we saw at Thanksgiving. Remember them?"

He nods.

"Nikko's been working with them. Helped them put a demo together. Daisy's representing them now. *Them,* not Hall of Fame."

I watch the information sink in, see the exact moment embarrassment starts flooding his features. "I'm an idiot."

"No," I say firmly because I need him to understand this. "You had reason to worry based on what you heard. I should have told you what Nikko was doing." My thumb traces the line of his jaw. "Which brings me to the second thing."

I take a breath, knowing this next part is important. "We're leaving the record label. Going independent."

"Independent?"

"Think of us as a less attractive foursome version of Taylor Swift. Complete creative control. We decide when we record, where we record, if we tour, and for how long." Excitement bleeds into my voice despite my attempt to stay calm. "For the first time in our adult lives, we get to have actual control over our schedules. We can build our lives around the music instead of the other way around."

I watch hope bloom in Taylen's eyes, tentative and beautiful. "So when you said you're staying…"

"I meant it." I cup his face, needing him to feel the truth in my touch as much as hear it in my words. "I'm expanding the studio here. We can record in Vermont. If we tour, it'll be shorter runs with real breaks in between. And you know what the best part is?" My smile grows despite myself. "We don't need permission from anyone to make those decisions anymore. The only partnership we have with the recording label is for distribution."

He closes his eyes, and I can practically see the fear draining from his body. When he opens them, I see something else. "Taylor Swift may be the boss, but you're way more attractive. And you're mine."

I laugh. "About that mold…"

His cheeks flood with color. "Forget I said that."

"Absolutely not." I can't help laughing, the tension of the last few minutes finally breaking. "That's the most romantic thing anyone's ever said to me."

"Shut up," Taylen mutters, but he's smiling now, his body relaxing into mine in a way that makes everything feel right again.

"I love you, Taylen Howard," I tell him, pouring every bit of what I feel into those words. "And I'm not going anywhere without you. Not for recording, not for tours, not for anything. We figure this out together, okay?"

His response comes in the form of a desperate "Thank fuck" before his mouth finds mine with an intensity that steals all the air from my lungs. The kiss quickly turns hungrier as his hands tangle in my hair. My grip tightens on his waist as I walk us backward until his back meets the workbench with a soft thud.

"Sorry," I manage when we break for air, though his laugh suggests he doesn't mind the rough treatment. "Got carried away."

"Don't apologize," he tells me, pulling me closer until no

space remains between our bodies. "I like it when you get carried away."

My hands slide lower, finding the gap between his shirt and jeans.

"Hmm, Bastian…"

"We…should stop," I manage, even when my mouth continues trailing kisses down his neck. His hands clench against my shoulders as I find a particularly sensitive spot.

"Probably," he agrees, but he hooks his leg around mine to keep me close. "Definitely. Any second now." But neither of us moves.

It's Gouta who finally breaks the spell, her imperious bleat making us both jump slightly. She stands a few feet away with an expression that clearly conveys her disapproval of our behavior in her domain.

"Come on," I tell him, taking his hand in mine. "I have something I want to show you."

His confusion is evident as I guide him across the property toward the studio, but he follows without protest.

Inside, I lead him to the couch, watching as he settles into the worn leather.

My acoustic guitar waits in its usual spot. I grab it, feeling the familiar weight settle against my body as I position myself on the couch beside him.

"Bastian, what—"

"Just listen, okay?" I interrupt gently, my fingers finding the opening chords to a song he's probably heard a thousand times. Our biggest hit, the one that plays on every radio station, the one that made us household names.

But as I begin to play, I change the words. Keep the melody that millions know by heart, but replace the lyrics with something I've never shared with anyone.

"*Winter lights reflecting in your eyes,*" I sing softly, watching his face as recognition dawns that this isn't the version he knows. *"Vermont snow falling like confetti from the sky, and I'm finally home where I'm meant to be. Right here beside you is where I want to stay."*

His breath catches, his eyes widening as he processes what I'm doing.

"No more running from what I feel inside, no more hiding from the truth I've tried to fight. You're my anchor, you're my home, you're everything I need. And I'm not going anywhere, I promise you, I swear it's true."

I continue through the chorus, transforming our band's anthem about life on the road into a declaration of everything I feel for the man sitting beside me. Every chord progression filled with the promises I'm making, every word chosen specifically for him.

The melody shifts as I continue.
There's a goat sleeping on my pillow
Chickens roosting in my bed
Got a rooster named Elvis
Who won't let you sleep in
And somehow you're still in my head

You brought chaos to my life
Turned my quiet into sound
But I'd take all your crazy gifts
Every last ridiculous bit
Just to keep you around

Taylen's laugh breaks free, genuine and warm, his hand covering his mouth as his shoulders shake. "You wrote a song about our animal warfare?" he manages between chuckles.

"About how you invaded my life with livestock," I correct, grinning as I watch joy transform his features. "And how I wouldn't change a single thing about it."

"Just thinking," he says, color rising in his cheeks as a smile plays around his mouth. "About how teenage me would absolutely lose his mind over getting a private performance from Bastian Hall." His hand slides higher on my thigh as he adds in a husky whisper, "My crush was so big that I used to jerk off to posters of you."

The air around us feels charged again as I watch desire darken Taylen's eyes.

"You know," I say carefully, watching as his pupils dilate at the tone of my voice, "I think I've earned a performance of my own." The suggestion draws a sharp intake of breath from Taylen that makes my blood run hotter.

"I don't sing."

"Wasn't thinking about singing," I tell him, running my hand up his thigh. "I was thinking I'd like to see you touch yourself for me. The real me."

The look he gives me contains enough heat to melt the polar ice caps. "Only if you play that song again," he counters, his voice dropping lower as he adds, "in your underwear."

"Deal," I agree immediately, already reaching for the hem of my shirt. His hands catch mine before I can begin undressing. "What?"

"Let me," he says quietly, his fingers sliding beneath the fabric, making my muscles contract beneath his touch.

His hands move way too slowly as he helps me undress, each newly exposed inch of skin receiving attention that sends fire through my veins. By the time I'm down to my boxer briefs, every nerve ending feels hypersensitive to the slightest touch.

The guitar feels different against my bare skin as I settle

back onto the couch. Taylen's eyes never leave mine as he begins his own slow strip, each movement a deliberate tease.

The opening notes of the song come less smoothly this time, my fingers slightly clumsy on the strings as I watch him touch himself through the remaining layer of clothing.

His underwear joins the pile of discarded clothing as I reach the chorus. The sight of him stroking himself while watching me perform sends such an intense wave of desire through my system that I nearly forget the words I wrote myself.

Before I throw my favorite guitar onto the floor, I set it on its stand with less care than it probably deserves. I need to touch him so badly, but Taylen's hand on my chest stops me before I can reach for him properly. "No touching," he says quietly, though the strain in his voice suggests he's fighting the same battle I am.

So I maintain the distance he's set, letting my hand mirror his movements. Our eyes lock as we pleasure ourselves, the connection between us feeling more intimate than any physical touch.

His breathing grows more ragged with each stroke, his chest flushing a beautiful shade of pink.

The sight pushes me toward the edge faster than expected. I fight to maintain control because I want to watch him fall apart first. His eyes are half-lidded as he gives in to pleasure, one hand stroking his cock steadily while the other seeks his hole. Every muscle in his body seems strained toward release.

When he finally comes, my name is on his lips sounds like a prayer. The sight proves too much for me, and I let go with my eyes pinned to his beautiful blues.

I grab my T-shirt from the floor and clean us both before pulling him against my chest.

"That was…" he trails off, his laugh carrying pure joy. "Definitely better than posters."

"Should hope so," I tell him.

"I vote for a jerk-off session at least once a month," he says, letting out a yawn.

"Agreed. One day," I say quietly, watching as his eyes find mine, "in the not-so-distant future, I'm going to marry the hell out of you, Taylen Howard." I run my hands over the warm skin on his back as I add, "Fill a house with mini Taylens who'll drive me completely mad."

His laughter fills the studio with pure joy. "Yeah?"

"Yeah," I say, cupping his face. "If you'll have me. You, me, a whole bunch of kids who'll probably be as stubborn as you and as musical as me. Sound like a future you might be interested in?"

"Ask the question, and you'll find out."

34

TAYLEN

THE SMELL of cinnamon and pine fills the air, mixing with the sound of carols drifting from speakers mounted on light poles. Even though it feels like the festival only started a few days ago, it's been two weeks, and so much has happened. So much has changed. A few more hours, and the lights will turn off, the music will stop, and in a few days, after Christmas, this piece of land will return to Bastian and me.

"I love being out with you like this," Bastian says, placing his arm over my shoulder and keeping me close. His eyes catch mine as we pause near a popcorn vendor. "Just being a normal couple enjoying a seasonal festival together."

"Still not a date," I remind him automatically, although my smile probably ruins my attempt at maintaining our running joke.

"Of course not," he agrees easily, using his hold over my shoulder to pull me even closer. "Just two friends who happen to be disgustingly in love, walking arm in arm at a Christmas festival," he whispers in my ear, making me shiver, not from the cold but from the memory of his voice in my ear as he pounded into me, making me come hands-free, just before we stepped out this evening. "Totally platonic."

"Taylen Howard, Sebastian Hall, is that a public display of affection I'm witnessing?" The familiar voice makes us both turn, finding Noëlle watching us with an expression of pure delight. Her girlfriend stands slightly behind her, amusement clear on her face.

Bastian kisses my forehead, giving us away.

"I knew it!" Noëlle practically bounces with excitement, her hand already extending toward her girlfriend. "Pay up, sweetheart. I told you they'd be official by Christmas." The twenty-dollar bill changes hands with the sort of ceremony that suggests this bet has been an ongoing topic of discussion.

"You were betting on us?" I ask, feeling all kinds of mortified. My crush on Bastian was supposed to be a secret, dammit.

"Honey, the whole town's been betting on you two," Noëlle informs me cheerfully, tucking the money into her coat pocket with a satisfied pat. "Though most people had New Year's Eve in the pool. I just had an inside track from watching you bicker at every opportunity and for every single reason known to humankind while we planned the festival. I even watched you argue over apple and honey muffins, although why you'd argue over that is beyond me."

Her girlfriend, Sam, rolls her eyes fondly. "What she means is that we're happy for you both. Even if some of us are now twenty dollars poorer."

"Thanks," Bastian says, the squeeze he gives my hand suggesting he's enjoying this more than strictly necessary. "Anyway, I should buy my wonderful boyfriend here a hot cider. We're on a date, you see?"

I roll my eyes as the girls head over toward the stage area.

"Kill me now," I mutter. "Whole town's been betting on us."

"Never mind that, let's grab some hot cider. I'm all about keeping my promises these days," he says, and I poke him in the ribs.

Bastian's arm remains steady over my shoulder as we weave between vendor stalls.

The festival lights continue twinkling overhead like stars brought close enough to touch, making the silver streaks in Bastian's hair glow. His smile holds the promise of a more private celebration later, but for now we simply walk together toward Joe's stall—not on date of course—letting the town we both love witness the happiness they apparently knew was coming long before we did.

Bastian's family clusters near the counter at the pop-up bar, steam rising from their mugs.

Finn notices us first. "Happy Christmas Eve!" he declares. His shoulders look looser somehow, the tension that normally radiates from him noticeably absent as he raises his mug in greeting.

"You look suspiciously relaxed, little brother," Bastian observes, accepting the steaming mugs Joe hands him without being asked. "Festival stress finally break you completely?" The teasing draws a laugh from Finn that sounds genuinely carefree, making his transformation even more remarkable.

I take a sip of the cider Bastian hands to me, enjoying the warm spiced drink.

"Tonight will be the first real sleep I'll have in weeks," Finn explains, satisfaction clear in his voice. "Everything's handled. No work until after Christmas when this whole shebang comes down." His smile grows slightly sheepish as he adds, "Though don't count on me showing up on time for

Christmas dinner tomorrow. I might actually hibernate until the new year."

Sylvie moves around her sons over to me, sliding her arm around my waist and pulling me into a warm hug that smells like cinnamon and a mother's love. "How are you, sweetheart?" she asks quietly, though something in her tone suggests she means more than a simple greeting.

"Good," I tell her honestly. "Really good."

"And your parents?" she asks, though the twinkle in her eye suggests she already knows the answer. "Have they made it to the festival yet?" I laugh as I picture exactly where they probably are.

"Somewhere on your farm," I confirm. "They said they wanted to visit the new calves first. As they say, you can take a Vermonter out of Vermont, but you can't turn them into flatlanders."

Henry's laugh carries genuine amusement as he joins the conversation. "Smart people, your folks," he says approvingly, pride clear in the way he discusses the recent additions to the herd. "Those calves are something special. Bastian did good work there."

The praise makes something warm bloom in my chest as I watch color rise in Bastian's cheeks. Because this is what we're building, a life where his different talents receive equal appreciation, where farming skills matter as much as musical ability.

"Speaking of appreciation," Finn says. "How amazing is it that the mayor is giving the band and Taylen an award for saving Winterberry's Christmas? You can all thank me on my birthday with a nice gift."

"It's really not necessary," Bastian protests. "We just did what needed doing. Anyone would have helped."

"It's time the town started rewarding its people," Finn

insists, passion clear in his voice despite his obvious fatigue. "People who step up when things look impossible, who put the community before personal gain." His eyes find mine with an intensity that makes my skin prickle. "Both of you deserve recognition."

Sylvie's arm tightens around my waist. "We're so proud of all of you," she says, her voice filled with warmth. "Of everything you've built here." Her eyes meet Henry's across our circle, their love clear in the way they share a knowing smile. "Some partnerships just make sense, even if it takes time for everyone to see it."

Joe chooses that moment to refill our mugs, so Sylvie gives me a peck on the cheek and goes to stand by her husband's side.

"To family," Henry says suddenly, raising his mug. "And for the grandchildren we can now start asking for."

I cough when my cider goes down the wrong hole. Did he just…?

Bastian laughs. "How about we enjoy the honeymoon period first, Dad?"

Henry winks. "That's the best time, son. You two enjoy it."

I hide my face in Bastian's coat while he and Finn collectively groan.

"Oh, you young people don't know how to have fun these days," Sylvie says. She pats Henry's butt and pulls him away from the bar toward the stage area where a DJ is playing Christmas dance music.

"I hope my sleep, when it comes, resets my memory," Finn says, shuddering.

Bastian whispers in my ear. "Do you think you'll be touching my butt when we're that old?"

I step away from him. "That's it. I'm out."

Bastian catches me, pulling me closer and stealing a kiss.

"Jeez, not you too. What's in the water around here?" Finn puts his empty mug on the bar and walks away from us.

"I think he maybe had a fight with his whatever, whoever he is," I say.

Bastian's eyes go wide. "Excuse me? What do you know that I don't? Couple rules state that all gossip that comes into the knowledge of one party must be shared with the significant other."

I snort. "You're my significant other now, are you?"

He lowers his face down to my level and whispers in my ear with that low, sexy voice I can't resist. "You bet I am. No take-backs, baby. We're it."

To prove it, and to prove we're on a date, Bastian drags me again to the ring toss booth. Thankfully, he doesn't ask again about Finn's...whatever it is...because I genuinely don't know. I'm trying not to let it bother me. Finn will tell me when he's ready.

"Watch and learn," Bastian tells me as the guy from the booth gives him a suspicious look. "This is what we call professional expertise."

"Pretty sure throwing plastic rings at bottles isn't exactly like performing sold-out shows," I observe dryly.

He lines up the first throw, the ring sailing through the air with perfect accuracy, landing around the bottle's neck with a soft clink. Another perfect landing draws a few oohs from the audience that's gathered to watch Sebastian Hall demonstrate unexpected carnival game prowess. His final throw completes the hat trick, the ring settling around the bottle like it was always meant to be there.

"Show off," I mutter as he picks the biggest plushy toy in the booth, a cow that looks a little like Miss Maple.

"For you," he says. "To keep you company when I'm busy with the real cows."

"You're ridiculous." But I still clutch the plushy against my chest, hiding my smile against the soft fabric of the Miss Maple lookalike.

We make our way toward the stage where the mayor is getting ready to do his closing speech, which, to my embarrassment, also involves me going up on stage to accept the award. I don't know how Bastian does it, being the center of attention when so many people look up to him.

We spot Stone and Nikko among the gathering audience. Stone's perfectly styled hair falls down in waves over his designer coat.

"Look at you two ticking all the cliché boxes. Falling for your brother's best friend and winning toys at a Christmas festival," Stone says, looking around the crowd. "Anyone spot the Hallmark film crew yet?"

I roll my eyes, but it's Bastian who delivers the best retort. "Speaking of Hallmark. Has the town vet, who happens to be your future neighbor, fallen for your charms yet?"

Stone pouts. A genuine, honest-to-god pout. "I'm starting to think he's straight."

Nikko's attention, which seemed completely taken up by his phone, suddenly turns to us. "Where's Fox?"

We all look at each other.

"Haven't actually seen him for a couple of days," Bastian says.

"That's because you've been fucking like bunnies to make up for lost time," Stone says. "I saw him this morning at Noëlle's."

Finn joins the group. "Why all the faces?"

"Have you seen Fox?" Nikko asks, and Finn's face falls immediately.

"No...I...no," he says with finality.

"Maybe check your phones in case he messaged," I suggest.

Nikko's the first one to react to whatever he sees on his phone, his expression filling with worry. "Looks like Fox has done another disappearing act."

BONUS SCENE
BASTIAN

Ten Years Later

THE MID-AFTERNOON SUN casts long shadows across the farmyard as I search for my son, though I already know where he'll be. Jackson has his dad's stubbornness and my love of animals. A combination that regularly leads to moments like this, when the quiet grows too suspicious and I have to track him down before his fearlessness gets him into trouble.

My boots crunch against the gravel drive as I head toward the barn, autumn leaves skittering past in the crisp breeze. The familiar smell of hay and livestock grows stronger with each step, along with the distinct sound of my five-year-old trying and failing to whisper. His high-pitched "good girl" carries clearly through the afternoon air, making my stomach clench with equal parts pride and concern.

I ease the barn door open slowly, not wanting to startle either my son or whatever animal he's befriended this time. The sight that greets me still manages to stop my heart for a moment. Jackson is perched precariously on young Dorothy's back, his small hands tangled in her fur as she shifts uncertainly beneath him. The heifer's eyes roll toward me, as if asking for help with her tiny human burden.

"Jackson," I say firmly, keeping my voice steady when I really just want to laugh. "The cows are not for riding. You are not a cowboy." My feet are already carrying me forward even as I speak, my hands reaching for my son.

"But, Papa!" he protests as I lift him off Dorothy's back, his little body squirming in my arms. "She likes it!" His face shines with the particular pride of a child who sees no danger in their accomplishments, only the pure joy of connection with an animal too gentle to buck him off.

I settle him on the ground but maintain hold of his hand, knowing his tendency to dart back toward whatever creature has captured his attention. "Dorothy is very patient," I tell him, crouching to meet his eyes. "But she's not a horse. She could have been hurt, or you could have fallen."

"I don't fall," he insists, his free hand already reaching toward Dorothy, who has drifted closer, curious about our conversation. "I'm good at climbing! And look—" He pats her flank with the gentle touch we've taught him since birth, "She likes me!"

My heart always skips a beat as I watch my son interact with the animals. He has the same fearless joy I remember from my own childhood, tempered now by adult knowledge of everything that could go wrong. "She does trust you," I acknowledge, because positive reinforcement works better than negative with him. "That's why we have to be extra careful not to abuse that trust."

His brow furrows in concentration as he considers this, his mouth forming the slight pout that means he's working through something important. "Like how I'm s'posed to be gentle with Bella?" he asks finally, drawing a surprised laugh from my chest at the connection he's made.

"Exactly like that," I tell him, using his distraction to guide us toward the barn entrance. "And speaking of trust, I think Grandma Sylvie was baking cookies earlier. Want to see if she needs a taste tester?"

The mention of his grandmother and potential sweets successfully diverts his attention from the animals, though he waves goodbye to each cow by name as we pass their stalls. His running commentary continues as we walk the short distance to the farmhouse, his small hand warm in mine.

Mom smiles as we enter the kitchen. "There's my favorite farmer," she calls, already holding her arms out to catch Jackson as he breaks free from my grip to run toward her.

"Grandma!" he exclaims, colliding with her legs with the particular enthusiasm of young children greeting loved ones they saw just hours ago. "I teached Dorothy to be a horse!" The declaration makes us both laugh, but my mom's eyes hold sympathy as she meets my undoubtedly frazzled expression.

"Is that so?" she asks, running her fingers through his perpetually messy hair. "Well, why don't you come help me with these snickerdoodles while Papa takes care of actual farm work? Then you can tell me all about your riding lessons."

"I'll pick him up before dinner," I say.

"Make it tomorrow morning and have some quality time with your husband."

I give her a kiss on the cheek. "You're the best, Mom."

She waves me off, and before she can change her mind, I take off toward our house.

The house Taylen and I built stands warm against the autumn evening. Every step up our porch carries the memory of decisions we made together. The extra-wide stairs for future children to play on, the comfortable swing where we've spent countless evenings watching the sun set over our land.

The door opens silently on well-oiled hinges, another thoughtful detail from a man who understands the importance of being quiet with small children. Inside, the air carries the scent of tonight's dinner, something involving garlic and herbs that reminds my stomach how long it's been since lunch. But it's the sight in our living room that stops me in my tracks.

Taylen stands near the window, our six-month-old daughter Bella cradled against his chest as he sways gently. His back is to me, but I recognize exhaustion in the slope of his shoulders. Bella's dark curls peek over his shoulder.

My sock-clad feet move silently across the hardwood floors we installed together, stepping carefully around scattered toys. The stuffed cow Jackson insisted his sister needed, the teething ring currently wedged under the coffee table, the soft blanket draped over the couch arm that Bella refuses to fall asleep without. It's a fight to remove it from her tiny but oh-so-very-strong hands every time.

I wrap my arms around Taylen's waist from behind, pressing my chest against his back as we both watch our daughter's peaceful face. His body relaxes into mine automatically, his head tilting back to rest against my shoulder in that way that makes my heart stumble even after all these years.

I trail kisses down his neck, smiling as his body reacts to my touch.

"Don't you dare," he whispers, a smile playing around the edges of his mouth. "Took me forty-five minutes of singing every farm animal sound I know to get her down." But his hands find mine where they rest against his stomach, our fingers tangling together.

"I can be quiet," I promise, my lips finding the spot behind his ear that still makes him shiver. "Very, very quiet." My teeth graze his sensitive skin gently, drawing a sharp intake of breath that he quickly stifles. "Besides, you deserve a reward for such dedicated parenting."

His laugh comes out barely louder than a breath, his body shifting slightly against mine in a way that suggests his resistance is already weakening. "You're impossible," he mutters, but he tilts his head farther back to give me better access to his neck. "She'll wake up the moment things get interesting."

"Then we'll have to be quick," I suggest, my hands sliding beneath his shirt to find warm skin beneath. "And careful." My fingers trace the familiar patterns across his stomach, feeling the muscles move beneath my touch. "I'm very moti-vated to make this work. Didn't I promise you a house filled with children?"

Bella chooses this moment to make a small sound in her sleep, causing both of us to freeze completely. But her breathing remains steady, her tiny fingers clutching Taylen's shirt.

"Nursery first," he decides after endless seconds of listening to ensure she's truly asleep. "Then maybe, *maybe,* we can discuss your ridiculous idea about quickies while children nap."

I grab the baby monitor from the coffee table as I follow, remembering too many interrupted moments before we learned the importance of advance planning. The small screen shows the perfect image of Bella's crib, technology that's worth every penny when it lets us steal moments like this.

Taylen moves with practiced grace as he settles our daughter in the crib, moving like he's trying to keep a small-but-very-loud bomb from detonating. Her dark lashes flutter slightly but don't open, her small body curling automatically into her favorite position. We both hold our breath until she settles completely.

"Bedroom," he says quietly, already moving toward the door with a haste that makes heat pool in my stomach. "Before I remember all the reasons this is a terrible idea." His hand finds mine as we slip into the hallway, our connection electric even after years of marriage.

Our bedroom door closes behind us with a soft click that feels like permission to breathe again.

"Where's Jackson?" Taylen asks as my hands work the buttons of his shirt, each newly exposed inch of skin pouring fresh heat through my system. But something falls as the fabric parts, making both of us pause to examine the small shower of crumbs that sprinkles across the floor.

"Eating in bed again?" I ask, brushing more evidence of his snacking habits from the soft cotton. "Thought we had a rule about that." My fingers continue their work despite distraction.

"Bella's morning nap," he explains, helping me shrug the shirt from his shoulders. "Needed a sugar boost to survive the afternoon shift." His laugh catches slightly as my hands find a particularly sensitive spot along his ribs. "Besides, you're one to talk. Found your coffee cup under the pillow yesterday."

"Different situation entirely," I argue between kisses that trail toward his collarbone. "Coffee is a necessary survival tool. Cookies are pure indulgence."

"You still haven't told me where you hid our son."

"Mom," is all I say when the only thing I care about right now is the sounds I draw from his throat. "Sleepover."

He sighs with such relief it breaks my heart. Being parents to two small children and farmers isn't for the fainthearted. We love every second of it as much as we love a break. Thankfully, now, in addition to my parents, we also have Taylen's parents, who moved back home almost six years ago when we announced we were having Jackson.

"Bed," I tell him, rising to capture his mouth in a kiss that has too much teeth to be entirely comfortable, but he responds with matching intensity, his hands already working to rid me of my clothing. We stumble toward the mattress together, neither willing to break the connection long enough to move with more grace.

"If you don't come while I fuck you," I promise against his throat, "you can fuck me after." His whole body shudders beneath mine. "Deal?"

His answer is his legs wrapping around my waist, drawing me closer with strength that still sometimes surprises me. "Less talking," he demands. "More action. Before small humans wake up and ruin the moment."

I comply eagerly, reaching for supplies we keep close at hand for exactly these stolen moments. His body welcomes me with a familiar heat that still manages to take my breath away every time, the connection between us feeling simultaneously new and perfectly known. Each thrust draws fresh sounds from his throat that I swallow with kisses, trying to maintain some semblance of quiet despite mounting pleasure.

I know exactly how to angle my thrust to make him see stars, just as he knows precisely when to shift beneath me to drive me completely mad.

"Taylen," I cry into his neck when my orgasm comes way too soon. "Fuck, baby."

I pull out of him slowly, noticing he didn't come. Instead of turning us over, I straddle him, using my cum to lather his cock. It's sexy and dirty, and sometimes we have to do what we have to do when we might get interrupted at any moment.

He holds my cheeks as I relax my muscles and slide down his cock. My husband fills me perfectly. His groan tells me he's not too far from his own orgasm, so ignoring my discomfort, I ride him in earnest.

"Jesus, Bastian," he cries. We hold our hands together, and then I lower myself to kiss him. With that angle, he touches my prostate with every thrust, and while I know I won't come again, it still feels fucking good.

"Are you gonna come for me, baby?"

"Fuck yeah," he cries, and it's almost too loud. He comes inside me, filling me up just like I did him.

Taylen Howard-Hall has my whole heart and body.

"So," he says finally, voice still rough. "That thing about the kids and filling this house with little Taylens." His fingers move softly across my back..

I laugh. "Do we have to go over the birds and the bees again?"

The baby monitor remains blissfully silent as we trade lazy kisses that gradually grow more heated again. Outside, the sun has set completely, leaving the room lit only by the small lamp beside the bed.

"So help me god, Taylen, if you start giving me presents again, I'll divorce you."

He laughs. "No, you won't."

No, I won't.

"I love you," I say into his mouth.

"Love you too, rockstar."

Dear reader, did you enjoy your introduction to Winterberry and the Hall Farm family?

I've enjoyed every second of Bastian and Taylen's story, and I loved even more teasing the next couple.

Are you ready for it? Midnight and Mistletoe will be here in 2026 but if you want to secure your copy when it releases, you can preorder it now here [readerlinks.com/l/5020379]

BOOKS BY ANA ASHLEY

Spencer Brothers

Three brothers, three fun but heartfelt love stories, each with an accompanying novella because side characters have to have their own happy ever after!

The Lost Fiancé Twist (book1)

The Christmas Roommate (Christmas novella)

The Fake Husband Deal (book2)

The Convenient Groom (novella)

The Best Man's Secret (book3)

The Fostered Promise (novella)

Single Dads of Stillwater

A spin off series from Chester Falls that can be read on its own. Each book features one or more single dads in this community of friends, family and found family. In this contemporary MM romance series you'll find heat, emotion and a guaranteed happy ever after.

Newcomer

Antagonist

Breakthrough

Heartstring

Bittersweet

Second Chance Series

A standalone series set across the Atlantic between New York and Portugal. Find your way home with this contemporary MM romance series with friends to lovers, star-crossed lovers and age gap with plenty of heat, feels and always a happy ever after.

Home Again

Together Again

Love Again

Complete Again

Room for 3 series

This is a high heat MMM contemporary romance series set in an island resort.

The Resort

The Vacation (novella)

Chester Falls Series

From a Prince to a Happy Ever After for all, enjoy this small town MM romance series that's as sweet as they come, with plenty of heat, humor and everything in between.

How to Catch a Bookworm (Prequel short)

How to Catch a Prince

How to Catch a Rival

How to Catch a Bodyguard

How to Catch a Bachelor

How to Catch the Boss (a Christmas novella)

How to Catch a Biker

How to Catch a Vet

How to Catch a Happy Ever After

How to Catch a Billionaire

Standalone books

Christmas Bubble: a low angst, standalone, Christmas novel featuring a petite but larger-than-life cheerleader, an older demisexual football coach and a winter cabin by the lake with only one bed. With cameos from Chester Falls and Stillwater.

Midnight Ash: a sweet Cinderella fairytale retelling with a sexy kinky twist on the side, and a cast who don't quite behave as you'd expect.

Stronghold: a sweet and sexy romance in Sarina Bowen's World of True North, Vino & Veritas series. This is a standalone story between two childhood friends who reunite after as decade apart, with some creative use of maple syrup.

Winter Wishes and Coffee Kisses: A shared-world, small town romance between a new-to-town coffee shop owner and the big, slightly-grumpy, next door neighbor.

With the highest percentage of LGBTQIA+ residents in Vermont, Maplewood is a town where everyone belongs. And with festivals year round, there's always something fun happening! This multi-author, low-angst queer series features ten standalone romances—each set against the backdrop of a different festival. Come for the celebrations, stay for the happily-ever-afters!

Sweet on the Royal Guard: This short story set in the fictitious country of Lydovia brings together Zeke, one of the palace's royal guards and a recluse media heir in hiding. What can go wrong when one of them knocks at the other one's door buck naked and holding a box of donuts?

AUDIOBOOKS BY ANA ASHLEY

Most of Ana's audiobooks are now available through her store.

Ana Ashley Shop

Spencer Brothers narrated by Alexander Cendese

The Lost Fiancé Twist

The Christmas Roommate

The Fake Husband Deal

The Convenient Groom

The Best Man's Secret

The Fostered Promise

Dads of Stillwater narrated by John Solo

Newcomer

Antagonist

Breakthrough

Heartstring

Bittersweet

Chester Falls narrated by Nick Hudson

How to Catch a Bookworm (a short prequel)

How to Catch a Prince

How to Catch a Rival

How to Catch a Bodyguard

How to Catch Bachelor

How to Catch the Boss (a Christmas novella)

How to Catch a Biker

How to Catch a Vet

How to Catch a Happy Ever After

Stronghold narrated by John Solo is available on Audible and wide stores as well as libraries.

Also narrated by Alexander Cendese:

Sweet on the Royal Guard

Winter Wishes and Coffee Kisses

ABOUT ANA

Meet Ana Ashley, your friendly neighborhood romance author!

Ana has been lost in the pages of books for as long as she can remember, taking a few amusing missteps with her childhood writing attempts. But everything changed when she discovered the magical world of LGBTQ+ romance—cue the confetti!

Ana's books offer sweet and sexy romance with a charming mix of humor and heart. Getting her guys together wouldn't be the same without the meddling but well-intentioned cast of secondary characters, who always insist on having their own story.

When she's not crafting heartfelt tales, you can find her indulging in her favorite pastime of baking delicious treats, enjoying quality time with friends, or staying up late immersed in the pages of a good book.

You can follow Ana on the usual social media hangouts.

For access to exclusive teasers, content, and general book and food related goodness you can now join Ana in her Facebook Group, Café RoMMance - Ana's Reader Group

Ana's VIP Readers - bit.ly/AnaAshley

Facebook Page - @anawritesmm

Email - ana@anaashley.com

Instagram - @anaashleyauthor

Bookbub - https://www.bookbub.com/authors/ana-ashley

Goodreads - https://www.goodreads.com/ana-ashley